Say hello to Skye Farrel, the eldest of the Farrel sisters—three strong, independent women who live by their celebrated mother's Holy Commitment Trinity:

- Shared interests
- Mutual respect
- And great sex.

According to their Harvard-trained sexologist mom, these are the only ingredients a couple needs for a satisfying, rewarding life together. But the Farrel recipe is due for a pinch of romance, and Skye is about to find out that no relationship is complete without love.

KISS ME ONCE, KISS ME TWICE

Kiss Me Once, Kiss Me Twice

Kimberly Raye

WARNER
FOREVER

NEW YORK   BOSTON

Copyright © 2004 by Kimberly Groff
Excerpt from *Sometimes Naughty, Sometimes Nice* © 2004 by Kimberly Groff

Cover design by Shasti O'Leary Soudant
Cover illustration by Jethro Soudant
Book design by Giorgetta Bell McRee

WARNER BOOKS

Time Warner Book Group
1271 Avenue of the Americas
New York, NY 10020
Visit our Web site at www.twbookmark.com.

Printed in the United States of America

First Printing: February 2004

10   9   8   7   6   5   4   3   2   1

This book is dedicated to the best agent in the business, Natasha Kern. For your continued support and understanding and professional insight. You are invaluable to me!

Acknowledgments

I would like to say an extra special thank you to an extraordinary group of writing friends: Nina Bangs, Lynn McKay and Donna Maloy, for their understanding and continued support through each and every writing project. Y'all are the best! I would also like to thank the wonderful women at *www.racehippie.com*. Female NASCAR fans rule! For personal encouragement and keeping me sane during the most stressful times, heartfelt thanks goes to my close friend, Debbie Villanueva, who's never too fearful to take on a group of screaming kids when I need her. And, as always, all of my thanks and love go to Curt Groff, who's always there to help and guide me when I need him the most. Thanks, babe!

Kiss Me Once, Kiss Me Twice

Chapter One

"Welcome to Girl Talk. For the next few hours we're going to learn the ins and outs of sex. Literally."

The moment the words left Skye Farrel's mouth, a wave of giggles floated through the enormous living room of the downtown Dallas high-rise that was overflowing with party attendees. Tonight's hostess, a corporate attorney who headed one of the biggest law firms in the city, navigated through the maze of women with a vegetable tray in one hand and a bottle of Ranch dressing in the other.

"Remember," Skye went on, "tonight is about expanding your arsenal of sexual knowledge. Nothing is taboo, from erotic fantasies to basic hand techniques for mindblowing masturbation." Another wave of laughter rolled through the sea of women, but Skye wasn't the least bit intimidated.

"To get the party rolling," she went on, "we're going to focus our attention on tonight's guest of honor. This"—she picked up the plastic replica sitting on the expensive cherry wood coffee table—"is Dinah the friendly vagina."

Skye watched as several faces fired a bright red. Sympathy washed through her. Once upon a time she had been just as uncomfortable. Six years ago to be exact, when she'd led her first Girl Talk workshop. By the time the evening had ended, she'd morphed into the poster girl for a sunburn ad.

A crazy reaction for a woman who'd learned early on from her Harvard-trained sexologist mother that sex was a natural experience and a woman's body, whatever size and shape and color, a beautiful thing.

"I say friendly because a vagina is nothing to be frightened of. It's a natural part of a woman's body."

"Can women really learn how to have multiple orgasms?" The question came from a redhead wearing tailored black slacks and a matching jacket. "I mean, I know it's possible," she rushed on, "but I never have. Even with my husband. We've been married for five years and he's really great in bed. He always waits for me and everything, but the minute it happens, he turns into Old Faithful."

"I have note cards for questions," Skye started, bolting to her feet and reaching for the stack of blank cards to her right. Normally, her assistant passed these out and collected the written questions so that Skye could review them during the breaks and give intelligent, thoughtful responses once the workshop resumed. But Jenny, her trusted sidekick and the only woman other than Skye's two sisters who could recite every Kama Sutra position without benefit of notes, had been MIA since her morning coffee date with Do-Right Duke the Dietician. She'd left only a voice mail a few hours ago stating that she was running late. "Let me just pass these around—"

"Mine, too," another woman blurted, mindless of the card Skye thrust into her hand. "I used to have multiple orgasms before I married my husband, but now he's so quick on the trigger that it's a miracle if I have one at all."

"I swear, it must be something in the water because my guy does the same thing . . ."

The comments echoed around the room as the women started to open up about their own experiences and express their needs. It was just such a conversation seven years earlier that had prompted the idea for Skye's wildly successful Dallas-based sex education company. Despite a master's degree in human sexuality education, she'd been barely scraping by as an assistant sociology professor at a nearby junior college when she'd been invited to a Home Interior party given by one of her colleagues.

She'd been eyeing the dècor and munching cheese balls when she'd noticed something interesting. Rather than discussing the latest home fashions, the party attendees had been dissecting one particular woman's failing relationship, and none too successfully.

Skye had known then and there that Tupperware and Pampered Chef were a thing of the past. To foster a healthy relationship with a man in today's society, a woman needed more than domestic knowledge. She needed to know how to sexually satisfy her man and herself, and so Girl Talk had been born.

No subject was off-limits, although Skye did tailor her talks to each individual group by handing out questionnaires ahead of time to make sure that she addressed everyone's hot topics.

Tonight's group ranged from twenty-somethings to a

few women in their mid-forties. Most were well-educated, attractive professionals who'd made it in the boardroom and were now eager to succeed in the bedroom, as well.

". . . Bernie's quick on the draw himself," one of the women was saying. "We've tried Viagra and everything, but it doesn't help anything except the size of his you-know-what. Surely there's something to help the hardness last."

"There has to be," another woman said. "What about vitamins? I hear they can do wonders."

Skye held up a blank sample card. "I know you all have lots of things to ask, so please jot down everything rather than calling out. We've got a lot to cover and the cards will keep us on track."

"What about a cock ring?" one woman asked. "I've heard it can squeeze the blood and hold it in the member so that the erection lasts longer?"

So much for staying on track.

"Or one of those penis pulsers," another voice added. "Don't they do pretty much the same thing?"

"Actually, they do—ugh." Skye bit her lip against a sudden burst of pain as she stubbed her toe on the way back to her chair. Her foot throbbed.

"There are many techniques," she managed to go on, limping the last few feet in her no-nonsense, low-heeled black pumps before sinking down, "to help excite you quicker and push you to the brink earlier, as well as some things you can do to draw out your man's pleasure." She grabbed her notes and zeroed in on the next part of the program.

Sex didn't make her nervous.

Questions about sex didn't make her nervous.

It was being caught off-guard that made her stomach

jump and her mouth water for the chocolate chip cookies sitting just to her right.

Not just store bought ones either. These were the homemade kind—big and bumpy and overflowing with chocolate chips, with an imperfect shape and slightly browned edges and—

Don't do it, her conscience whispered. *Think of all the sexy lingerie samples sitting in your briefcase. Teachers teach by example. Cookies and thongs can be a deadly mix.*

It wasn't as if she actually wore thongs in her own everyday life. No woman wore such skimpy underthings for the sake of comfort. They were sexy, period. Skye's job was all about sex, so she promoted thongs to her clients as a seductive tool.

Skye summoned the courage to resist a cookie and forced a steady breath. She had a cup of Earl Grey in front of her, as well as a plate of wheat crackers and carrot sticks. Life was good. Painful with her throbbing toe, but she could deal with it.

Slipping off her shoe, she drew in a deep breath. "We'll explore as much as we can tonight," she went on, "but before we can learn how to drive the car, we have to know a little about how it runs. Now"—her gaze shifted around the room—"who can tell me the most important aspect of a woman's sex life?"

A forty-something woman wearing a severe navy blue suit rose to her feet. "Grace Philburn, here. Defense counsel for Walker and Hughes."

"Loosen up, Gracie," the woman next to her said. "We're not in court."

Grace ignored the comment and focused her gaze on Skye.

"Yes," Skye prompted.

"Why did you name the vagina Dinah? Couldn't you call it something like Margaret or Elizabeth or Gretchen?"

"I suppose you could call it anything you want. Dinah just happens to be my choice. It seems very upbeat and sex should be fun. Not to mention, it rhymes."

"Oh." The woman nodded and sank back into her seat.

Skye took a sip of tea and smiled. "Okay, now what is the one thing that every woman must have in order to experience great sex?"

"A husband who doesn't spend every waking second watching the Outdoor Channel."

"A babysitter who'll pull an all-nighter with the kids."

"A guy who doesn't ask 'Who's Your Daddy?' "

"A Junior Jelly Number Five with a rotating tip."

"Brad Pitt."

Skye smiled. "All very good answers, but believe it or not, the most important aspect of great sex for a woman is a positive body image." The comment met with a surprised murmur. "The better you feel about yourself, the better you'll feel about sex, and the better sex will feel."

She went on. "The ultra hot spot for any woman is always the—"

"Is it made in Japan?"

Grace's voice rang out and halted Skye mid-thought. "I beg your pardon?"

"The vagina. Where is something like that made? Probably overseas. They have a much freer sense of self over there. Why, in a lot of countries I hear that they don't even have to wear clothes in public."

Who cares? Skye bit her lip against her first thought as her brain scrambled for an answer. "Actually, it's made right here in America by a company called Wild Woman, Inc. They're famous for erotic toys, but they also do educational models for workshops such as these."

At Grace's nod, Skye re-directed her attention back to Dinah and the . . . What had she been saying? Yes, the hot spot. "Okay, the clitoris is the ultimate pleasure point and it's located right—"

"Does it come with a warranty?"

"Thirty days," Skye replied. "Satisfaction guaranteed or your money back." If there were this many questions about the small plastic model in her hands, the place would go nuts when she pulled out the three dozen rubber penises packed in her briefcase. "Now, about the—"

"What about replacement parts? Do they make those?" Grace's voice rang out again and Skye's stomach gave a traitorous grumble. Her nostrils flared and the delicious aroma of chocolate chips baked to their finest stirred her senses.

Maybe she would have one teeny, tiny cookie after all.

Skye had managed to limit herself to small nibbles and was only on her third cookie when Jenny finally arrived a half-hour into the program.

Skye had passed out the penises and was giving the women a chance to get acquainted with their new friends when her assistant collapsed on the sofa next to her.

Jenny's face glowed and her eyes danced and she looked anything but deathly ill.

"I thought you were sick."

"I never said I was sick. Just that I was going to be late."

"I assumed you were sick. You're never late."

"I was right in the middle of something that couldn't

wait." Her gaze caught Skye's and she smiled. "Guess what Duke did?"

"Let's see . . . He finally worked up the nerve to hold your hand." Skye savored the last nibble of her cookie and rubbed her hands together. That was it. She was done. She'd fallen off the wagon, but now she was climbing back up into the driver's seat. Jenny was here and it was business as usual.

"He did that weeks ago," her assistant said. "This is better."

"He kissed you on the cheek." Skye started gathering crumbs from her tailored cherry red suit and placed them in her napkin.

"Last week, and it's much better."

"He kissed you on the lips."

"Day before yesterday." Jenny smiled. "Better."

"He French-kissed you."

"Yesterday and way better."

"Okay, I'm going to throw all my cookies onto Duke's plate and give him a great big vote of confidence. I say he finally found his nerve and felt you up either above or below the waist. Maybe both."

Longing filled Jenny's gaze. "If only." She shook her head and excitement brightened her eyes again. "Still, this is much, much, much better."

"If he's barely put a hand on you upstairs or downstairs, I'm sure this next answer will be wrong, but what do I know?" Skye was riding a chocolate chip high, her nerves buzzing so pleasantly that she hardly felt her aching toe. "Maybe you two got really creative and actually had sex."

When Jenny gave her a *get real* look, Skye added, "I know the whole waiting for sex thing seems romantic, but this is the twenty-first century. Don't you think his reluctance screams major hang-up?"

"You've been a sexpert too long. You're too analytical. It's the way he was brought up. He's got certain standards and beliefs, that's all."

"Or maybe he's got a limp willy."

"He calls it Captain Long Dong, and believe me, it's not limp. Now, come on and guess. I'm dying here."

"Just tell me."

"That spoils the fun. Guess."

"Okay, he talked to you about having sex."

"Better."

"He wrote you a letter asking you to have sex."

Jenny gripped Skye's hand and blurted, "He asked me to marry him."

"He—he *what*?"

"We're getting married." Jenny dropped Skye's hand and stared dreamily at her ring finger, which glittered with a rock the size of Gibraltar.

"Married?" Skye's stomach churned. "You're getting married? Married?"

"In two months." Jenny shrugged. "I know marriage was never really my thing, but then the right man never asked me until today."

"Married, as in walking down the aisle and saying 'I Do'?"

"Can you imagine me in a white dress? With pink roses. I have to have lots of pink roses."

"Pink?"

"A soft, dewy pink, not the Pepto-Bismol kind. With lots of tulle. Tulle looks so elegant and moves so beautifully during ballroom dancing."

"You don't ballroom dance."

"Duke and I are going to take lessons. Ballroom dancing is so romantic and we want the older people at the wedding to feel comfortable. We'll have a big band. Maybe even an orchestra. And a sit-down dinner with assigned seating and one of those waterfalls flowing with champagne and an ice sculpture shaped like a cauliflower."

"A cauliflower?"

"Duke being a dietician and all, I want something that says healthy, and cauliflower is one of the healthiest vegetables in the food group."

"I didn't know that," Skye murmured, eyeing the remaining platter of chocolate-chip satisfaction.

"And guess what else?"

"I can't imagine." She didn't want to. She was already in a state of shock. Jenny. Single-loving, let's-play-180-Ways-Around-the-Bedroom-on-the-first-date Jenny was actually getting *married*.

"You're going to be my maid of honor. Isn't that wonderful?"

"I . . ." The words died on her lips and Skye did the only thing a single woman with a deep-seated aversion to weddings and an even greater fear of pink tulle could do.

She reached for the cookies.

Chapter Two

Two months later . . .

"The wedding is off," Skye declared. "Over. *Finis.*"

"You can't do that. You're the maid of honor, not the bride. She's the only one who can call it quits."

"But I can't wear this." Skye stared at her massive reflection in the mirror. Massive because Jenny had decided to go with a traditional southern theme, complete with hoop skirts and parasols. "I look ridiculous."

"You don't look ridiculous. You just look . . ." Xandra Farrel swept a gaze from Skye's head to her toes and back up again. "Purple," she finally declared. "Very purple."

Skye stared pointedly at her youngest sister, who sprawled in a nearby chair. Wearing faded blue-jean overalls, worn tennis shoes and a baseball jersey, Xandra looked more like a Little League coach than the owner and head designer for Wild Woman, Inc., America's leading manufacturer of erotic toys and sensual aids for women. It was a fashion statement that had started back in grade school when Xandra had been chubby, and one that had continued despite the fact that she'd slimmed down and shaped up over the years.

She had her long, thick blond hair, a shade darker than Skye's, stuffed up under her favorite Houston Astros ball cap. A pair of Ray-Bans perched on the hat's brim.

Xandra shrugged and smiled. "Okay, so you look a little ridiculous. But it's for a good cause. Not to mention, five other women will be wearing the same thing, so you won't look ridiculous all by yourself."

"Yeah, right." Skye gave her sister a look. "Actually, the dresses are all different colors. Each custom-dyed to match a specific fruit featured in Fresh Fruit Fantasy. I'm the grape."

"Fresh Fruit Fantasy?"

"From Potent Produce, this vegetarian diner near Jenny's gym. One day, she ordered the Fresh Fruit Fantasy, but they got the topping wrong. Jenny went to complain and this man walked up holding a plate of the same thing, only with her topping. It was Duke. He'd gotten her order and she'd gotten his. So she's using Fresh Fruit Fantasy as her wedding colors, since it's their favorite dish and how they met."

"Well, you make one knockout grape." Xandra blew out a deep, frustrated breath. "Boy, I could use a cigarette."

"You can go out into the mall." They were at the Galleria in the heart of downtown Dallas. "I think they have a designated smoking area somewhere near the garden quad."

Xandra shook her head. "I'm trying to stop. I went cold turkey, but that didn't do it, so I'm trying the patch."

"That must have been awful. How long did you do the cold turkey thing?"

Xandra glanced at her Nike sports watch. "About an hour this morning. I've been doing the patch"—she lifted the sleeve of her T-shirt—"about two hours now."

"Two hours. I'm impressed, not to mention I can see you much more clearly without the usual pack-a-day fog hanging around."

"You're funny."

"I'm trying to ease the pain."

"Nothing but a Camel and a lighter could do that."

"Nonsense. You're strong. You're fearless. You're a Farrel." Skye turned back to the mirror and gave herself another once-over. "I look like Barney."

Xandra narrowed her green gaze, the exact same shade as Skye's. "You know, you sort of do."

"You're here to make me feel better, remember?"

"Actually, I'm here because I'm the boss and I can take a few days off to fly from Houston to Dallas on a moment's notice. Otherwise, you'd be on your own."

"You're here for a convention. That's why you're staying at a hotel and not at my place. Because it's the convention hotel and you're running a booth."

"True, but I'm also doing you a favor by being your date for the wedding since there's no hot male prospect in your life right now."

"I don't even have a cold one," Skye grumbled. Her last relationship had ended over five months ago, and at thirty-three, she'd outgrown the one-night stand phase.

"Exactly. You need your baby sister to keep you company, which I'm happy to do when I'm not working. But if you want a side order of moral support with the date, it'll cost you."

"I'll buy you dinner."

"I'd rather be included in your will." She grinned. "Because at the rate you're going, you're liable to die of a heart attack before you make it out of the boutique. Your face is red and you're breathing much too heavily." She grinned. "Relax, Sis. Just think of this as a new experience. A grand adventure. Like picking an exotic locale off the top of your head and rushing off for the weekend."

But that was the problem. Skye didn't rush anywhere for the weekend. She researched. She planned. She prepared for her weekends, and every day in between.

And it didn't help that the dress was for a wedding. Not that she had anything against a good celebration. It was the ritual itself and what it stood for that gave her the heebie-jeebies. From this day forward. Forever and ever. 'Til death do us part . . . Bye, bye freedom.

No, thank you.

A woman didn't have to sell her soul and sign a piece of paper to guarantee a lasting relationship. Her mother and her father—a quiet, conservative sociology professor and conservationist—had been together for over thirty-six years. They had a mutually gratifying, committed, monogamous relationship and three healthy daughters. A formal license hadn't figured in, and never would.

As if on cue, Jenny floated into the room wearing bike shorts, a tank top and running shoes. She took one look at Skye and her lips curved into a huge smile. A huge, silly, dreamy smile. The sort of look reserved for teenage girls who spend their class time pining away for the captain of the high-school football team.

A tear slid down Jenny's cheek and Skye's heart pounded even faster.

"What's wrong?" she asked.

"Nothing. It's just so . . ."

Awful.

Overdone.

Wrong.

Skye awaited the response she knew would come. After all, Jenny was always open and honest and fashionable. Thankfully.

"It's absolutely perfect," Jenny announced, pulling a tissue from her pocket and blowing loudly. She smiled and touched the layers of purple tulle. "Don't you just love it?"

"I . . ." Skye licked her lips and forced a smile. "Love doesn't begin to describe what I'm feeling right now."

"I'll admit, at first I was thinking it might be too much, but after seeing you in it," Jenny told Skye as she sniffled back a tear, "I know I made the right decision. You look just like a fairy princess."

When Skye's eyes widened, Jenny added, "I know, I know, it sounds cheesy. I never thought I would feel this way about a wedding, but here I am going through the motions like a real bride."

"You are a real bride," Skye told her. "And a beautiful one."

Jenny smiled and wiped at her eyes. "You're the best maid of honor in the entire world." She gave Skye one last look, then went in search of the salesperson who'd been helping her.

"Looks like you're not as bad at this wedding stuff as you thought," Xandra said. "Especially for a wedding virgin."

Skye turned back to the mirror and sucked in her tummy. "I may say the right things, but I'm a nervous wreck. I've gained at least five pounds already. The Cookie Connection over at the mall named me their customer of the week."

"Maybe I should just wait to give up the cigarettes until I get back to Houston." Xandra licked her lips, an anxious light in her eyes. "I mean, what's one more week, right?"

Skye whirled and pinned her sister with a stare. "You talked to Mom, didn't you? You're nervous and you're never nervous unless you talk to Mom."

"I always talk to Mom. In fact, lately, I'm the only one who even answers my phone when she calls, which is why I'm her favorite, and why I'm *this* close to having a brain meltdown. I *really* need a cigarette right now." She put a hand on her hip. "It's not fair that you and Eve don't help divvy up her attention and her time. Lately I've been her sole focus and it really sucks."

"You know Eve hibernates when she's working on a project."

Skye's middle sister was the producer and director for Sugar & Spice Sinema, a West coast company that produced how-to videos to help couples reach their true sexual potential. Eve was the typical L.A. artsy type—very creative and eccentric. When she started a new series, she went virtually underground, holing up in her apartment with her research books and her computer until she'd perfected a step-by-step script.

"So what's your excuse?" Xandra's voice drew Skye's gaze. Her youngest sister arched an eyebrow, a knowing look in her eyes. "Mom's been trying to get you for the past month."

"I talked to her just last week."

"For about five seconds and then you made up some excuse to let her go."

Skye shrugged. "I've just been so overwhelmed by the wedding, and so rushed since Jenny put this whole thing together in such a short time to accommodate some long lost cousin's busy schedule. I haven't been myself. You know Mom. She's a mind reader, at least when it comes to me. More than five words with her, and she'll know something's up. Then she'll ask me. I've never been good at lying to her."

"So don't lie."

"And tell her I'm smack dab in the middle of matrimonial hell, and I'm participating? Tell her I've read *Weddings for Dummies* twice?" Skye shook her head. "I'm neck deep in an archaic tradition that Mom loathes. She would totally freak if she knew."

"Just don't mention it. I never mention anything about my personal life. When she asks, I simply steer the conversation back to her, and everything is cool. That's what you should do."

Skye turned back to the mirror and surveyed her reflection. "I can't believe I'm actually going to wear this out in public."

"Atta girl." Xandra smiled. "Keep the faith, Sis. It's almost over. Besides, it's not all doom and gloom. The bachelorette party is tonight, isn't it?" She wiggled her eyebrows. "At least you know what to do when it comes to a single girls' night out."

"True."

"My trunk is loaded with goodies. And this," she added, pulling out what looked like a tube of lipstick from her purse, "is an exclusive. Fresh off the production line and guaranteed to not only liven up any party, but seduce any and every man in eyesight."

"It's shaped like a miniature penis," a petite, blond Kate Hudson look-alike and Jenny's only sister declared later that night. She sat opposite Skye at a long rectangular table filled with Xandra and ten of Jenny's closest female friends.

They were at Whiskey Dicks, a male version of Hooters where the waiters wore nothing but tight, faded jeans and a smile as they served up beer and hot wings to the all-female clientele. The atmosphere was festive and fast, with No Doubt blaring from the speakers. The sound of laughter and voices rose just above the music and the *clink-clink* of glasses and plates.

"It's called a lipdick," Xandra told her. "Get it? Lipstick. Lipdick. But that might not be the final choice. The name is still in the research phase." Xandra slathered her lips with the creamy crimson before handing it to Skye, who sat next to her.

"I like it." Jenny was wearing a makeshift white veil decorated with glow-in-the-dark packages of condoms, and a white T-shirt decorated with real pink Lifesavers that spelled out SUCK FOR A BUCK.

Rocko, their buff waiter, had been the first to suck for a buck. Since then Jenny had earned an entire twenty dollars.

Skye smiled. She was definitely in her comfort zone now. No hideous dresses. No talk about cakes or vows or what dressing to serve on the salad at the sit-down dinner.

All was right with the world.

Jenny put on the lipstick and licked her lips. "Mmm . . . Mine tastes like strawberry."

"We're working on cherry and raspberry and watermelon, too," Xandra said. "Oh, and I've got a fuchsia one that tastes like pink lemonade."

"Pink lemonade? I just love—I don't believe it! *That's it!*"

"What?" Skye spewed a mouthful of margarita and glanced around. "What? Where?"

"Pink lemonade. That's what I need at the reception. A lemonade fountain to sit next to the champagne fountain. It's so much more creative than just tea and coffee and it's the perfect alternative for a non-alcoholic beverage. Not to mention we can do it with a low-calorie sweetener so that it doesn't pack too many calories. Just plenty of Vitamin C. I have to tell Duke right now."

Before Skye could protest, Jenny wiped wing sauce from her fingers, pulled out her cell phone and pressed a number on her speed dial. "I hope he picks up. His oldest brother was taking him out to do after-hour laps at Dallas Raceway."

"You're so lucky, Jenny," one of the women said. "You're not just going to meet Clint MacAllister. You're going to be related to him."

"Yeah," another girl agreed. "You're so lucky."

"Clint MacAllister?" Skye asked. "That's Duke's oldest brother, right?"

"And NASCAR's pride and joy," Jenny's sister added.

"NASCAR?" Skye asked. "*The* NASCAR?" When the woman nodded, Skye glanced over at Jenny.

"I told you he raced," Jenny said.

"But you didn't say anything about NASCAR. I was

thinking you meant a Saturday night hobby at the local track. Not an honest-to-goodness NASCAR driver."

"He's more than a driver," Jenny's sister added. "He's *the* driver. He's won more Winston Cup championships in fifteen years than most drivers win in an entire career. He won Rookie of the Year his first season in Winston, and he's broken I don't know how many records. *And* he's good-looking and sexy."

"Definitely sexy," one of the women agreed.

"You said it," another woman chimed in.

"And how."

"You don't know anything about NASCAR," Jenny told Skye as she punched in the number a second time. "That's why I didn't make a big deal."

"I don't know *about* NASCAR, as in details, but I have heard of it. And I know it's a big deal."

"And so is Clint," Jenny's sister added. "He's famous, and not just because he drives. Everybody's seen his picture at one time or another, whether or not they follow stock car racing."

"Even you," Xandra said when Skye shook her head. "Remember back in high school? The picture of that guy in his underwear at Billy Bob's Honky Tonk?"

Skye's memory rushed back to her senior year and the girls' locker room. There'd been an entire group of oohing and ahhing females hovered around a copy of a well-known tabloid magazine, their attention fixed on the twenty-year-old on the cover.

He'd been completely naked except for a pair of white briefs, cowboy boots and a straw Resistol. He'd sat astride a mechanical bull smack dab in the middle of the largest honky tonk in Texas, one hand gripping the rope, the other poised up in the air while a throng of fans cheered him on.

The picture had been legendary, showing up first in the tabloids and then in a series of ads selling everything from western wear to auto parts to fast food.

"The half-naked cowboy is Duke's brother?"

Jenny nodded. "And best man. And he's not really a cowboy. He just likes the hat and boots and—Duke? Thank God you picked up, honey. I've got the perfect answer to the beverage dilemma . . ."

Jenny spent the next hour going back and forth between Duke, Jiles the wedding planner and a platter of hot wings, while Skye looked on and thanked the Big Lady Upstairs that she would never have to endure such torture.

Men had their place in the world. That much was true. She liked the companionship and the sex, but not enough to even think about saying the dreaded *I do*.

Okay, *like* was too mild a word. She adored companionship and sex. She enjoyed them. She craved them. She lov—

Uh-uh.

Skye Farrel didn't believe in the infamous L word. She'd never seen it up close and she'd certainly never experienced it. Thankfully.

"No daughter of mine would ever fall for a concept invented by men to keep women submissive and needy." So sayeth the infamous Jacqueline Farrel and, as usual, she was right.

Skye knew that, but it didn't stop her from smiling as she watched Jenny talk to Duke on her cell phone. Jenny grinned and laughed and blushed, and Skye couldn't help but wonder what it would be like to have someone in her life who made her so happy.

Even more, she couldn't help but want her own somebody for more than a measly six months—the duration of her longest relationship to date.

Not for marriage, of course. Skye Farrel was thirty-three and single and, as much as she hated to admit it, a little bit lonely. But she wasn't crazy.

She was definitely crazy.

Skye came to that conclusion when she stumbled into her apartment at four in the morning. Only a one hundred percent certifiable loony toon would schedule a bachelorette party the night before a mid-afternoon wedding.

She yawned, dropped her purse on the coffee table, grabbed a nearby quilt her grandmother had made, and sank onto the sofa. Her small, white, two-year-old Shih Tzu, Skipper, jumped up and settled herself on Skye's lap while Skye turned on the TV and punched the Rewind button on her VCR. Since she frequently worked in the evenings, Skye didn't get a chance to catch *Get Sexed Up*, her favorite talk show, which aired after hours. So she'd resorted to taping the show and watching it when she came in.

Two years and she'd yet to miss an episode.

The screen flickered and lit up with a talk-show set decorated in various shades of red. The intro theme— George Michael's fitting classic "I Want Your Sex"—blared as the camera spanned the rows of excited audience members.

"Good evening and welcome!" the announcer's voice rang out. "It's that time again, ladies, so relax and release those inhibitions, because you're about to *Get Sexed Up*."

The audience applauded and the camera zeroed in on a door at the rear of the set where a familiar woman appeared.

Jacqueline Farrel was tall and thin and professional in beige slacks, a matching suit jacket and low-heeled, no-nonsense beige pumps. Silvery gray streaked her shoulder-length blond hair, which had been cut into a stylish bob. Only the barest hint of makeup accented her pale skin. She wore a pair of silver-framed glasses that seemed slightly too large for her narrow face. They slid down her nose and she pushed them up as she stepped out onto the set and rounded a red leather sofa. She walked the length of the stage and waved at the three hundred die-hard Farrel fans packed into the audience, who were ready to digest any and everything she had to say.

Jacqueline Farrel hadn't always been so popular. Her theory that relationships endured because of three key ingredients—great sex, shared interests, and mutual respect—was outlined in her groundbreaking book, *The Lifelong Orgasm*, back in the early sixties. While the infamous Holy Commitment Trinity had struck a chord in some women, the idea hadn't really taken off until a few years ago.

Thanks to the rising divorce rate and a special segment on *Oprah*, a movement had exploded, triggering a re-release of the book, a wave of publicity for Jacqueline, and an offer from Lifetime to host a special late-night segment where women would dish about being women. The trials. The tribulations. The victories. She'd accepted, thrilled at the prospect of bringing her female empowerment doctrine to women all across the country, even if she had to do it on an extravagant red set that looked like Skye's worst Valentine's Day nightmare.

"Ladies, ladies, thanks for joining me tonight." Jacqueline sank down into a red leather armchair. "We've got a great show planned. The topic is underwire bras and why we, as women, should reject them. It's not just a matter of comfort, ladies. It's a matter of pride. We women no longer have to sacrifice ourselves to fit male-inspired ideals of what we should or shouldn't look like. Perky breasts? If you've got them, great. But if not, rejoice!" She cupped her bosom with both hands and gave an affectionate squeeze. "But first, we'll do our audience question. And the winner is . . . " She reached into a bowl sitting on the coffee table and drew a name. "Cheryl Anderson from Wisconsin."

A round of applause sounded as a short, timid, middle-aged woman with mousy brown hair and trembling hands got to her feet.

"I, um," the woman blushed and reached into her pocket. "I wrote my question down because I knew I'd be nervous." She cleared her throat and unfolded the paper. "My husband is always telling me that he's better than me. He says it's because man came before woman, therefore women are second best. Dr. Farrel, what do I tell my husband when he says that to me?"

"First off, you have to speak to him in language the male creature can actually understand, which means you don't talk feelings. You talk business. Just tell him he's the prototype and you're the finished product." A wave of laughter went through the audience. "From a creationist standpoint, man did come first. But once God, in all of her infinite wisdom, realized her mistakes, she promptly corrected them and created woman."

"I never thought about it that way," the woman said.

"That's what *Get Sexed Up* is all about. Broadening the female mind. Realizing that your existence doesn't revolve around your partner." Jacqueline smiled.

A round of applause went up and the music started. The announcer's voice came over the speaker. "For your question, Cheryl, you'll receive an autographed collection of Dr. Farrel's books. And we'll be right back after this message from our sponsor . . . "

The music faded into a commercial and Skye let her eyelids drift shut. She knew the topic and the opening question. If her mother asked—and she always asked—Skye could respond openly and honestly and completely guilt-free. She'd done her duty as the eldest and most supportive daughter of Jacqueline Farrel.

"I need the maid of honor." The high-pitched voice rang out above the steady chatter that filled the small dressing room and made Skye's temples pound.

"Over here." Skye popped two Tylenol and slid her hand into the air. The sea of women parted and she spotted the petite man dressed in a tailored Evan Picone black suit. He had a shiny bald head and wore small, wire-rimmed spectacles and a frustrated expression.

"I need you over *here*." Jiles Carrington was Dallas' most sought-after wedding coordinator. He was neat with impeccable taste in clothes. He'd also been featured in every major wedding magazine and was a virtual genius when it came to turning a young bride's matrimonial dreams into reality.

But most of all, Jiles was a pompous, bossy pain in the ass who got the job done.

"Where have you been?" He reached her in three

quick strides. An overflowing box of flowers sat in his small, thin arms. He clutched a decorated cake knife in one hand, and a serving spatula in the other. "I've been looking for you forever."

"I've been right here."

Except when she'd slipped away for a trip to the ladies' room. She'd needed to after drinking a six-pack of Diet Coke throughout the morning to wake her up.

Not that Jiles would be the least bit understanding.

"You are the maid of honor. You have responsibilities. You have to be accessible and reliable."

"I've been right here," she insisted.

He gave her a *Do I look like I just stepped off the boat, Sister* look before shoving the box at her. "These bouquets need to be distributed to each bridesmaid according to ribbon color." He gripped the cake knife and spatula with one hand and snapped his fingers at her. "Well? Don't just stand there. Get going. We haven't got all day. I want everyone lined up for a personal inspection in thirty minutes or else."

"Or else what?"

"Or else you'll suffer the consequences." He held up the cake knife and waved it at her. "I don't like tardiness."

"Even if it can't be helped?"

"*Especially* if it can't be helped." He gave her the Evil Eye. "So I suggest you go get everyone together."

"Or else?"

"Exactly."

Skye only hoped that the *or else* was swift so that she missed all the blood. She didn't do blood very well.

He snapped again and barked, "Chop, chop."

Skye stifled the urge to bop him over his head with one of the bouquets or, worse, turn and bolt because he was obviously not playing with a full deck. He was a wedding coordinator, for heaven's sake. Not a character from *The Sopranos*.

You can do this. You're in the home stretch. Just a few more hours.

A few deep breaths later, she worked her way through the dressing room filled with females and spent the next ten minutes matching dress color with the appropriate ribbon until she'd distributed all of the bouquets, except for the yellow.

"Where's the banana?" she asked.

"That would be Cheryl," one of the bridesmaids—the peach—called out from a few feet away. "She's our second cousin."

"Where is she?"

"Beats me. The last time I saw her, she was in the parlor puffing away on a cigarette."

"She still smokes?" the cherry asked.

"Like a chimney," the peach replied.

"And she still drinks," the kiwi offered. "But hopefully she'll behave herself tonight. No trysts in the men's bathroom like last time. Duke warned her last night."

"Since when does she listen to Duke? She needs to grow up."

"She needs a good spanking."

Skye looked at her watch. Twenty minutes to Jiles' inspection and counting . . .

Skye walked out of the dressing room, damning herself for not stuffing a few Chips Ahoy into her purse before she'd left the house that morning. But she'd been determined to make it through today without indulging. After all, it was just one day. She was in the home stretch, trudging toward the finish line. She could make it. She would make it. Without a sugar fix.

She glanced around, then picked a direction at random. How hard could it be to find a girl wearing a monstrous, blindingly yellow dress?

Damned hard.

She came to that conclusion ten minutes later after she'd searched almost the entire first floor of the Southern Oaks Plantation.

Skye shoved open the last men's room door and muttered, "Where in the hell is she?"

"Can I help you?" The deep male voice came from behind her.

She whirled around and saw a broad back outlined by a crisp white shirt. He stood a few feet in front of her, his back to her as he faced the urinal. His pants sagged around his hips, the black material accenting a firm, muscular rear end—

Zippp . . .

The sound sent a bolt of reality through her and ended her speculation. Her gaze shot to the mirror on the opposite wall and a man's smiling reflection.

Familiar. He looked so familiar with his lips crooked in a cocky grin and his eyes dancing with amusement.

"Can I help you?"

The deep, smooth voice echoed in her ears and sent a hum pulsing along her nerve endings.

A reaction she'd felt many times before with many attractive men, though not quite this intense. Intense enough to scramble her common sense for several frantic heartbeats.

"I'm looking for a banana," she finally blurted.

He grinned. "That's what they all say, sweetheart."

Chapter Three

Clint MacAllister had heard some really great pickup lines in his thirty-six years, and so he considered himself somewhat of an expert. They were a hazard of the job for one of NASCAR's hottest drivers, not to mention the Most Eligible Bachelor in Comfort, Texas—a title he'd owned for the past fifteen years thanks to the good citizens of his hometown, half of whom were related to him.

He'd heard everything from *You have really great eyes* to *Wanna go back to my hotel and play hide the salami?* Some lines were tasteful, some downright raunchy. Some were shy and demure, others as straight as an arrow. Some tasted as stale as his momma's day-old biscuits, while others were as fresh as the women delivering them.

He wasn't sure how to categorize this one. While there was nothing new about the banana line, the desperation in the woman's eyes gave it a sincere edge.

Definitely a first for Clint. He'd met many women during his career, but very few he'd been able to take at face value thanks to his high profile image as a hotshot driver.

Then again, he wasn't as hot as he'd been in years past. He'd stepped down after the opening Daytona 500 this season thanks to a crash and burn that had left him with a dislocated shoulder and a hell of a lot of pain.

The shoulder had been fixed and he no longer screamed with every deep breath, but he still wasn't the same.

"It's all about confidence, folks. And it seems that Clint MacAllister may have lost his."

That's what the press was speculating, but Clint knew better. He hadn't lost anything. Hell, no. He'd gained an insight into his life. Namely, that he didn't have one. He'd been so busy with his career for the past fifteen years that he'd had little time for anything else. No wife. No kids. Nothing but a gigantic house on the outskirts of Dallas filled with boxes that he hadn't had time to unpack in the two years since he'd purchased it.

But all that was changing. He'd taken the retirement he'd planned for the following year. He'd found another driver for his race team and now he watched from the sidelines.

As an owner, he had a lot more time and energy to devote to other things, like unpacking, getting a Blue Heeler named Jezebel, and noticing the bright green eyes of the woman standing in front of him.

But while he had time to notice, he didn't have time for anything more. There was a roomful of rowdy groomsmen who needed some organization, not to mention a nervous groom desperate for a little moral support. Clint was the best man. Better yet, he was a reformed man since the shoulder injury that had changed his life and put him on the straight and narrow path to the altar.

He'd hosted his last bachelor party. Next time around, Clint intended to be the guest of honor.

He grinned. "I'd like to help you out, but this banana's spoken for. If you want to let me go get my jacket, I'll hook you up with an autographed picture." That usually did the trick for most women.

She gave him a puzzled look before realization seemed to hit her. She shook her head. "No, no, that's not what I mean." Another shake and the soft blond curls framing her face trembled. "I mean, that *is* what I mean. Sort of." She blew out a deep breath and licked her bottom lip, drawing his full attention to her mouth.

She had a really great mouth with full, pouty pink lips. The kind a man fantasized about feeling against his own.

"Where's a cookie when you really need one?" she murmured.

"I thought you wanted a banana?"

"I do, but not your banana."

Okay, it was one thing to be too reformed to get picked up, and quite another to be told he wasn't worthy of the effort.

He frowned. "What's wrong with my banana?"

"Nothing." Her cheeks flooded. "I'm sure your banana's fine."

"As if you don't know. I saw you checking me out."

"I was not checking you out."

"You stood here a full minute just staring."

"I was not staring."

"Forget a minute. It was more like two. Maybe even three."

"Maybe I was staring." She blew out an exasperated

breath. "But you caught me off guard. I didn't expect to find anybody in here."

"Right. You probably followed me in."

"I did not follow you in."

"You still checked me out." He eyed her.

She eyed him back. "Maybe I did and maybe I didn't. But it's not your banana I'm after right now. It's Jenny's."

"Jenny's banana is this close to tossing his cookies, so I'd keep my distance if I were you."

She shook her head again and blinked frantically. "Not banana as in male member, though I can see how you would be confused by the phallic symbolism given our present situation. I'm looking for Jenny's banana *bridesmaid*. The girl wearing the yellow." At his confused look, she added, "She didn't choose just one color. Instead, she went with a fruit theme for everything."

"That should make for some interesting pictures."

"You're telling me—Ohmigod!" She glanced at her watch and panic lit her eyes. "It's almost time for the inspection and I'm still missing the banana!" She whirled and reached for the door.

"The patio out back," he called after her.

She paused. "I beg your pardon?"

"The guys are on the back patio watching the Busch Series. They race on Saturdays. Winston races on Sunday. That way drivers can race in both series if they want."

"That's very informative, but what does it have to do with the banana?"

"My guess is you'll find her out back since she obviously likes keeping company with the men, otherwise you wouldn't have been raiding the men's room."

She looked so grateful and relieved that he heard himself say, "And it isn't time. You still have a few minutes."

"What are you talking about?"

"Jiles always bumps the inspection time up by a half-hour to give himself a safety net for just this sort of situation." At her puzzled expression, he added, "It's my eighth wedding in the past five years. Jiles has been the wedding planner for five of them."

"You've been in *eight* weddings?"

"Actually I've been in sixteen, but the other eight were back in my twenties. I was just a groomsman in those. In the last eight, I've been the best man."

"This is my first wedding and first time as maid of honor and—Ohmigod. You're him." She looked as if he'd grown two heads. "You're that cowboy guy."

He shrugged. "I'm not really a cowboy, but if that floats your boat, all the better." What the hell was he doing?

You're flirting, buddy.

Hell and damnation, he wasn't supposed to be flirting. Flirting led to other things, *naked* things, and he'd promised himself no more when he'd popped the question to Darla, his intended and the best damned media contact at Daytona International Speedway.

So what if she hadn't exactly said yes.

"I'm really flattered, Clint. I like you so much. You're a master behind the wheel, but in the bedroom . . . I'm afraid the sex just isn't that great. But hey, I still want to be friends."

Most men would have crawled away with their tail between their legs, but Clint had never gotten anywhere by letting others keep him from what he really wanted.

Darla was the woman for him. They had the same things in common. He could talk to her about his latest transmission adjustment or the new shock he'd just developed and she didn't look at him as if he'd just sprouted a second head. Even more, Darla was down to earth. Simple. She wasn't one of those uppity-up types who thought they were better than everyone else. Darla was real and she didn't look down on him because of his dyslexia. She treated him like everyone else.

That's why he intended to come up with a strategy and approach her again when his race team returned to Daytona in a few weeks for the Pepsi 400. He just wasn't so sure what he intended to say, much less do.

Yet.

"I can't believe you're him. He's you. And you're right here."

"Listen, don't take this personally, but I can't do this. I'm practically engaged. *This* close to tying the knot myself."

"Can't do what?"

"Waste time with flirting."

"Waste time . . . ?" The words seemed to strike a chord and she glanced at her watch. "I—I really need to go. Jiles is going to freak."

"Maybe this will help." He reached into his pocket and pulled out an individually wrapped peppermint. "The male equivalent of a cookie. Actually, a cigarette would be the equivalent, but I gave up those last year." He held out the candy to her. "Try it. It's not too bad."

"It's not chocolate, but it does have the prerequisite sugar." She popped the mint into her mouth and smiled at him again. "Thanks and I'm sorry I walked in on you. I don't usually bust into men's rooms unannounced."

"What sort of announcement do you usually use?"

Her smile widened. "I don't bust in at all. It's a day of firsts all the way around."

For Clint, as well, because for the first time in his life, he let a beautiful woman desperate for a banana simply walk away from him.

"Angel food cake?" Skye blinked and eyed the eight-tiered wedding cake towering in front of her. It was a spectacular display of light, fluffy white cake covered with low-fat whipped cream and topped with a mound of fresh, sliced fruit. It was a health nut's wet dream. "Isn't there a groom's cake somewhere?"

The waiter smiled and pointed to a nearby table.

Skye's gaze shifted to the mountain of trembling green gelatin decorated with dollops of white whipped cream. "That's a Jell-O mold, not a cake."

The man shook his head. "That's what the groom wanted."

"What happened to the chocolate cake? The groom always has a chocolate cake. It's tradition." That much she'd committed to memory from her *Weddings for Dummies* book.

"Chocolate is full of sugar and caffeine and the groom *is* a dietician."

She sighed. "No chocolate."

"Would you like powdered sugar sprinkled on your fruit? Or maybe a dollop of low-fat whipped cream?"

"Both."

"Both?"

"A double dose of both."

A few moments later, Skye juggled two plates and made her way toward one of the round tables set off to the side. She'd spent all of dinner sitting at the head table with Jenny on her left and the peach bridesmaid on her right. Not a bad spot since they'd been served dinner—

yummy sesame balls dipped in tofu sauce with a side of steamed cauliflower—before the other guests.

If only the banana bridesmaid hadn't insisted on leaning forward and flirting down the table with Clint, who'd been on Duke's left.

Her gaze went to Clint MacAllister. He was standing on the other side of the dance floor near the giant cauliflower-shaped ice sculpture. A petite redhead clad in a severe brown jacket and skirt flanked him. She looked to be in her mid-thirties, her expression calm, her gaze serious. Unlike the endless line of smiling women that wound its way around the ballroom and out the door—thanks to Celibate and Loving It, a local women's group whose annual dinner was taking place in the second ballroom opposite the reception. They'd invaded the reception, eager for a picture and a chance to talk to Cowboy himself.

The Cowboy. She still couldn't believe it was actually him. *In the flesh.*

And boy, what flesh.

At least from the posterior vantage point. She'd memorized that in the few frantic moments she'd been in the men's room.

The front looked equally impressive. He had short, cropped brown hair, a strong jaw, a smooth, perfect nose that wasn't too small or too big, and lips that hinted at fullness. Not too full, mind you. Just enough to make her think about how they would feel nibbling at her bottom lip, trailing down her neck, skimming her collarbone.

Broad shoulders accented a trim waist. He had an athlete's body that filled out the tuxedo to perfection. In fact, she would be willing to bet there wasn't an ounce of body fat anywhere on him, and she would also be willing to conduct the search for said fat herself.

Skye fought back the urge.

Despite the fierce attraction she felt, she wasn't about to act on it. He was engaged and while she didn't believe in marriage for herself, she certainly wouldn't infringe on another woman's territory. Another woman's marriage-minded territory.

But while he was off limits lust-wise, there wasn't anything to stop her from approaching him and thanking him for steering her in the right direction.

She'd found the banana smack dab in the middle of the half-dozen groomsmen and ushers glued to the television watching this week's Busch Series race.

Not that Skye had known the Busch series from the Winston Cup series before Clint had clued her in. Her own father had spent most of his time off somewhere promoting animal conservation or preparing his latest paper. He'd let Jacqueline Farrel set the example when it came to their three daughters, and she'd shown them only the things important to her—her passion for literature written by and for females, her zest for preaching equality of the sexes, and her mission to emancipate all women from the invisible chains of male domination.

Right now, Skye's mission was all the way around the other side of the dance floor.

Chapter Four

"This is not in my job description."

Clint glanced at the petite redhead to his left. She held a stack of pictures in one hand and dangled a hotel room key in the other, courtesy of the adoring fan he'd just handed a picture to.

He grinned. "You're my personal assistant, Lindy. That room key is personal, therefore you're obliged by law to assist with it."

Back in high school, Clint had been a stupid kid struggling through Mr. Montgomery's eighth-grade English class, a heap behind on his assignments thanks to his dyslexia, and Melinda Beckendorf had been the geeky honors student who'd never had to struggle with anything except the zipper on her Gloria Vanderbilt jeans.

He'd helped her out one day after school when some of the "in" girls had been picking on her. In turn, she'd agreed to help him out with his assignments.

Since they'd both been fanatics for ice cream, they'd met at the Tasty Freeze after school at least three days a week for vanilla cones and reading. The meetings had continued until the day after their graduation when Clint had driven his souped-up '69 Mustang out of the city limits and she'd headed for San Antonio and St. Mary's University.

Five years passed before they bumped into each other at the same Tasty Freeze while visiting their folks, but it might well have been five minutes. Lindy was still Lindy—crazy about vanilla cones and always willing to listen to his problems. And help, if possible.

And so she'd taken the job he'd offered—he'd needed someone smart and honest to assist with the business end of his race team—and she'd been his assistant ever since.

She was as nice a woman as she'd been a young girl. And just as prim and stuffy.

"I'll handle it right into the trash," she said.

"At least it's just a key. These women are celibate, remember? All that deprivation probably has them ready to spew like a volcano. I'm surprised that no one's ripped her clothes off and attacked me right here."

"You are so full of yourself."

"It's called confidence, and women like it."

"There's a fine line between confidence and cockiness. You're definitely riding the fence with a comment like that."

"Have I told you you're fired today?"

"If only." Lindy blew out a disgusted breath and passed him another picture to hand to the next woman who gushed and blushed and stepped up in line. "Just hurry up," she said under her breath before calling out, "Next!" to the line of women.

"I just love you, Mr. Clint," a woman gushed. "You're so wonderful. I just know everything the press is saying isn't true. Why, I know you're not afraid of anything."

" 'Course not, sugar." Clint forced a smile and winked.

"Can I give you a kiss?" Before Clint could respond, the woman planted one right on his cheek. "Ohmigod," she exclaimed as she stumbled back a few steps. "I did it. I kissed Cowboy MacAllister. I actually *kissed* him!"

"Don't these women have any pride?" Lindy grumbled when the kisser had retreated to her group of friends a few feet away. "This is a wedding, for heaven's sake. A sacred time in a couple's life. Don't they feel the least bit embarrassed about crashing the reception?"

"Jenny and Duke haven't even noticed. Besides, I like being busy. It keeps me away from my family and saves me from having to hear 'So when are you tying the knot?' *Again*." He took a sip of champagne. He never touched the stuff, but he needed something to numb the pain of several dozen nosy relatives.

"Such is the curse of being single in a big family. At least your family cares."

"So does yours."

"Let's not even go there."

Clint knew from the closed expression on Lindy's face to let the subject drop.

He grinned. "I think Uncle Jack, there"—he motioned to his sixty-something-year-old uncle who was also a retired security guard—"is hoping for a riot so he can flex a little muscle."

"Men," Lindy muttered. "Always looking for an excuse to act like a big shot."

"Lighten up. Hey, there, darlin'," Clint said to the next woman. Another grin and a wink and he handed over a picture. "It's all in good fun," he told Lindy.

"It's not supposed to be fun. It's business. Why, there was a time when you would only see drivers do sports interviews with real reporters or serious news anchors. Now they've got Dale Jr. on MTV, not to mention your golden boy, Tuck Briggs. He was a guest VJ just last Friday night. A *Friday* of all nights. There he was shaking his ass to the new Beyoncé tune when he should have been focused on the next day's qualifier."

Tucker Briggs was the hot young rookie currently driving Clint's infamous #62 Chevy. Tuck wasn't just gaining popularity by winning race after race, however. He was also gaining a reputation as one of the wolf pack—a line of hot, hip drivers who brought NASCAR into mainstream culture. And Clint was the leader of the wolf pack.

"MTV boosts awareness which increases the fan base which puts more money in all of our pockets."

"I know, I know," Lindy grumbled. "It's not your dad's sport anymore," she repeated the mantra she'd heard him say time and time again when it came to marketing. "It's just I think the focus should be on driving, not on the driver and how cute he is and how well he can shake his ass."

"Lindy. It's publicity."

"It's bad publicity."

"There's no such thing. Hey, there, Grandma Jean," he said to the little gray-haired woman who stepped up in line. "You don't have to stand in line for a picture. I'll send you as many as you want. Lindy, make a note to get my Grandma Jean a nice big stack of pictures."

"Pictures?" The ninety-something woman pushed her glasses up onto her nose and stared at Clint, then Lindy. "I thought this was the buffet line." She studied the autographed picture. "I'd rather have some shrimp."

"No shrimp, Grandma," Lindy said in a loud, pronounced voice reserved for toddlers and anyone with a hearing aid. "But I hear they have some meatless meat-balls over by the champagne fountain."

"Meatless meat?" Grandma wrinkled her nose.

"Meatless meat*balls*," Lindy emphasized. "Tofu. It's a healthy alternative."

"When you tie the knot, young man"—Grandma wagged a finger at Clint—"and you'd better make it soon because you're not getting any younger—you make sure to serve some decent food if you want me to come. I declare, I've never in all my life seen such a travesty . . ." Her words faded as she hobbled off.

"Excuse me." The voice followed by a small tap on his shoulder drew Clint around. He knew who it was even before he saw the bright green eyes glittering back at him.

Before he could open his mouth, Lindy leaned in and handed a picture to the woman.

"Don't compromise your beliefs for this man. He's not worth it, and he's not sleeping with you."

The woman smiled and held the picture with slim fingers. "I know. He already told me. He's engaged."

"He is?" Lindy's gaze made a beeline for him.

He shrugged. "I was going to tell you when all the details were ironed out."

Lindy frowned. "It's a shotgun wedding, isn't it? I knew this whole bad-boy image was bound to get you into trouble. Some poor girl is claiming you knocked her up, banking on the fact that you're some hot playboy who sleeps around and—"

"It's not a shotgun wedding and nobody's claiming anything. It's just . . . it's pending, that's all."

"You have an engagement that's *pending*?" She shook her head. "It's too late for me to be hearing this. I can't think when I'm tired. Or stressed. I *really* need my bunny slippers," she muttered as she turned to gather her things. "I'm calling it a night. Give Duke and Jenny my love." She snatched up her briefcase and stalked out of the ballroom.

"I didn't have a chance to introduce myself earlier. My name is Skye Farrel."

"The maid of honor."

"Only for the next hour or two." She reached up, her fingertip dabbing at his cheek. "Nice shade of lipstick."

He grinned. "Thanks."

She pulled her hand away. "You were right about the banana. She was right where you said she'd be. Thanks. Otherwise, I would be a chalk outline on the floor right now."

"Jiles is just a little high strung. He's really harmless."

"So sayeth the wedding expert. He likes you. You know what to do. You're an old pro at all of this."

"You'll get there. It just takes time."

"Not for me. Once is enough. I've had my fill. No more weddings. Not ever. I'll send a gift, but that's it. Speaking of which, good luck with your own." She glanced at the black-and-white publicity shot she held. "Nice picture." And then she handed it back to him.

"You can keep it," he told her as she turned. "I've got plenty more."

"That's okay. I'm not really into NASCAR."

Not into NASCAR? Right. She'd followed him into the men's room earlier and made a point of singling him out here at the reception. She was into NASCAR, and she wanted to be into him. She was playing hard to get, thinking that if she acted uninterested, he would be just the opposite.

Either that, or she was for real.

He weighed the notion as he watched her walk away from him for the second time that day.

Nah. She wanted him, all right.

Too bad he couldn't oblige her, but Clint MacAllister had his mind set on something, and he wouldn't change it, no matter how hot the chemistry.

He was tying the knot and settling down. It was just a matter of time.

She'd touched him.

The thought stuck in Skye's head as she made her way back to the small table where she'd left her cake plates. She hadn't meant to touch him, but then she'd seen the lipstick spot and it had only been natural that she reach up. She'd always been a touchy, feely person. She would have done the same with any man.

But he'd been warmer than she'd expected, his skin slightly rough thanks to a five o'clock shadow that made him look all the more dark and delicious.

Not that she was interested.

She had her principles, after all.

Skye had just retrieved a glass of champagne and slid into a seat when Xandra collapsed beside her.

"You haven't danced one dance."

"I'm drinking instead." She held up her glass of champagne. "I'm too stressed to dance. Besides, you're dancing enough for the both of us."

"That's because I love to dance but Mark doesn't." Mark was Xandra's on-again, off-again boyfriend of seven years. They were currently on-again, but he was out of town on a business project. "I don't want him to feel left out, so I keep my dancing shoes in the closet when he's around."

"Suppressing your own desires to please a man. Mom would be so proud."

She pinned Skye with a stare that said *you're not changing the subject*. "The wedding's over. You survived. You should be rejoicing like everybody else."

She should have been, but the only thing she felt like doing was diving into the mound of low-fat whipped cream that topped her angel food cake.

Her gaze shifted to the overflowing dance floor. It was the typical hodgepodge of guests found at family events. There were couples of all ages swaying to Shania Twain's "Still the One". Jenny's two great aunts, who'd lost their husbands eons ago, waltzed with each other. Duke's great-grandmother held the hands of the five-year-old flower girl and twisted side to side as if Chubby Checker himself were on the stage dictating the movements. Every few seconds a shriek sounded as children darted through the maze, chasing each other while their parents enjoyed the music.

Skye's attention focused on the bride and groom, who were plastered together, arms wrapped around each other as if they'd been permanently welded into position.

"You miss Jenny," Xandra stated as she dipped her finger into Skye's whipped cream and took a taste.

"She's just going to Jamaica for two weeks. I can make do until then."

"That's not what I mean. You miss the old Jenny. The single Jenny."

But Skye didn't miss Jenny. She envied her.

Not because she'd said "I Do". Skye had no intention of stuffing herself into an overdone dress to stand in front of her friends and family and trade her freedom for a wedding ring, even if it were a platinum gold band with a two-carat marquis diamond surrounded by baguettes.

Skye Farrel could buy her own ring. What she couldn't buy was a man.

"Uh-oh."

"What?" She glanced at Xandra, who scooped another finger full of whipped cream.

"You've got the fever," she said as she licked the white fluff.

"I feel fine, with the exception of a pounding heart and a frantic craving for some real sugar, but those are stress-related."

"Not that kind of fever. Wedding fever."

"Impossible. I'm anti-wedding."

"It doesn't matter. It's the whole love and commitment thing. It makes all of us singles feel like there's this big club and we're not allowed inside because we haven't found it."

"It?"

"Him. Mr. Right. Some guy to fulfill all of our dreams and make us supremely happy."

"Men don't make us happy," she recited the mantra she'd heard time and time again growing up. "We make ourselves happy."

"True, but having the right man by our side adds a heap of happiness."

The comment stuck in Skye's mind over the next half hour as she watched the newlyweds. Jenny's eyes glowed and she had this silly smile on her face that wouldn't seem to go away. A smile that said supreme happiness and told the entire world she'd finally found a man who fulfilled the infamous Holy Commitment Trinity.

Skye couldn't help but want her own Commitment man.

The hot sex had never been a problem. She was a firm believer in chemistry and she never pursued a man who didn't press her lust buttons. Ditto for mutual respect. The men she dated were nice guys with decent jobs and big hearts. She respected them and they always respected her.

But shared interests . . .

There was the kicker because Skye Farrel was a victim of Darwin's Theory. She tended to gravitate toward macho, he-man types. Guys who oozed testosterone.

A man's man.

A man like Clint MacAllister.

Her gaze zeroed in on him and she watched as he handed out yet another picture. She'd been honest with him. She didn't follow NASCAR or any other male-dominated sport.

She collected teacups and spent her off-time cruising shoe stores and trying on everything that was skimpy and sexy and high. Not that she bought any of them. Skye had a serious, professional image to maintain and so she stuck to practical. But she did like to look.

Most certainly there were men out there who enjoyed either of her two favorite activities. The trouble was, she wasn't remotely attracted to them. What she really wanted was a hunka-hunka man like her last boyfriend, Dirk the Fireman. And the one before him—Dwayne the Policeman. Then there was Curt the weight lifter and Brock the construction worker and Steve the high school football coach. All strong, smart, handsome and great in bed—all NASCAR fans, by the way—and not one of them had lasted longer than six months. Once the new romance rush had slowed down, she'd realized they didn't share enough interests to make things last.

She didn't really blame the men, though. It was the proverbial I-wouldn't-belong-to-a-country-club-who-would-have-me-for-a-member syndrome. She didn't want a man who collected teacups in his spare time, or who went all soft inside at the sight of a slinky pair of Anne Kleins.

She wanted a 'til-death-do-us-part of her own, minus the license and the ceremony, of course. A man to come home to, grow old with. A man with whom she could have a committed, long-term relationship.

Holy Commitment Trinity Nirvana.

Since that was about as likely as Jacqueline Farrel hosting an episode of *A Wedding Story*, Skye settled for the next best thing.

Another slice of cake and another glass of champagne.

She needed a bathroom *now*. The six glasses of champagne she'd drunk demanded it.

Skye eyed the line of women stationed outside the two-stall ladies' room and frustration welled inside her.

Why was there never a line outside the men's room?

Before she could change her mind, she pushed through the men's room door. A quick visual sweep confirmed that the place was empty. It was small with only one stall and one wall urinal and . . . Yes! A lock on the door.

After throwing the lock, she wedged herself into the stall. If only she could get the dress up and the blasted panties down . . . Ah, there.

Her relief lasted only until she finished, stood up and tried to bend to retrieve the panties that had slid to her an-

kles. There just . . . didn't . . . seem to be . . . enough . . .
room . . . to actually . . . *move*.

Bam, bam!

"Someone's in here," she called out, her fingers frantic, her heartbeat furious. "Just a minute!"

The minute turned into several before she finally managed to get the panties up and her dress down. But then she tried to turn and there was simply too much dress and not enough space.

"Everything okay in there?" came a muffled voice, followed by another loud knock.

Okay? *Okay?*

She was tipsy *and* dizzy *and* alone *and* in desperate need of a cookie. Everything was far from . . . *rippp!*

She glanced down to see a huge slash in the side of her dress where it had caught on the toilet-paper holder when she'd exited the stall.

She blinked back a surge of ridiculous tears—she was drunk, but not that drunk. Not enough to cry over the loss of such a hideous dress.

Bam, bam, bam—

She threw open the door to find one of the groomsmen standing on the other side. He was twenty-something with dark hair and dimples and great eyes and . . . cute. He was majorly cute. Especially when he smiled at her the way he was doing right now.

"I'm sorry. I had to go," she explained.

His smile faded and his expression grew anxious. "I know the feeling." He wedged past her and then dropped a bomb that destroyed what tiny bit of self-control she'd managed to recover. "Excuse me, ma'am."

She was tipsy and dizzy and alone and in desperate need of anything close to a cookie *and* she was a *ma'am.*

Tears welled in her eyes and she blinked frantically as she started down the main hallway toward the reception. She was not going to cry. She never cried. Real women didn't cry over their problems, they looked for answers. They acted rather than reacted. They—

The mental spiel stumbled to a halt when Skye glanced inside an open set of double doors, into the ballroom opposite the reception area. She stared past clusters of women, to the far side of the room. On a white, linen covered table sat the answer to at least one of her problems. Mounds of chocolate-dipped strawberries topped a five-tier, fudge-frosted cake drizzled with white chocolate sauce and . . . *yum*.

She closed her eyes and tried to calm the sudden pounding of her heart. Here she'd spent the past three hours torturing herself with low-fat whipped cream, when relief had been just across the main hallway. She should have known. Where there were celibate women, there was sure to be chocolate.

Before she could stop herself, she made her way over to the cake, lured by its sweet promise and driven by her pounding heart and frazzled nerves. She swiped a piece and walked calmly toward the exit.

A few seconds later, she slipped through an open pair of French doors that led to a small, isolated garden. Blessed darkness swallowed her up just as she shoved a forkful of cake into her mouth. Taste exploded on her tongue and sent a rush of pleasure through her. She took another bite and her anxiety eased enough for her to actually breathe again. Another and she actually groaned. There was nothing like dark, sweet, rich choc—

"That must be some piece of cake." The deep, familiar voice came from behind and sent a jolt of awareness through her. Her fingers faltered and her fork clattered to the ground as she whirled.

She found herself face-to-face with none other than Clint MacAllister. Moonlight played over his features as he stared down at her. An amused smile curved his lips. His eyes twinkled. "Looking for another banana?"

She swallowed the mouthful that had lodged in her throat. "Banana?"

"I knew the picture thing had to be a put-on." He sounded tremendously relieved. "You followed me out here."

"I didn't even know you were out here."

"Look, you don't have to pretend." His eyes took on a sympathetic twinkle. "I know most women in your situation get nervous and act a little nuts, but it's totally understandable. Still, I'm a person like anybody else. You should just come straight out and tell me what you want."

"The only thing I want right now is another fork." Her stomach grumbled for more of the goodie on her plate.

"Not that I can give you what you want. You're good-looking and all, but I'm through with good-looking women."

She eyed him. "So you're going after good-looking men now, is that it?"

"What?" He shook his head, his expression hardening as realization seemed to hit him. "No. Hell, no."

"It's okay. I've got a thing for good looking men, too." She smiled.

And then she frowned.

Her stomach whirled from the sudden mix of chocolate and champagne. Heat fired her cheeks and her mouth went dry.

"Are you okay?"

No. "Yes, I—I'm fine." She stumbled toward a nearby wrought-iron patio chair and sank down as a wave of dizziness swept through her.

"You don't look okay." He sat down in the chair next to hers.

"I'm fine," she murmured again as she settled the plate on her lap and waited for the ground to stop shaking. "I really am." She blinked and swallowed and fought for a deep, calming breath. "It's just the champagne."

"I've had several glasses myself." He held up a flute.

"And this wedding," she went on, the words tumbling out in a rush before she could stop them. "It's really getting to me. I'm not big on weddings and then there's this dress and I ripped it and then this young Freddie Prinze Jr., Justin Timberlake, 'N-Sync looking *guy* called me *'ma'am'* and it's been months since I've had a date, much less an actual relationship and . . ." The words trailed into a huge sob and she blinked frantically. She was *not* going to cry. And she certainly wasn't going to cry in front of anyone. Particularly Clint MacAllister.

Cripes, what was she doing?

Reality hit and she swiped at her eyes as embarrassment flooded her. "I'm sorry." She sniffled. "You don't want to hear any of this."

"Sure I do." He sounded so nice and sincere, that she actually believed him. Or maybe she was just drunk and her judgment slightly impaired.

"You should be inside with your family and your fans." She sniffled again.

"True." He reached into his pocket, pulled out a hand-kerchief and offered it to her. "But a guy can only take so much."

"Thanks." She dabbed at her eyes.

He downed the rest of his champagne. "Don't get me wrong. I love my family, but I get tired of hearing, 'It's time for you to settle down, Clint,' and the ever-popular 'You're not getting any younger, son.' I know all of that, that's why I'm trying to do something about it."

"Aren't they happy about you getting married?"

"They don't exactly know about it yet. I was waiting until we ironed out a few details."

"Until you set a wedding date?"

"Until she actually says yes."

"You haven't proposed yet?" The ground settled and her face started to cool.

"Actually, I have. She said no, but that's just temporary. We have a few issues to work out, then she'll say yes. We were made for each other. She knows as much as I do about racing and she wants a big family. I want the same."

"It sounds like you have a lot in common. That is *so* important, and so hard to find. I've got it covered on the hot sex and the mutual respect, but it's the common interests where I keep coming up short."

Now why had she said that?

Because she was going on a full thirty-six hours with hardly any sleep and she'd just had the most stressful, unbelievable day of her life. She'd worn the most god-awful purple dress and endured Jiles and chugged six glasses of champagne and now she was sitting next to none other than Cowboy MacAllister, NASCAR wonder boy. It was unbelievable, all right. Downright crazy, even, and Skye didn't react well to crazy.

Or to such a quiet, serene ambience. The only light drifted out from the double doors just off to their left and small twinkling lights situated throughout the garden.

Crickets buzzed and the sound of music filtered out from far away. Everything seemed so . . . distant. As if she were far removed from reality and caught in a dream. And so it didn't matter what she said.

"Do you know that I didn't recognize you at all?" she told him. "You're a NASCAR icon, and I had no clue. I'm single and thirty-three and I haven't got a clue when it comes to men. Sure, I know them biologically, but that's it. I don't know what they think. What they like. No wonder I'm alone with nothing but a dog for companionship. I'll never have a real relationship if I can only ace two of the Holy Commitment Trinity."

"I think I saw something about that Trinity thing on TV."

"It's been on the news, on talk shows. It's even been mentioned on *Will & Grace*, which really boosted my mother's popularity."

"Your mother?"

"Jacqueline Farrel. She's the one who came up with the theory when I was two years old. She's been preaching it ever since. She hosts her own late-night segment called *Get Sexed Up*."

"I've seen that show. The doctor's really your mother?"

"The one and only."

"She's a little stiff."

"She's just strong in her beliefs. And she firmly believes the Trinity is the way to ensure a successful relationship."

"My parents have been married for over fifty years. They've got ten kids and lots of respect for each other, and they do both love golf."

"There you go. The awesome threesome in action,

minus the marriage part. My mother doesn't do marriage. Neither do I. But I would like to have one special some-one in my life. I just can't seem to find someone who likes the things I like. Not that I would want someone who likes the things I like, anyway. I want a guy who likes guy stuff. Stuff like football and wrestling and rac-ing."

"That shouldn't be too hard to find. I know a few dozen of them myself."

"They're not hard to find. The problem is, I don't have the same interests. The only thing I'm good at is shopping and spotting rare pieces of china—namely tea cups. And sex. I'm great at sex, but then it's my job."

"*What*?"

"Not job as in having sex. Job as in talking about sex. Teaching it. I own Girl Talk. I give private parties and conduct lectures that teach women how to find the ulti-mate pleasure. Jenny's my assistant."

"Duke mentioned something about Jenny working for an educational company, but I was thinking more along the lines of academics. Not that I can't see the need for a sex company. I can. Sex can be a tough subject. I've spent all these years more focused on quantity, only to find out it's more about quality."

"You're having quality control problems?"

His shoulders squared and he seemed to stiffen. "I wouldn't exactly call it a problem. More like a few unan-swered questions. I know I'm good in bed." He seemed to think about his statement. His voice grew deeper and he added, "At least, I thought I was good in bed. Every-body I've ever been with said so, but how does a guy *really* know? I thought the sex was good between me and Darla—not that it happened very often with my busy schedule and the fact that I only raced Daytona twice a year, which means I only saw her twice a year—but she obviously didn't think so."

"She won't marry you because of the sex?" When he cleared his throat and muttered yes, she smiled. "That's lucky for you."

"What do you mean?"

"Sex is important, but it's the least worrisome of the Holy Commitment Trinity. You can learn how to have great sex. I teach women how to achieve the ultimate sexual pleasure in a simple four-part workshop."

Teach.

The word stuck in her head and an idea sparked.

A crazy, ridiculous idea that didn't seem nearly that crazy or ridiculous while sitting outside in a huge purple dress.

Instead, it seemed the answer to both their problems.

Skye smiled as she murmured, "Have I got a proposition for you."

Chapter Five

"So do you want to be on top, or on bottom? Personally, having the woman on top is my favorite position, but I like missionary, too."

"Who *is* this?" Skye demanded as she held on to the phone while struggling into an upright position.

Not an easy feat for a woman still wearing last night's purple dress and nursing a monster of a headache. She pushed and pulled at her favorite three-hundred thread count, cream-colored linen sheets and did her best to ignore the pounding in her temples and the sinking feeling in the pit of her stomach. Meanwhile, Skipper barked her dissatisfaction with being upended off the edge of the dress where she'd fallen asleep.

"Clint," the deep, masculine voice declared. "Clint MacAllister."

NASCAR's finest and the star of last night's hot dream.

He'd been naked except for his cowboy hat and Skye was naked except for a pair of red stiletto heels that would have done Barbie herself proud. They'd touched and kissed and had wound up facing each other on the back of a giant mechanical bull.

"There's always doggie style. That's a personal favorite, too."

Skye forced the sexual image aside and tried to concentrate on his words. Not very easy since it was his voice itself that sparked the image. He sounded so deep and sexy, as if he were *this* close, whispering a few naughty suggestions in her ear.

"But I'm open to new positions," Clint went on. "I know this is supposed to be a learning experience."

She blinked away the fog and focused on reality. "What are you talking about?"

"Our agreement."

The minute he said the word, the past night rushed full force through her head.

The men's bathroom.

The garden.

Her proposal.

His acceptance.

The exchange of phone numbers.

The stop at the twenty-four-hour Get-N-Go around the corner from her apartment for a bag of Chips Ahoy.

Her gaze shot to the nightstand and the empty bag. Crumbs littered her dress and the sheet and she knew beyond a doubt that she hadn't been dreaming. She'd actually propositioned Clint MacAllister.

Worse, she'd eaten a whole bag of cookies.

"Hello?"

"I'm here. Sort of. Could you hold on for a second?" Before he could reply, she reached for the half-empty Diet Coke sitting on the nightstand next to a mangled purple napkin with *Jenny and Duke* printed in rainbow foil.

She chugged the lukewarm contents. There wasn't enough caffeine to clear the cobwebs and so she shook her head and blinked her eyes several times.

"Hello?" he prodded.

"I told you to hold on."

"Yeah, but you're still there. I can hear you breathing. Or maybe you're panting. I knew you were hot for me."

"I'm not panting and I'm certainly not hot for you. That's my dog. She's hot for a treat. I'm merely doing something and I can't talk."

"Don't tell me you're eating another cookie?"

She glanced around. "How do you know I ate cookies?"

"I drove you home. You had a little too much to drink at the wedding and your sister was busy dancing, so I offered to give you a ride. After watching you swipe another piece of cake from the celibate ladies, I didn't think you could put away any more sweets. But I swear you ate half the bag before I left you at your apartment."

"You were here? In my apartment?"

"I suppose I could have just driven by and shoved you out the door. I was tempted after you started spilling crumbs all over my Hummer. But I've got a reputation to uphold."

"Cocky and arrogant and stuck on yourself?"

"Confident and self-assured and comfortable in my skin."

"Same thing."

"Despite the lack of sexual skills, I'm known as a ladies' man. A charmer. A roaming cowboy who stops off for a good time then rides off into the sunset. Dumping women on their front porch doesn't exactly fit with the image. Maybe if I dumped them after sex, but we haven't had sex yet so it just doesn't seem right."

She didn't miss the humor in his voice and she knew he was teasing her.

Charming her, and living up to that irresistible bad-boy image.

She thought back to last night, to the craving in the pit of her stomach and the way he'd looked the first moment she'd spotted him—so dark and handsome and hungry as he'd stared back at her. As if he'd really wanted to take a bite out of her.

Not a possibility. Clint MacAllister, for all his good looks, didn't have bite potential. Not as the biter or the bitee. He and his marriage-minded ideas put him at the top of her hands-off list.

"So you brought me all the way home?"

"All the way."

"Up the elevator and into my apartment?"

"And straight into your bedroom."

"You put me to bed?" She wiggled, feeling for her undies. There. Present and intact. Relief swamped her. He hadn't been completely teasing when he'd said they hadn't had sex. They really hadn't.

Yet.

The word rooted in her head as his voice slid into her ear. "Actually, I poured you into bed and left the rest of your cookies and your picture on the nightstand."

"Picture?" She eyed the black-and-white photo sitting next to the empty bag. Clint stood in his racing uniform, his helmet in his hand. "I told you I didn't really follow racing."

"Once I accepted your proposal, you told me how great I was and begged me for a picture."

She searched for the memory and came up with a very fuzzy version. "I did not beg."

"It sounded like begging to me."

She could practically hear his smile over the phone. No doubt the same cocky expression he wore in the picture.

Her heart did a double thump. She shifted her gaze to the scribbled CM in the lower right-hand corner. Her thumb brushed over the ink, which wasn't ink at all but part of the actual picture. "A pre-printed autograph?"

"It saves time. So when do you teach me how to go at it?"

She set the picture aside and plopped her Diet Coke can on top. "I'm not going to teach you how to *go at it*. I'm going to teach you how to pleasure a woman. There's a big difference."

"Sure. So which position do we start with?"

"Girl Talk is an information source, not a call-girl service. You'll receive an in-depth education on everything from the female anatomy to what to do to with said anatomy. We do have some hands-on exercises, but those are with educational tools. It's up to you to take the knowledge you acquire and apply it in practice." What was she saying? She wasn't really going to do this. No way was she going to coach Clint MacAllister on how to pleasure a woman.

And why not?

He was a guy, for heaven's sake, and her clientele were all women. She educated women, not men.

And why not?

Because her entire career had been geared toward providing women with information to make them sexually independent. To put them in charge of their own bodies and their own orgasms and their own pleasure. She couldn't sell herself out and change her entire mission statement just so she could learn firsthand how a man crushed a beer can against his forehead and avoided a concussion.

She had ethics. She had principles. She had . . . *a huge bedroom all to herself.*

Her gaze swept the room, from the sheer white curtains embossed with pink roses, to the white vanity table overflowing with makeup and perfume and flavored body gel courtesy of Xandra and her company, to the king-sized four-poster canopy bed where she half-sat, half-sprawled amid a pile of cookie crumbs and a Shih Tzu.

And you were saying?

Okay, so she had a frilly room that made men uncomfortable. That was still no reason to take on Cowboy Clint MacAllister as a client.

He was too exasperating with his slow, lazy smiles. Too infuriating with his twinkling, strip-you-bare blue eyes. Too intimidating with his in-your-face attitude.

Too much her type.

Which was the entire point. Who better to help her get the inside scoop on an alpha male than the poster boy himself?

At least that had been her thinking last night. But today, in the bright light of day with her answering machine blinking with a dozen messages, a few of which were sure to belong to her mother, it seemed so . . . traitorous.

She could practically hear her mother now.

"No daughter of mine would sacrifice her time studying a bunch of typically male-oriented subjects just to find a man. Why, it's the man who should be learning your interests. Think, Skye. No daughter of mine would change for a man. The man should be changing for you."

But she hadn't planned on actually changing who she

was. She just wanted to expand her interests, broaden her horizons, add a few more layers to her personality.

"So when do we get started? I really need to have this stuff down in the next three weeks, in time for the Pepsi 400. The race is at Daytona Speedway where Darla works as a PR rep. It'll be the perfect opportunity to get together with her and prove her wrong about the sex. I'll show off my newfound skills and she'll reconsider my proposal."

"You sound really sure of yourself."

"She said it was the sex. I fix that and it's all good. We've got two out of the Holy Three. Darla's the perfect woman. She knows everything about racing and she loves the sport. She can name every team in the NFL. She loves fried chicken."

"Your favorite food, I take it."

"Actually, chicken fried steak is my favorite food. But the point is, it's fried."

"You can both grow old and clog your arteries together."

"Exactly." The Texas accent faded as his voice took on a more serious note.

Skye had a sudden thought that maybe Cowboy MacAllister wasn't the one hundred percent good ole bad boy he pretended to be. He had a serious side.

The deep, self-assured ring to his voice sent an added thrill through her, even more than his charm-you-out-of-your-panties drawl.

"My schedule is hectic," he went on. "As the owner, I'm still as responsible for the team and its success as if I were actually driving the car. This week I can do Monday—tomorrow—and Thursday. Next week my schedule is pretty much the same, but I'll be home Wednesday night. We'll get together then and—"

"I really need more notice than this. I already have several private bookings both this week and next." She crawled out of bed and tried to ignore the sensation in her chest. He had such a deep voice and with every word, she felt a flutter. The reaction made her forget about adding layers to her personality and, instead, made her think about peeling a few layers off her person and getting completely naked with the handsome race-car driver on the other end of the phone line.

You're crazy. You can't do this. You don't have to do this. A man will come along who shares your interests. He'll be handsome and caring and macho enough to ride a mechanical bull. All you have to do is be patient and proud. You're a vibrant, mature woman.

"Cancel something," Clint said.

"I can't cancel." *You're a woman who knows who she is and where she's going.*

"So work me in."

"Easier said than done. I need time to get a decent lesson plan ready." *A woman who doesn't have to sacrifice her sense of self just to find a man.*

"You probably know this stuff by heart. Just wing it."

"I don't wing it."

"Why not?"

"Because . . . because I don't. Sure, I know a lot about sex, but I still have to stay up on all the new studies. Speaking of which, I've got a seminar at the University of Dallas on Saturday that I'm still preparing for. I'll be busy every day this week." *A woman who doesn't need a man to validate her self-worth.*

"We'll get together in the evening."

"I've scheduled late afternoon sales meetings with the

people who supply my educational materials." *A woman who makes and plays by her own rules.*

"We'll get together at night."

"I'm a contributing writer for the local paper and I've got a column due next Monday. I do a question-and-answer thing on women and sex and relationships. Not that I'm currently in a relationship." *A pathetic, desperate woman who makes and plays by her own rules all by her lonesome.*

"The week after the weekend after next? I suppose we can do it if we cram—"

"Tomorrow," she blurted. "We'll get together first thing tomorrow."

"I think it's a great idea," Xandra said around a mouthful of Tic Tacs. She leaned back in a beige chair situated in the middle of Crosby's, one of the biggest and most elite shoe boutiques in Dallas, and popped another mint into her mouth. "I don't know why you didn't think of it before."

Skye eyed the mountains of boxes that surrounded her own chair before reaching for one. "Because I've never been a tipsy, nauseous maid of honor before." She pulled a pair of black satin, three-inch heeled sandals from a box and slid one on her right foot. "Oh, and did I mention lonely and desperate and depraved?" She shoved her left foot into the second and stood. "No wonder Mom's antiwedding." She took a few steps, came back, and, ignoring a twinge of longing, reached for a pair of red slingback pumps. "Weddings can definitely be hazardous to mental health. They give people unrealistic expectations about marriage. When real life doesn't measure up to the ideal, couples call a lawyer. No marriage, no lawyer, no expensive divorce. Non-marriage keeps things simple and sane."

"So sayeth the good, obedient eldest daughter. You've been watching way too much *Get Sexed Up*."

"The marriage spiel isn't from one of her shows, it's from Mom's second book."

"Oh." Xandra shrugged. "Okay, so I don't watch or read her, but at least I talk to her." She sucked a few seconds on her Tic Tacs—her new quitting smoking strategy—then pinned Skye with a stare. "You can talk to her now, you know. The wedding *is* over."

"But her oldest daughter doing something she would totally disapprove of is not. Mom would freak if she thought for an inkling of a second that one of her daughters was taking macho lessons in order to find a long-term relationship."

"I see your point. But I'm sick of being the only one she can actually get a hold of. That gets me all of her attention and her advice. If I hear one more time about how she gave Dad flowers for their non-anniversary rather than the other way around and how I should be the aggressor with Mark and just come out and tell him I want his sperm, I'm going to explode."

"You want Mark's sperm? As in, Mark's baby?"

"Not Mark's necessarily. Just a baby. I went to seven baby showers last month alone and in a weak moment I mentioned to Mom that I might actually like to have one of my own someday."

"I wouldn't mind a baby of my own, either" Skye said, eyeing a nearby pair of yellow pumps with small square heels. "Someday. Maybe."

"I never would have figured you for the maternal type."

"Why not? I'm an older sister. I've changed plenty of diapers in my day, including yours. Not that I really enjoyed it, but I know how to do it. And someday, I wouldn't mind doing it for a child or two. Maybe even three."

"Three." Xandra let loose a low whistle. "That would be a big responsibility."

"Responsibility's my middle name. Unlike some people." She pinned Xandra with a stare. "Couldn't you have given up a few dances to see your oldest sister safely home?"

"And deprive said oldest sister—single, lonely oldest sister—of the company of a really hot stud? The man is hot, and you propositioning him was a stroke of genius."

"I hope so." Skye reached for another box with a pair of tan slide-on mules with turquoise beading sewn onto the soft leather. "Wow. Look at these. Too high, huh?"

"Way too high, and do I detect a second thought?"

"No. Yes." She shook her head. "I don't know." She paused. "I am doing this, because it is the right thing to do. I'm just not so sure I *can* do it."

"Nonsense. You've taught sex to a zillion people."

"Women. I've taught sex to women. Clint hardly falls into that category."

Xandra seemed to think. "I see your point."

"I'm afraid I might feel uncomfortable."

"Maybe you should try that technique where you picture someone in their underwear. It makes them less threatening."

"I doubt that will work in this case."

"So picture him in ballet shoes and a tutu, and get on with it." Skye smiled and Xandra added, "And make sure you take lots of notes and pass them on to me."

Skye grabbed another box and unearthed a pair of high pink platform shoes. "Look at these."

"Barbie shoes if I've ever seen them," Xandra said.

Skye's passion for all things Barbie, particularly her shoes, stemmed from their childhood when Barbie had been a forbidden item in the Farrel household. Skye could still remember going to the local toy store and walking down the Barbie aisle coveting the different versions of the doll and all the accessories. Furniture. Clothes. Shoes.

Just as she was coveting Clint MacAllister now.

The intense physical attraction she felt for him and the lusty craving threatened her sanity, but made him all the more perfect. If she wanted to find and keep a man as macho as Clint MacAllister, a man who could scatter her thoughts and leave her speechless with just a glance and a smile, then she had to learn as much as possible about the activities he enjoyed.

Of course, in return, she had to teach him about females and their pleasure. That would be the easy part. She was a female, after all, and she knew what made for great pleasure.

Even more, she was a professional on the subject, and the next two weeks would be purely business.

She gave the pink platforms a last, long look before shoving them back into the box and reaching for the first box, which contained a pair of chunky, low-heeled black pumps that were on sale. Pumps that were practical and professional and comfortable and well within her budget.

"I'll just take these," she said, handing them to the salesperson.

Chapter Six

"I think Tucker's nervous," Jeep McGraw said as Clint took the phone from Lindy on Sunday afternoon. Since it was Sunday and a typical work day for him, Clint sat behind his desk going over the contracts Lindy had previewed for his approval. She stood a few feet away in front of a wall of file cabinets, a stack of paperwork in her hands.

"Forget think," Jeep went on. "I know he's nervous."

Jeep was the car chief responsible for the now infamous #62 red, white and Texas blue Chevrolet sponsored by Big Tex Motor Oil. Winning car of the past seven Winston Cup series championships, and a current contender for number eight if Tuck kept up his current winning streak.

"Naturally, he won't admit it," Jeep went on. "He's got that *it's-all-good* grin on his face like always. But he's pacing up a firestorm from one end of the garage to the next, and he *never* paces."

"He's nervous, all right." And with good reason.

Tuck was one of the youngest drivers to ever hit the

Winston Cup Series, and one of the best. Clint had spotted him the previous year in his first Busch Series, where he'd won a few races and shown a great deal of raw talent. But he hadn't been much of a contender for the championship thanks to a reckless streak and a rebellious attitude that had overshadowed his remarkable driving skills. After the Busch team fired him, Clint found him racing the short, local tracks in Texas and offered him the chance of a lifetime.

The chance to drive a winning car in the most prestigious NASCAR cup series, and the most lucrative.

"He's never raced Pocono before—only in test laps and that isn't even close to the real thing. You and I both know that it's one of the most difficult and frustrating tracks in NASCAR."

"I don't think that's it, boss. When he found out that you weren't flying in for the race, he had this strange look on his face. Like he was pissed off and hurt at the same time. Now he's acting like he couldn't care less. He didn't even give us any feedback to make final changes after yesterday's qualifier. Said the car was perfect right off the truck and he's good to go."

"Maybe he is."

"Maybe, and maybe he's going back to his old ways where he didn't give a shit. You know what they say, you can't teach an old dog new tricks."

"He's probably just wired because it's a difficult track," Clint replied as he punched the remote control and the big-screen TV that took up half his trophy wall flickered to life.

"Probably."

"You'll just have to reassure him."

"I don't think I like where this is going."

"Keep things as routine as possible."

"I really don't like where this is going."

"Just do what I do before each and every race so this doesn't seem like a bigger deal than any of the others."

Silence stretched for several long seconds before Jeep grumbled, "I'm *not* reading the menu from Buck's Barbecue and Babes. I'll adjust the throttle, restrict the air pressure, give the fuel system a tweak here and there. That's it. That's the end of my job."

"You're there to do anything and everything to bring home a victory. Just read it. It'll make him think about having lunch there tomorrow, which will make him think about flying to his home in Austin tonight, which will make him think about Victory Lane and all the press stuff that follows, which will make him think about the race. It's all about focus."

"Forget it. I'm a car chief, not a waiter."

"It'll work, and we've got ten wins so far to prove it."

"You don't pay me enough for this," Jeep grumbled before he hung up.

"The menu from Buck's Barbecue and Babes." Lindy gave him a disbelieving expression. "That's what you do those few seconds before he lines up in pit road?" She shook her head. "And here I thought you guys were praying or discussing strategy or something normal."

Clint shrugged. "It's his favorite restaurant."

"Buck's Barbecue and Babes is a gentlemen's club, not a restaurant. The biggest gentlemen's club in Austin, Texas, as a matter of fact. And the sleaziest. I heard Anna Nicole Smith got her start at Buck's. And her finish. One of the tabloids spotted her just a few days ago. A lot of her, if you know what I mean."

"I thought you didn't read the tabloids."

"Only when they feature this race team."

"You don't mean . . ."

She slapped a copy of the *Texas Tattle-Tale* on the desk in front of him. "You're the cover story."

Clint grabbed the article and stared at the blazing headline. *Is Clint MacAllister the leader of the wolf pack, or the wuss pack?*

Anger coiled inside him and his fingers tightened on the paper.

Stay calm. Controlled. Focused.

Lindy went on. "The press on you would probably die down if our driver weren't attracting so much attention. The *Tattle-Tale* is sure to spot him at a place like Buck's."

"What can I do? He likes the food."

"Speaking of dying down, I'm doing what you said and telling the press that you're not doing any interviews." She gave him a pointed stare. "But TNN Sports keeps calling. And so does ESPN. They really want to talk to you."

"About my retirement?" She nodded and he shook his head. "I'm retired. What's there to talk about?"

"Maybe why you started out as hot as ever in the Daytona 500, only to call it quits before the end of the day."

"I was injured."

"You've been injured before. That's no reason to throw away a fifteen-year career behind the wheel."

"I'm fed up with it. That's it."

"Then why haven't you sold the team and washed your hands of it?"

"Maybe I will."

"And maybe I'll win Miss Texas this year."

He eyed her, from her bright red hair pulled back into a tight braid, to the drab navy dress she wore. It did nothing for her figure, if she had a figure, and he really couldn't say because he'd never seen her wear anything that didn't hang on her small frame like a large sack. She wasn't ugly, but she wasn't an eye-catcher either. She was just Lindy, responsible and dedicated and so serious most of the time that he felt certain her face would crack if she didn't lighten up.

He grinned and tried to draw a smile. "I'd vote for you."

Her frown deepened. "You're deranged."

"But you still like me."

"I don't like you." She didn't smile, but the lines eased a little. "But you're the boss and it's your call. Personally, I think you should talk to the press. Set them straight."

"Do you really think if I give an interview and tell them I just decided it was time, that they're going to believe me?"

"Probably not."

"Definitely not. The real reason isn't exciting enough. It's better to look for an ulterior motive. Something deep and dark and terrible." Like fear. "It's human nature."

Clint knew that better than anyone. He'd heard the worst prognosis for his learning disability every time he turned around. There'd been no maybe or possibly. It had always been "You'll never amount to anything." End of story. He'd heard it so much, in fact, that he'd started to believe it.

Until his love of cars led him in to the driver's seat at his local track. In racing, he'd found his strength and realized that he called the shots. Soon he was driving with the big boys in NASCAR's Winston Cup series. He'd amounted to something, all right, and he'd proven everyone who'd ever said a negative word about him wrong.

So do it now. Talk to them. Show them.

Clint shook away the thought, walked around his desk and collapsed into a nearby chair just as the pre-race show started. He'd concentrated on his career long enough. It was time to turn his efforts to his personal life, starting tomorrow.

He and Skye had worked out the details. She would give him four detailed lessons based on her four-part ultimate pleasure workshop—the body, foreplay, sex play and after-sex play. In return, he would give her four lessons based on common guy interests—football, wrestling, fishing and cars.

He would get the first lesson, since he was racing against the clock and had a certain performance level to achieve in time for the Pepsi 400 at Daytona and his next meeting with Darla. They would alternate from then on out. She would give him lessons at his place and he would give her lessons at her place. That way they would each be in their comfort zone while trying to beef up their knowledge of the opposite sex.

Sex itself being his particular area of interest, and Skye was just the woman to teach him. She had all the credentials.

Not that she looked the way he would expect a woman in her profession to look.

She was attractive in a quiet, classy, conservative way with her soft blond hair pulled back in a simple knot and her minimal makeup. Not the made-up Playboy centerfold type he would have expected given her profession.

Clint took a long draw of his raspberry iced tea and tried to concentrate on the race. But all he could think about was Skye.

A fluke, he told himself. The idea of her—woman

teaches sex therefore woman is extremely good at sex—turned him on in a major way.

No way was he actually attracted to her.

Okay, so he was attracted to her.

In a superficial, this-isn't-going-anywhere kind of way. But attracted nonetheless.

He admitted that to himself Monday night as he stood in the doorway separating his kitchen from his den and stared at the woman who sat on his sofa.

A feeling that had nothing to do with the fact that she was holding a very large rubber penis.

He watched as she slid her hand down the thick piece of rubber, tracing its shape before setting it down and reaching for another. The second was larger, thicker. Long, slender fingers wrapped around the width in a grip that made him catch his breath.

Okay, so maybe it had a little to do with it. He was only human, after all, and seeing her handle the fake penis with such intensity made his own member stand at attention and cry *me, me, me*!

"Nice technique," he murmured as he walked into the room with a glass of raspberry iced tea and her requested glass of water.

Her fingers tightened and the penis popped from her grasp. "Oh," she said, glancing up at him. "You startled me. I was just setting everything up." She retrieved the wayward penis and set it aside. "We'll start with the female body during the first half of the lesson, and then discuss the male in our second half."

He set the drinks on the coffee table and sat down beside her as she rummaged in her briefcase.

After fingering through several files, she finally pulled out a set of neatly typed notes and handed them to him.

"What's this?"

"A handout. So you can follow along. We have a lot to cover in a short amount of time. I don't want to get ahead of you."

He glanced at the paper before setting it aside. "Don't worry about me. I race for a living. I'll keep up." He grinned and eyed the display of erotic models sitting on his coffee table. "Just wave the checkered flag and lead the way."

Chapter Seven

"I'm a little out of my element here," Skye said several moments later after Clint had given her the go-ahead. "I mean, you don't actually *have* a vagina."

"True, but I've got three sisters, four females on my crew pit, a woman publicist and a Blue Heeler named Jezebel." Clint gave her a slow, wicked grin that did nothing to ease the trembling in her hands. "I'd say that makes me guilty by association."

Skye's attention shifted to the large dog curled up on a doggie bed in the corner of the room. "I never really thought about it that way."

Hold on a second. Trembling hands? What was wrong with her?

She snatched Dinah off the coffee table and busied herself by making sure all the removable parts were thoroughly in place. Trembling hands were just one step away from a major craving.

Don't even go there, Sister.

"I know your usual audience is female." Clint's deep

voice drew her attention and she stared at the six foot plus of tall, dark and delicious male sitting next to her.

Close. So temptingly close . . .

"But the idea is the same," he went on. "Women want to learn how to receive the ultimate sexual pleasure and I want to learn how to give it to them. Just lay it out the way you do during one of your workshops. My being a man is just a technicality."

Man being the key word. He wasn't a two-headed dragon or an alien or an ultra-conservative Republican, for heaven's sake. He was just a man and she knew men from the inside out. Sure, she was lacking when it came to male interests, but she knew the nuts and bolts. She'd studied the male animal as thoroughly as she'd studied the female. Men were just flesh and blood. Human. They did not make her nervous and jittery and . . . breathless.

Unless they happened to be sitting next to her, so close she couldn't help but drink in the intoxicating scent of fresh soap, raw male and wild recklessness. An aroma that conjured an image of Skye completely naked on the back of a giant mechanical bull with a certain cowboy . . .

A burst of heat zipped from her head to her toes, pausing at several major erogenous points in between. A gnawing started in her stomach and Skye bolted to her feet.

Dinah in hand, she crossed several feet of plush carpet until she reached the opposite side of the room where trophies and plaques lined the massive wall.

She forced her fingers to relax before she broke off a major piece of the model in her hands. Dinah was fragile. Expensive.

And Skye was in complete and total control.

She was a professional, a *teacher*, and Clint was her

student until tomorrow night when the roles reversed. Then the burden of control would rest with him.

In the meantime . . .

The chemistry might be strong, nearly overwhelming, but she had certain rules. Clint had a significant other—sort of—and she didn't do attached men.

She chanced a glance over her shoulder to see him sitting on the couch. He didn't spare her a look as he leaned forward, his elbows on his knees. He peered at the variety of educational tools that sat on the coffee table.

Okay, so come tomorrow night, the burden of integrity might not be much of a burden at all. He seemed to be breathing quite easily. He didn't appear nervous or torn or the least bit turned on by their close proximity or the subject at hand.

The thought was depressing enough to calm her racing heart and kill her craving. Not that she wanted him to want her, mind you. It was simply the principle of the thing. No woman liked to think her lust was a one-way street, no matter how inappropriate the object of that desire.

She turned her attention to the room, her gaze sweeping the interior. A big-screen television overwhelmed one corner of the room. An entertainment center spanned the entire length of one wall and contained several DVD players, a home theater system complete with massive speakers and an impressive array of digital lights, and the biggest multi-CD player Skye had ever seen. The room overflowed with dark colors, electronics and shiny trophies. Definitely an alpha guy's wet dream.

Far from her airy living room with its cream-colored sofas, mint green throw pillows and overabundance of plants. Why, there wasn't a sign of any living, breathing thing besides the two of them.

One woman and one man.

It was the classic case of opposites attracting. But while opposites attracted, they rarely stayed together. She knew that firsthand. A dozen alpha boyfriends, and not one relationship longer than six months.

Never again.

She was going to learn as much as she could from Clint and broaden her range of interests. She might even go all out and redecorate her living room a little. Maybe get her own multi-CD player complete with a couple of Nickelback CDs for good measure. With careful preparation, the next Mr. Alpha who happened by would stick around long enough to break her current record.

This was business, plain and simple, and she was not turned on. More importantly, she did *not* want a cookie.

"Come on," he said, drawing her attention and giving her a wink and that heart-stopping grin. "Sex me up, teacher."

Okay, so maybe she could go for a few animal crackers, but those didn't really qualify.

"I'm holding in my hands Dinah the friendly vagina," she managed, launching full force into her presentation. "I say friendly because a vagina is a woman's best friend. As a man, the more you know about her best friend, the better lover you'll be. If you know just where to touch her—"

"Don't you think this thing is a little too flexible to be realistic." Clint's voice drew her around and she turned to see him holding the Cattle Boss. He wagged the eight-inch rubber penis in the air. It flip-flopped from side to side. "Shouldn't it be more stiff than this? Harder is definitely better."

"That's a first."

"What do you mean?"

"Size is usually the issue for most men, not rigidity."

He shrugged. "Hey, no issues here. Just asking."

"Then to satisfy your curiosity, it's supposed to be rigid enough to hold its shape, but supple enough to be comfortable. Now," she rushed on, eager to get back on track. "While a vagina isn't the Bermuda Triangle, it can be the eighth wonder of the world to your woman *if* you learn when and where and how to touch each and every part—"

"Don't you think this one is a little small?"

She turned this time to see Clint holding the Cow Poke.

"Actually, that's closer to reality than the other two."

He grinned and arched a black eyebrow at her. "Whose reality would that be?"

"Seventy-six percent of all men."

He nodded. "That many?"

"Yes, the next eighteen percent fall closer to the Ranch Hand and the last six percent make up the Cattle Boss category." For a split second, she had the incredible urge to ask him where he fell in the statistical range.

"Of course," she cleared her throat. "There have been much smaller sizes recorded. And much larger ones, as well." *Not that he was one of them and not that she cared one way or the other.*

"How much larger?" The Devil himself danced in his dark eyes and she felt an all-too familiar stirring in her stomach.

"Exceptionally larger." She licked her suddenly dry lips while her traitorous stomach grumbled. "The basic parts," she blurted, eager to get back on track. "There's the labia and the vulva and here you have a woman's hot spot. Her clitoris. Now, the clitoris is very sensitive and—"

"Do you really pass these out at your workshops?"

She turned to see him waving the Cow Poke and the Ranch Hand.

"They help with demonstrating proper hand and mouth techniques." She turned her attention back to Dinah. "The clitoris has a small hood that retracts when the area is stimulated—"

"Do you pass them out randomly or do women get to choose which one they want?"

"Sometimes I pass them out, sometimes they choose. The clitoris will swell with stimulation and—"

"Do women ever fight over which one they want?"

"What are you talking about?"

"I've seen my sisters at a shoe sale. They can get vicious over a pair of Gucci pumps. And what about this color?"

"What about it?"

"Did you pick the colors for these, because I've never seen a neon purple di—"

"Who cares about the color?" she cut in, her aggravation boiling over. "I thought the whole purpose of these lessons was to beef up your knowledge of women. So far, all we've done is debate the penis and the last I looked, most women don't have them. They have Dinah here, who takes care of pleasure and her sister Ula the Uterus, who's responsible for the reproductive end."

At the mention of the big R, his grin faded into a determined expression and he set the penis on the table. "I'm ready. Keep going."

He looked so serious that her aggravation faded into a wave of admiration. While she didn't understand his whole obsession with marriage, she could relate to his desire for a child.

Someday . . .

Right now, however, the only thing she *really* wanted was a . . . *Don't even think it.*

She drew in a deep breath and fixed her gaze on the wall of plaques. Anything to get her mind off the infuriating man on the sofa and the fact that she didn't find him half as infuriating as she found him sexy.

Read. Her gaze rushed from award to award for everything from the fastest qualifying time to most starts for the year. The more she read, the slower her heart beat until her gaze touched on one in particular given by his sponsor.

All-around exceptional driver for 2002.

The word rooted in her mind and conjured an image of a convertible car roaring down a lonely stretch of highway on a moonlit night. She sat in the front passenger seat, naked and very aroused. Clint sat behind the wheel, just as naked and just as aroused and—

"Are you okay?" His voice shattered her thoughts and she whirled.

"I . . ." The sentence stalled as she found him standing a few inches away, so close she could see the faint laugh lines around his eyes and a tiny feather-like scar at the corner of his mouth.

A really great mouth with strong, full lips.

An exceptional mouth for an exceptional man.

"You don't look so good. Can I get you some water or something?"

"A cookie," she blurted before she did something exceptionally stupid like press her lips to his and see if he tasted even half as delicious as he looked. "A really big cookie."

Chapter Eight

"Where's the handout?" Skye perched on the edge of her sofa the next afternoon and stared across the room at Clint.

He popped a DVD into her player and pressed the Close button. "This is just the basic stuff. No handout required."

He punched a button on the remote control and her small television flickered on. "I know we agreed about each of us being in our own place during our lessons, but we should have done this at my house. To get the full effect, you really need a big screen."

"I've never really had the need for one. I don't watch much television."

"Neither do I, but when I do, I like to be able to see what I'm looking at."

"I can see just fine."

"Bigger is always better."

"Do we have to go over this size business again? I told you, women don't care. The bigger myth is typical of a man's perspective."

"Isn't that the point of all of this? For you to get a man's perspective?"

"On football. Not on the size of my television."

"I bet if you took a poll, you would find that the majority of big-screen TVs are purchased by men." He eyed her. "Men who like football. Macho men who like football, and wrestling and fishing and—"

"I'll get a bigger television."

"Good girl." He grinned and sank down to the edge of her cream Victorian sofa. His knee bumped the edge of her antique cherry wood coffee table when he tried to get comfortable. A crystal vase trembled and he reached out, barely catching it before it toppled and lost its bouquet of tiger lilies.

"Let me get those." She grabbed the vase and deposited it on a nearby divan that held a collection of teacups.

She walked back to the sofa as he leaned back and squirmed around. "Not much cushion on this sofa."

"It's an antique. I love antique furniture almost as much as I love antique teacups." Her attention shifted to the large glass curio cabinet that housed her treasures. A spotlight reflected off the glass, making the china glitter.

Clint frowned and patted the sofa next to him. "Don't they have any antique La-Z-Boy recliners? Something with a little cushion? I feel like a bull in a china shop. There's no place to get comfortable."

"I'm thinking about redecorating. Maybe something a little more man friendly."

"Good idea." Another squirm and he gave up. He leaned forward, his elbows on his knees as he held the remote control. "Now," he hit the Play button and the DVD launched into the pre–Super Bowl highlight show.

"Say hello to one of the biggest spectator sports in the world."

She watched as a three-hundred-plus-pound player plowed into a mob of equally large men. The group crashed in on each other and she winced. "I know it's popular, but personally, I really don't understand the appeal. Other than the tight pants, that is. Those are definitely a plus." She eyed another tackle and watched a player take a hit right in his middle that sent him doubling over. "Otherwise, it looks painful."

"It is, but pain can be good. Motivating." At her skeptical look, he added, "It's a guy thing."

"In other words, women aren't insightful enough to get it."

"Actually, women are too insightful. It's a guy thing because it's so simple. It goes back to the caveman days. Men are motivated by the basic male instinct—survival. The more you push a strong man down, the more he fights to get back up."

"It looks more like showing off to me." She indicated the screen, where a man took the ball to the goalposts and stopped to do a booty-shaking dance that earned him a roar from the crowd.

"That's a victory dance, and he deserves to showoff. He just won the championship for his team."

"And earned a few extra million that he doesn't need. Don't you think the salaries that these guys command is a little ridiculous? Why, we could eliminate the national deficit and bump up social services with what these guys make. Better yet, we could give equal pay to deserving women in the workplace."

"Spoken like a true, sports-hating, bra-burning feminist."

She frowned and took a deep easy breath. She was used to this. She'd faced the same reaction time and time again while growing up and it no longer bothered her. She merely informed the other person that they were wrong and talked calmly, informatively, to steer them in the right direction.

She didn't let the comment get under her skin and she never, ever slapped the smug look off anyone's face, no matter how badly her fingers twitched to do just that.

Like now.

He grinned. "Not that I have anything against bra burning. Bare is definitely better when it comes to women."

She clasped her hands together and drew in another deep breath.

Her nostrils flared as the scent of clean soap and warm male filled her head. Mmm . . . not too bad.

He shifted his feet and the edge of his boot brushed the side of her foot. Her toes tingled and warmed.

Tingling? Warming? She wiggled her digits and tried to ignore the sensation by focusing on her anger.

"First off, the bra burning was a show of liberation. Most feminists I know actually do wear a bra."

"I wasn't talking about most feminists and their bras. I was talking about you and yours."

The heat spread through the arches of her feet and up into her ankles. "I have never burned anything but a few marshmallows during a fourth of July bonfire one year, and the occasional cup of hot chocolate."

"That's too bad."

"I don't burn it every time. Just when I turn my fire too high. Milk scalds so easily."

"I wasn't talking about the hot chocolate."

"I know." His grin widened and the warmth seeped up into her calves, past her knees and into her thighs, obviously headed for higher ground.

"Secondly," she tried to focus on her words instead of her body. Her warm, tingling body. "Most feminists do not hate sports. They hate the good ole boys club that is perpetuated by most sports. Third, I am not a feminist. I'm a womanist. There's a big difference."

"Feminist. Womanist." He seemed to weigh the two. "Yep, I can see the difference."

"Good because they're both really very unique . . ." She eyed him and saw the humor dancing in his eyes. A look that made her want to smack his cheek again. Or kiss it.

She pursed her lips and glared. "You're clueless, aren't you?"

"Yep, but I bet you're going to enlighten me before I can blink my eyes, aren't you?"

"I wouldn't be much of a sports-hating, bra-burning feminist/womanist if I didn't." Her statement earned her a smile, and while the urge to slap him faded, the need to touch her lips to his only intensified. "Actually, womanism has its roots in feminism. All womanists support feminism by definition."

"Which is?"

"Political, social and economic equality of women. But over the years, many feminists lost sight of the fact that they were trying to be equal to men. Instead, they tried to hide their emotional, nurturing characteristics behind the strong, stoic façade perpetuated by males in the workplace. That meant no crying on the job. No letting the kids interfere with work. No compassion or sympathy for fellow co-workers," she said, repeating the spiel she'd heard time and time again while growing up. "The womanist evolved from the feminists who grew tired of suppressing who they were in order to gain respect. A womanist embraces all things feminine."

"I know some men who fit that bill."

"Those are called players," she said. "And I know a few, too, who I'd rather not know. Anyhow, a womanist doesn't hide her emotional side for fear that it will make her appear weak. If she wants to cry, she cries. If she wants to stay home with her kids and bake cookies to her heart's content, she can. So long as she bakes because she wants to," she stressed. "Not because she has to, or because it's expected of her."

"So you like to bake cookies?"

"Actually, I like to eat them." She'd tried her hand at baking once before, but it hadn't worked out as she'd hoped. Of course, she'd been motivated not by her own hunger for homemade cookies, but by her hunger for a seventh-grade hockey player named Matt.

She'd been appointed Matt's study buddy in algebra class. Instead of finding the value for *x*, however, she'd spent more time studying him. He had had the bluest eyes and the most muscles of any boy in the seventh grade, and by the time Valentine's Day had rolled around, Skye had wanted nothing more than to have Matt as her sweetheart. And she knew just how to get him. Two dozen homemade goodies oozing chocolate chips—a surefire way to Matt's heart.

She'd been so excited to give him her Valentine, until her mother had seen her packing the goodies into a shoe box lined with wax paper and decorated with heart-shaped foil cut-outs.

"Baking cookies is fine, dear. I enjoy baking myself.

But baking for a boy? You need to think, Skye. No daughter of mine would ever enslave herself in a hot kitchen and sacrifice her integrity just to catch some boy's attention."

Her mother had been right, of course. Skye would rather jump through fire than sacrifice her integrity, and so she'd done what any self-respecting daughter of the leading womanist in America would do—she unpacked the cookies and tossed the box. The next day, she watched while Matt left school with a cheerleader who had big blossoming pom-poms and a giant heart-shaped, homemade fudge brownie.

Her lips twitched and her mouth watered. "Um, could we stop talking about cookies and get back to the subject?"

"Bra burning?"

"Further back."

His eyes twinkled. "Panty burning?"

"We never talked about panty burning."

"We should have. It sounds interesting."

"Womanists don't burn their panties. No one does."

"That's too bad." That cocky, teasing grin crooked his mouth and her heart did a double thump.

She stiffened and tried to focus. "I fail to see how my underwear has anything to do with guy stuff. We're here for football, remember?"

"Football?" He winked. "Oh, yeah." A serious expression fell over his face and his eyes danced with excitement. "Now, you probably know more about pro ball than you realize. An NFL game isn't that different from the tag football we all grew up with."

"Tag football?"

"Yeah. When the guys get together and toss around the football at the local park."

"I spent every Sunday afternoon at the park at Southwestern University near my grandmother's house."

"There you go."

"It was generally pretty quiet. People studied or just lazed around in the sun and watched the birds. There were never any impromptu sporting events. Except croquet. I've seen that played before."

"Forget tag football. What about high-school ball? They had a football team at your high school, right?"

"Of course."

"There you go. Now high-school ball is just like pro ball except—"

"But I never actually went to a game."

"Never?"

"I babysat for the head coach. It was always too cold during football season for his girls to be out and they weren't into the game anyway. We stayed home and watched the Cosby show. And played paper dolls."

"What about college? I know you went to college." He smiled as if he'd thought of something brilliant.

She nodded. "The University of Texas."

"A-ha!" He clapped his hands. "The Longhorns are a great football team."

"That's what I've heard."

He eyed her. "Don't tell me you went to UT and *never* took in a football game?"

She shrugged and tried to ignore the hollowness in the pit of her stomach. "I was too busy with classes and when I wasn't in class, I was volunteering at the Austin Women's Shelter."

"You never saw the Horns play?" He pressed as if he

couldn't quite believe her. "Not even once? Not even *the* game of the season against their arch rival the Texas A & M Aggies?"

"That's Thanksgiving weekend and I always do Thanksgiving at one of the shelters." She balled her fingers and ignored the urge to reach for the plate of graham crackers she'd set out for lack of cookies to go with the pot of tea she'd brewed. She'd cookie-proofed the entire house just that morning, determined to curb her craving.

She licked her lips. "It's good to help other women less fortunate. It helps you remember what you're thankful for. Tea?"

"Don't drink tea."

"But you drank tea at your house last night."

"That was iced tea."

"But tea's tea."

"Not to a man. Men don't drink hot tea."

At least not men like Clint.

She not only needed to redecorate, she needed to revamp her pantry, as well.

"So you never saw an Aggie/Horns game? *Never?*"

"No."

He didn't look convinced. Instead, he stared at her as if she'd just confessed to crashing his favorite car. "What about your dad? Didn't he ever watch a football game? Any football game?"

"My dad's more of an intellectual. He watches A & E. Besides, he wasn't home very much when I was growing up. He's a research scientist for UT and he was always away somewhere collecting data for some project or another."

"So you only had your mom around?"

"Well, my mom was always off lecturing or giving

seminars when she wasn't promoting her books. My sisters and I lived in Georgetown, Texas, with our grandmother who spent most of her time growing vegetables, canning vegetables and reading *Reader's Digest*."

"Your grandfather?"

"He passed away before I was born. It was just us girls."

"A group of girlie girls."

"I'm probably going to hate myself for asking this, but what is a girlie girl?"

"A frilly girl. The kind that wear puffy dresses."

She frowned at him before shrugging. "I may have had a few puffy dresses."

"And ruffled panties."

"What's wrong with ruffled panties?"

"Nothing except they're not really practical for climbing trees and making mud bombs and doing fun stuff like that."

"I fail to see the fun in a mud bomb."

He eyed her. "I bet you cried every time you got dirty."

"Not every time. Once I fell and I didn't cry at all." She'd been too mad to cry. Ronnie Samson had called her names as usual and pushed her down, straight into a huge mud puddle.

"Why didn't you cry?"

"I was too busy punching to cry."

"*You* actually punched a guy?"

"He was a boy then. A hateful bully and I knocked out three teeth." The smile Clint gave her was enough to make her forget the lecture that had followed.

"I'll not have a daughter of mine rolling around on the ground like some testosterone-driven male. You're better

than that, Skye. Smarter. Remember, boys punch. Girls think."

Clint stared down at her, into her as if she'd just bench pressed three hundred pounds, and the feeling of euphoria she'd experienced after hitting Ronnie came rushing back. The elation. The pride. The satisfaction.

The attraction.

Not to Ronnie, mind you. He'd been ugly and mean. But Clint . . . He was handsome with the greatest eyes she'd ever seen, eyes as blue and iridescent as the Caribbean on a hot summer's day.

Skye swallowed and cleared her throat. "I've watched *Coach* a few times."

"What?"

"The sitcom that features the college football coach. You asked about my football experience and I'm telling you that I watch the reruns sometimes when I'm up late preparing for the following day's work." She smiled.

Clint shook his head, punched the Pause button on the DVD and the room went silent. "Maybe we should just start at the beginning with a few basics and work our way up to the video."

"Perfect." She reached for her notebook and pen, flipped to the first page and scribbled a quick heading.

"What are you doing?"

"Taking notes since there's no handout. After we're done, I would appreciate it if you'd look everything over and fill in any blanks I may still have."

He grabbed her notebook. "Forget notes. This isn't economics class. It's fun. Easy." He leaned his elbows on his knees. "You've got two teams each running the opposite direction for a touchdown that scores six points.

Then, if all goes well, the kicker comes in and scores another point to make seven."

"Which position does the kicker play in the game?"

"The kicker plays the kicker. He's a specialty player only on the field when he needs to kick. Or punt."

"What's a punt?"

"When you don't make a first down, you have to punt."

"What's a first down?"

"You're telling me you don't know what a first down is? You've never even heard of it?"

She shook her head. "Not the first or the second. Is there a second?" The question sparked a thought and she jumped to her feet. "I need to give my dog her second pill. She's had stomach problems."

"You have a dog?"

She nodded as she walked toward the bedroom. The minute she opened the door, a ball of white fluff darted past her, headed for the living room.

"Hell's bells, even your dog is frilly."

"She's not frilly," Skye said as she snatched up the ball of fur and headed for the kitchen. "She's a Shih Tzu."

"Don't tell me her name is Fifi or Foofoo or something girlie like that." Clint followed her.

"Her name is Skipper."

"Why Skipper?"

"When I was a little girl, I wanted a Skipper doll more than life itself. Actually"—she retrieved the dog's medicine from a cabinet—"I wanted a Barbie doll more than life itself, but that was out of the question."

"I would have thought your house would have been packed with wall-to-wall Barbies. You played with dolls."

"Baby dolls. Barbie was different. She was tanned, blond, with breasts out to there and legs up to here, and totally and completely politically incorrect. Barbie was and still is a poor role model for young girls according to my mother, so I set my sights on her younger, more realistic-looking sister. She still had the tan and the long blond hair, but her breasts weren't as big and her waist wasn't nearly as small."

"Did you get one?"

"Still too close to the whole Barbie image. I got a Hippy Harmony instead. She was this doll created by one of my mother's professor friends. She had short brown hair, chubby cheeks and an equally chubby body." *Why the hell was she telling him this?* Even as the thought registered in her brain, it did little to stop the flow of words.

"My mother had the right idea, I just didn't see it at the time. Besides, I like this Skipper much more than any old doll. Isn't that right, baby?" She rubbed the dog behind the ears and set her on the floor. "Look, if you don't want the hot tea, can I get you something else? Something cold?"

"That would be great." He leaned against the edge of the kitchen island and waited.

Skye turned toward the refrigerator. "Alcoholic or non-alcoholic?"

"Non-alcoholic."

She retrieved two different cans. "I've got Diet Coke and Diet Seven-Up."

He glanced around, his gaze skimming the giant sunflowers painted on the opposite wall before shifting back to the island and her sunflower burner covers.

"I like sunflowers."

"I can tell."

"So?"

He glanced at both drinks and shook his head. "What the hell? Go ahead and give me something alcoholic. It's after noon."

She turned around and retrieved two bottles. "I've got a peach-flavored Seagram's wine cooler and a Zima." She held up both bottles.

"Maybe you ought to take notes after all. This is going to be a lot harder than I thought."

"You're killing me, Tuck," Clint said into the phone later that day.

"I'm killing you? I'm the one who almost crashed and burned."

Yeah, but Clint was the one who had to deal with Vernon Simmons, the head of Big Tex Motor Oil and sponsor of the MacAllister Magic race team. It wasn't going to be pretty. Vernon liked to win.

"It was the tunnel turn," Tuck told him. "I was trying to pass and then we went into the turn and I didn't fall into place in time."

"You don't pass before the tunnel turn. You have to do it single file. You know that."

"I saw the opportunity, so I took it."

"You should have anticipated the turn before the pass."

"It was the fuel system. If I'd had more power, it would have been a piece of cake."

"The fuel system was perfect. It was the driver who malfunctioned. You didn't listen to the spotter." The spotter was the team member up in the box, watching the race from above. He communicated with Tuck via a headset. "He's your second set of eyes. He sees things you don't.

You have to listen to him. I know. The same thing would have happened to me back at Pocono in '96 if I hadn't been listening."

"It felt really weird not having you there," Tuck said before an expectant silence ensued and Clint got the feeling that Tuck wanted to say more. "Not that I need you there. I don't need anybody."

"You need your spotter, and don't forget it. That's what he's there for."

"Sure thing," Tuck said. "But I'm telling you, it wasn't me. It was the fuel system. That and some bad juju."

"I'll have Jeep go over the fuel system. You just make sure you're focused on Sears Point this weekend. It's a road course and it can be tricky."

"I'm ready," he said, a trace of resentment in his voice. As if he had no desire to listen to Clint's advice. "I know what to do."

"Good. Make sure you do it."

"No problem."

"Speaking of problems"—Clint reached for the *Texas Tattle-Tale* and stared at the black-and-white photo—"I'm looking at a picture of you in the paper right now. At first, I didn't think it was you. After all, you lost yesterday, which means—if you're sticking to our agreement—you didn't get to go out and party it up, and you're definitely partying judging by the shot glass in your hand."

"I think it was a body double. You know we all have one somewhere."

"You're wearing a Big Tex cap and your racing jacket."

"We not only look alike, we must have the same taste in clothes."

"It's you."

"I needed to unwind."

"You need to keep your focus."

"Not possible if you keep bringing up the past."

Clint let loose a heavy sigh. "Stay focused," he said. "It's all about Sunday in Sonoma from here on out."

"You're going to be there, right?" Tuck seemed to think better of his question. "Not that it matters. Either way, I'll have it under control."

"Make sure you do." Clint hung up the phone and turned to Lindy, who handed him a glass of raspberry iced tea and stacked autographed pictures on the corner of his desk. The familiar CM blazed in blue ink from the corner.

"He gave you the juju excuse, didn't he?"

"First you read my mind day in and day out, and now you're reading Tuck's." He took a long draw of the iced tea.

She planted her hand on her hip and glared at him. "Why do you like this guy so much? He's cocky, pretentious and he never admits fault for anything."

He shrugged and sank down into his desk chair. "He reminds me of me when I first started out."

She seemed to think about that for a minute. "You know, you're right."

"Why *don't* you like this guy?"

She slid the stack of mail directly in front of him and frowned. "Because he reminds me of you when you first started out."

Chapter Nine

"Now that you've learned the actual parts of a woman, it's time to learn what to do to those parts to guarantee a quality orgasm." Skye retrieved a neatly typed sheet from her briefcase and handed it to Clint, who sat next to her on his overstuffed sofa.

A throw pillow and at least two handspans of dark brown leather separated them. There would be no legs grazing during tonight's lesson. No accidental brush of arms. No touching, period. Skye needed her space for adequate concentration and so she'd made sure to spread out her working tools, namely her notebook, her lesson plan and several books on the art of kissing, fondling and stirring a woman's passion. Textbooks, not picture books—much to Clint's dismay—to keep tonight as completely non-sexual as possible despite the fact that she was teaching him about—hello?—sex.

She pulled a container of Tic Tacs from her briefcase and popped one into her mouth. Xandra had been right. The sucking took the place of chewing which had helped with her cookie cravings. Then again, she'd only been doing the mints for—she glanced at her watch—a full thirty minutes. But so far, so good. She sucked and drew a nice, easy breath.

That's what tonight would be. Easy. She'd given this lesson more times than she could count, and she had nothing to feel inhibited about. She certainly had nothing that might, in the least, make her feel nervous or anxious or hungry.

And if so, she had her Tic Tacs.

"So?" she asked him after several silent moments while he looked over the neatly typed sheet of paper. "What do you think?"

He stared at the handout another moment. "There aren't any positions on here," he finally said. "I think if we're talking orgasm, we need a good position, don't you?"

Yeah, baby.

She forced the thought aside. "We're not talking about doing the actual deed. Tonight is all about the pre-liminaries."

"But you said orgasm."

"Quality orgasm," she corrected.

"That's right. And if we're talking quality orgasm, we need a quality position. One that insures deep penetration."

The words slid into her ears and vibrated along her nerve endings and Skye swallowed. *Easy*, she told herself as she popped a Tic Tac. So the man had said *penetration*. Big deal. It was just a word.

One she'd heard many, many times.

One that had never before conjured a very vivid image of Clint leaning over her, cowboy hat shading the upper half of his face. Hands stroked down her sides and her thighs opened to accept him. Her legs wrapped around his waist and he slid inside in a smooth move that guaranteed maximum penetration . . .

She popped one, then two mints into her mouth. It was a word. Just a word. And she was *not* hungry.

"That's the next lesson," she managed, licking her lips. His dark eyes followed the action and her stomach hollowed out. "Tonight, um, isn't about the actual sex act," she said again. "It's about foreplay."

She fixed her attention on her notes, mentally skimming the high points. "So what are your thoughts on the subject?" She glanced up at him. Glancing was okay so long as she didn't let her gaze linger, or shift to certain, more nerve-wracking territory such as his mouth, or the strong column of his throat, or the small dip just above his black T-shirt where his Adam's apple bobbed.

She retrieved another mint and popped it into her mouth. The peppermint settled on the inside of her cheek and the scent filled her nostrils, temporarily blotting out the smell of warm male coupled with faint cologne coming at her from his side of the sofa.

He set the handout aside, leaned back and stretched his legs out, hooking his worn brown cowboy boots at the ankles. His arms slid into a fold beneath his head. "To be honest, I'm usually too hot to think."

"Most men usually are, which is why lack of adequate foreplay is the chief complaint among women." A truth she'd fallen victim to several times in her own past.

It seemed that the men who bragged the most about their ability to satisfy a woman were the fastest. Not that she'd actually read a study on the subject.

Her gaze slid to Clint. He liked to brag about everything which meant, based on her own past history, that he was probably very quick on the draw. The notion should have killed her fantasies.

It didn't.

"To really satisfy your woman," she went on, "it's not what you do after you enter her that counts, such as the position or the speed of your stroke. It's what you do before. If you've worked her up adequately, you won't have to pace yourself as much."

"Makes sense."

"But a man who really wants to give his woman pleasure will do both. He'll rev her engine and then he'll just drive around for awhile."

"Driving's what I do best."

"We're not talking a fast finish like one of your races. Pleasuring a woman should be like a leisurely scenic cruise around the block. It's about the trip itself and the sights and sounds along the way, not how fast you get to where you want to go."

He eyed her. "So how long is this trip? Just give me a ballpark figure."

"It depends on the woman, but from a professional standpoint you should aim for at least an hour." As soon as the words left her mouth, surprise registered in his gaze. "I'm assuming your goal usually isn't an hour."

"Fifteen minutes usually works."

"Fifteen minutes is a coffee break. We're talking a fully satisfying lunch here. Anything quicker than that and you run the risk of leaving her behind, and that is a definite no-no."

"An hour." He seemed to think. "Does that include foreplay?"

"It may, or it may not. It depends how serious you are about setting off the fireworks. A really hot lover will start the foreplay hours before the actual act. He'll draw it out over an entire day sometimes, building the anticipation until the object of his desire is practically steaming." *Speaking of steaming . . .*

Skye shifted her position. The lower part of her thighs stuck to the leather and she made a mental note to wear slacks to the next lesson.

Clint's gaze went to her legs and something dark and completely inappropriate gleamed in his eyes.

"There," she blurted, determined to stay on track and keep their attention focused on the lesson itself. "That look is exactly the sort of look you should use when looking at your lover. It says heat and hunger and *I want you bad.*" She swallowed what was left of her current mint and popped another. "Hot looks can add tremendously to a healthy love session."

She shifted again. "Now, if she's really on fire, you can probably go a little quicker with the actual act. But not too quick. You have to wait for her."

"Easy for you to say." He glanced at the noticeable bulge in his jeans. "He sometimes has a mind of his own." *Like now.*

She forced the thought away. Maybe she noticed him more because his pants were tighter tonight. A rip in the jeans gave her a glimpse of one hair-roughened thigh and she had the insane urge to lean over and touch her lips to the spot to see what he actually tasted like. To feel the tickle of hair against her lips.

"Focal point," she blurted. "When things get a little hot." She tugged at the collar of her light blue silk blouse. "You just choose a focal point and concentrate." Her attention fixed on a trophy just over his left shoulder. "It's all a matter of mind over body. You're an athlete. I'm sure you've been in situations," *such as this one*, "where you have to push yourself to do something extremely difficult."

"Like doing an extra lap at the track." He leaned just to the left, blotting out her view of the trophy and drawing her attention to the sparkle of his eyes.

He really did have great eyes. So deep and blue, fringed with dark lashes.

Her stomach grumbled and she shifted. The sofa groaned, masking the sound and she sent up a silent thanks. While she knew she was having trouble, he didn't have to know.

Trouble? No, she wasn't having trouble. She was focusing, concentrating, *sucking*.

"I remember days when I've been dead tired after a race and all I want to do is pack it up and go home," he went on. "But I knew a win on the following Sunday would be impossible if I gave up too soon."

"So what did you do? How did you keep going?"

"I listened to the roar of the engine and let all that power feed the need inside me."

"Sex is no different. It's all about finding a focal point and staying fixed on that one thing. For instance, what are you thinking about when you're having sex?"

He grinned and her heart did the traitorous double thump. "I'm thinking that it feels damned good."

"Because you're fixated on the sensation, which increases the sensation, which brings on a climax. But what if you think about something else?"

"I generally do, but that doesn't help matters."

"I'm not talking about *someone* else, as in the typical fantasy. I'm talking about something else that doesn't involve your own penis. For instance, fixate on your partner's eyes or her mouth or the sound that she makes when you slide a little deeper."

"That usually draws a scream."

The naked cowboy image rushed to the front of her mind and her cheeks burned.

Hello? You're not in grade school. You're all grown up now and you're a professional. This stuff doesn't embarrass you anymore.

"I'm serious."

"So am I."

That's what she was afraid of, almost as much as the sudden urge to find out for herself. "The point is, you need a focal point other than your own pleasure. You know you're going to come. That's always a given." A thought struck her and she eyed him. "It is a given, right? Your only problem is lack of knowledge, not a matter of plumbing?"

The question wiped the grin from his face. "My plumbing works just fine."

"Good." *Great*, a voice whispered and she popped yet another mint. "Then for you and sixty-two percent of men your age, achieving an orgasm is a given. But what about the woman? Sometimes she does and sometimes she doesn't." She looked straight at him. "Think how good your ego will feel if you make sure that she does. Then you've got an emotional rush along with the physical elation, and *bam*, you've doubled your own pleasure and satisfaction while giving your woman a good time, as well. Slowing down and working a little harder isn't the sacrifice that most men think. It's a win-win for everyone."

"Sounds good to me."

"Good. Now." She drew in a deep breath. "Kissing is

one of the main elements of great foreplay, and great foreplay usually guarantees an equally great orgasm."

"Kissing?"

"Most men don't think of kissing as a part of the actual sex act. Of course, they often kiss during sex, but it's not mandatory for them. Women, on the other hand, rarely climax if it's their genitals alone that are stimulated. They need all-over stimulation to really get going. That's why it's very important to understand the basics of kissing and the various sorts of kissing." Just saying the word drew her attention to his mouth.

Like his eyes, he had a really great mouth, his lips not too full, not too narrow, but just right. And the way he moved it, curving it into one of those cocky smiles that made her heart rev and her blood pressure leap to dangerous heights. Or tilting it just so in a grin that warmed her blood as much as it irritated her.

"Kissing," she said again, fixing her attention on her lesson plan. "A kiss is so potent because it sets off a chemical rush in the body that speeds the pulse, blots out stress, increases blood flow and body temperature." Her gaze lifted to meet his.

"Sounds pretty powerful to me."

"Kissing also packs a powerful whammy because taste and touch are directly intertwined. When we kiss, it's not only an exploration of touch, but a thorough dissecting of our lover's scent. During a kiss, neurons in our brain sort through odors and pick out pheromones—the body's individual perfume—and carry this information to the brain. It's this information that triggers the chemical cocktail and gives something as small as a kiss the power of an atomic emotional bomb."

"You really know your stuff." His gaze drilled into her and she felt her body warm again.

"It's my business."

"Since you know so much, you probably have to be pretty good at the actual act itself." She'd heard the comment so many times from so many different men.

But coming from this man, it didn't stir her anger. Instead, she thought of all the things she wanted to do with him, to him, and her own body temperature rose several degrees. "I, um," she cleared her throat and the Tic Tac slid to the back and took a nosedive down.

The mint lodged itself in her throat before she could take a breath and she coughed, her eyes watering. "Could you excuse me for just a second?" she croaked. Before he could reply, she bolted from the sofa and made a beeline down his hall into the kitchen.

A few vicious coughs and the Tic Tac rearranged itself and slid down the right pipe. She sucked in a deep breath, her throat burning as she leaned against the counter.

"Are you okay?" His voice carried down the hall.

"Fine," she called out. "I'm just getting a glass of water." She turned on the faucet and let the water run, but she didn't take a drink. Instead, she fished the second pack of mints from her pocket and popped several onto her tongue.

They did little, however, because the problem had nothing to do with hunger and everything to do with *hunger*. The nipple-tingling, weak-in-the-knees kind of hunger that made her want to lean into him and taste his lips with her own.

"Hey." His voice sounded from the doorway and she whirled. He stared expectantly at her. "Where's your glass?"

"What?"

"You said you were getting water." He glanced at the flowing faucet. "Are you planning on ducking your head under?"

"I . . ." Her lips tingled and she licked them. A bad move when her mouth was already sensitive and wanting and—

Talking.

She needed to talk, to do something with her mouth other than what she wanted to do at the moment. Since sucking wasn't doing the trick, maybe talking would.

Talking about a totally neutral subject, of course, that had nothing to do with plundering mouths or trailing tongues or getting naked and sweaty and *hot*.

"Don't you think your fans deserve an actual auto-graphed picture instead of those pre-printed things?"

"What?" He stepped closer. The heat from his body drew her. His scent filled her nostrils.

"Your publicity shots." She darted past him and headed down the hallway back to the den. "They're pre-printed."

"No, they're not," he said as he followed right behind her. So close that if she were to stop they would collide.

"They most certainly are." She reached the safety of the den and walked around the coffee table. Her gaze went to the wall where a framed version stared back at them. "See?"

"That isn't printed. It's an actual signature."

"That's printed. You don't actually sign each picture. Don't you think you're cheating your fans by not signing it yourself?"

"Cheating? I'm not cheating anyone. I give these away to anyone who wants one. Most drivers I know sell them.

They don't foot the bill for the picture themselves the way I do. That's not cheating. It's caring."

"It's cocky. You're assuming the fan wants your picture in the first place."

"There's nothing wrong with a little cockiness every now and then."

"And smug."

"I've got a lot to be smug about. I've worked damned hard to get where I am."

"And narcissistic." When he just glared at her, she went on. "Why focus on your own picture? Why, you could give away matchbooks imprinted with your name or car posters or autographed cans of Big Tex motor oil. I bet your sponsor would love that."

"Fans want pictures."

"So you assume. Maybe they just want a memento."

"They're always asking to take my picture."

He had her on that one and her mind raced for a comeback. "Pictures are too easy," she finally blurted. "Thoughtless. Especially when they're signed by someone else. And this isn't even a full signature. It's just your initials."

"Initials are fast and easy."

"What do you care? You're not the one signing them in the first place. They're printed. P-R-I-N-T-E-D." She knew she sounded juvenile, but from the dark, thunderous look on his face, she was pressing his buttons and that was good. Anger was good. Then he wouldn't look at her like he wanted to lap her up.

No, he would look at her like he was this close to wringing her neck.

Like now.

"Who the hell cares?"

"You should."

"I do," he growled.

"So why not use the full name?"

"Because that's what I used to sign in the beginning when I did them myself. Initials are my trademark."

"Because you're such a busy man. Much too busy to waste your time on a fan who's just one of millions. A fan you'll probably never see again. One who worships you—"

"Initials are all I could do," he cut in.

"What are you talking about?"

"I started signing my initials because I had to." His voice softened as he shrugged. "I can't write very well."

"I don't understand."

"Actually, I can write okay, just not very fast." His gaze met hers. "I have dyslexia."

"But you designed and built your own race car."

"Dyslexia is a learning disability. I have trouble learning. It doesn't mean I'm not smart."

"I know that."

"Some dyslexics tend to be very mechanical. Where they lack in book smarts, they make up for it in other areas. This is my area."

"I'm sorry."

"Don't be. It's not a big deal. I had trouble signing autographs after the races in my early days, so I started doing just the initials. As my fan base grew, so did the media attention and the number of autographs, and so I came up with the complementary autographed picture promo instead. My fans were happy with it. They would much rather have me hand them a picture than stand for hours in line to shell out a few bucks only to stand in line even longer to get me to sign it."

"I never would have thought about it that way."

"Because you're not dyslexic. I know it seems impersonal, but it's not. I care about my fans. They're everything to me. I even remember the very first time someone asked me for an autograph. His name was Dillon and he was eight years old. I'd just won my first race ever and he stared up at me with this huge smile on his face and his eyes twinkling. Like I was really somebody instead of some dumb-as-dirt special ed kid who'd always been on the outside looking in. I wasn't outside when he looked at me. I was actually *in*." His eyes glittered at the memory and her chest tightened.

"I know how you feel. I was the only girl in the first grade who didn't get invited to Tracey Burg's slumber party," she blurted. "There were twenty girls in the class, including Shauna Summers who still wet the bed, and I was the only one sitting home on Friday night with my grandmother and my two sisters. My mom was off at one of her seminars and my dad was spending the year in Arizona researching a paper he was writing. So, my sisters and I were stationed at our grandmother's in Georgetown, as usual."

"Nice little town. I've passed through a couple of times."

Skye shrugged. "It's a typical small, close-knit college town. Population 1,042. Tolerance level—zero, at least when it came to me and my sisters. To all the non-intellectuals, we were the outcasts because we didn't come from a traditional family. Not that we would have been any more accepted had my mom and dad been home twenty-four-seven. They were free-spirited activists more interested in raising awareness than raising cattle like most everybody else in Georgetown."

"What does all this have to do with dyslexia?"

Nothing. It was on an entirely different plane. Except for the way it had made her feel. She'd been ostracized herself. She knew what it felt like to be on the outside always looking in.

"You shared something personal with me, and so I thought I would share with you. To, um, make a point. Real pleasure is all about give and take."

"Really?" He stepped toward her.

"What are you doing?"

"I'm giving you a kiss. Or taking a kiss. Depends on how you look at it I guess."

And then his lips touched hers.

"Where the hell *are* they?" Skye stared at the kitchen table where she'd set the box of graham crackers leftover from her very first football lesson. They were several days old now, but it didn't matter. She needed a fix in the worst way, and while it was nowhere near a full-fledged cookie, it was at least close in the processed food chain.

Gone.

She glanced around the kitchen before spotting the mangled box on the floor near the pantry. She walked over and picked up what was left. There was no mistaking the soggy uneven edges where tiny doggie teeth had ripped through the cardboard.

Something brown caught the corner of her eye and she turned and spotted a piece of brown wrapper. A few inches away sat another shred. With what was left of the box in hand, she followed the trail across the kitchen, down the hall and into her bedroom, a sneaking suspicion growing in her mind.

She reached the doorway and spotted Skipper hovering over the last of the package of graham crackers.

The dog glanced up. Her whiskers, guilty with crumbs, twitched at the thought of gobbling up the last goodie.

"Don't even think it," Skye warned as she stepped into the room.

Skipper eyed her before placing her paw on the edge of the graham cracker and pulling it close.

"Skipper," Skye said, her voice a tad softer. "Please. I need it."

Skipper seemed to think for a moment before her whiskers twitched a second time and she leaned down, *this* close to gobbling up Skye's last chance at salvation.

"Skipper!" Skye warned, her voice as deep and commanding as the obedience trainer who'd given Skipper her potty lessons.

Skipper stopped hovering and leaned up to look at Skye. "Skipper is the best girl in the entire world and her mommy loves her. Speaking of which, I bet Skipper loves her mommy, too, doesn't she?" A tail wag answered the question. "That's right. Skipper loves her mommy and so Skipper would want to help her mommy. Mommy is not herself right now. She needs a fix." Skye eased down to her knees and crawled a careful inch toward the dog. "I know you're hungry, but I've got an entire box of dog biscuits in the cabinet. The real biscuits. They taste much better than those old graham crackers."

Skye crawled the last few inches and carefully reached forward. "Good girl. That's my—" The words stumbled into one another as Skipper gave another bark and wolfed the graham cracker down.

"I hate you," Skye grumbled, snatching up the dog and

the empty wrapper. "Okay, so I don't actually hate you," she said when the dog licked her cheek. The smell of dog breath mingled with graham crackers filled Skye's nostrils. "But I don't like you. You're a bad girl. Now what am I supposed to do?" She walked back to the kitchen and opened the pantry. Her gaze hooked on the gourmet dog biscuits she'd bought for Skipper.

Okay, she was hungry, but not *that* hungry.

Not after one kiss. Albeit one really great, hot, wet, thorough kiss that had made her knees go weak and her insides melt. While she'd kissed many men in her past, nothing had quite prepared her for the feel of Clint MacAllister's lips on hers.

He'd pressed and plundered and swept his tongue along the seam of her mouth and coaxed her to open up to him. She had. She'd parted her lips and caught her breath as his tongue had swept inside to deepen the kiss.

It was the best kiss of her life, and the worst. Because it had left Skye wanting more.

The thought stirred an image of Skye draped across the front of Clint's #62 Chevy. Naked. Naked and panting and ready for the man leaning over her. This time he didn't just kiss her. He kissed *and* touched *and* licked *and* sucked *and* . . .

She slammed the pantry door and marched to retrieve the Tic Tacs from her purse. Five mints later, she sank down onto her bed and chomped away as she reached for her day planner. If she sucked long and hard enough, surely . . .

Ugh. Long and hard were not words to be thinking of at the moment.

Then again, why not? She was a grown woman with needs. She could think what she wanted and she could get worked up and she could indulge herself if she wanted. She didn't need a man. All she needed was her imagination and one of the various hand techniques she'd perfected in between boyfriends.

She closed her eyes and counted five deep, easy breaths before she touched her left breast. Just a small caress that soon grew to an insistent rub that made her skin tingle and her nipples pebble and her thighs ache.

She trailed her touch lower, but in her mind's eye she didn't see Tarzan or George Clooney or Troy, the better-looking half from Montgomery Gentry.

Instead, she saw Clint MacAllister. She smelled him. She felt him.

But he wasn't there, and damned if the thought didn't bother her enough to kill her hunger and shatter the mood.

Her movements stilled and her eyes popped open and the fantasy ended. And Skye Farrel did the one thing she'd criticized every man in her past for. She rolled over, closed her eyes and went to sleep.

Chapter Ten

"The sun is shining, the weather is clear and it's a great day for a smooth bottle of wine and some fast and furious racing. We're at Sears Point Raceway in Sonoma, California, at one of only two road courses in the NASCAR Winston Cup series. It's going to be an exciting day full of sharp turns, lots of dips and a great view from the beautiful hills surrounding the track—cut!" Bobby Dupree, the host of MTV's newest Sunday night segment called *Race Daze*, motioned to the cameraman.

"There's Clint MacAllister!" He started after Clint and Lindy, who picked up their pace and headed for one of the enormous garages set up for each racing team beyond the pit area. "Hey, Cowboy!" Bobby wasn't just good looking with his short brown hair and Ricky Martin looks. He was fast. The microphone came over Clint's left shoulder. "Are you really out for good?"

Clint kept walking, his cowboy boots slapping pavement as he picked up his speed and moved faster.

Not faster, as in he wanted to get away. Faster, as in busy. His plane had been delayed in San Francisco, and the drive north had taken an hour and a half instead of the usual forty-five minutes, thanks to some construction and two different funeral processions.

He was late. And tired thanks to last night's kiss.

Christ, he'd actually kissed her.

Not that the fact surprised him. He'd known since the first spark of attraction that he would eventually kiss Skye Farrel. What he hadn't anticipated was how that kiss would make him feel—all hot and bothered and so damned needy, as if he hadn't had a woman in years. Or that he would want another, so much in fact that he'd tossed and turned the entire night thinking about another kiss and more.

Like touching and licking and working them both into a frenzy. And then parting her smooth thighs and sliding so deep he forgot where he ended and she began.

"Come on, Clint. Give us the scoop. The race fans want to know," Bobby kept on, dogging Clint's every step. "What's the real story behind your retirement?"

"I'd love to answer all your questions, but Lindy, here"—he motioned to the woman keeping time to his right— "would skin me alive. She handles all the press interviews and she's a stickler for protocol."

"Come on," Bobby persisted. "Rumor has it you're running scared. Is that—"

"Have a good one," Clint cut in, pushing through the door and leaving Bobby to face off with a narrow-eyed Lindy, who turned on him in the doorway.

"You heard the man. You want an interview, you have to go through me."

"I already did. You turned me down."

The door rocked shut on the rest of Lindy's words and Clint found himself surrounded by the roar of a motor.

The smell of oil and hot metal filled his nostrils and he inhaled, drinking in the familiar scent. Relief washed through him, short-lived when he spotted Vernon Simmons, a newspaper in his hand and a look blacker than oil that needed to be changed, talking to Tuck.

". . . making a mockery of this race team and that makes a mockery of Big Tex, and that makes me mad."

"I was just having a little fun. It was harmless," Tuck said with his usual easy grin. But there was nothing easy about the look in his eyes.

He was wary and worried that he'd made a mistake.

Clint knew, not because he knew Tuck all that well, but because he knew the look. He'd worn it a time or two in his younger days when he'd been wet behind the ears and a little too big for his britches.

"What's up?"

"It's what's off." Vernon handed Clint the sports section of the local newspaper.

Clint stared at the latest picture of Tuck. He had a beer in his hand and a smile on his face. If Lindy had been offended by the last picture of Tuck out on the town, she was definitely going to go ballistic over this one.

A woman's bra dangled from around Tuck's neck, while another draped over his head. Two attractive blondes—obviously the respective owners of the lacy lingerie—stood on either side of him. Minus their shirts, of course. The newspaper had printed black bars over their ample chests, but it was still painfully obvious that they were completely topless.

"While all the other drivers were meeting and greeting the reporters," Vernon went on, "Tuck, here, was out back with the Budweiser girls."

"They were the Bud Lite girls." Tuck winked and took a long pull of his bottled water. "And they were fans."

"I think that's obvious."

"I was just having a little fun," Tuck said again.

"Your fun is going to cost us money."

"Lighten up."

"Listen here—"

"Tuck's got a driver's meeting to go to." Clint motioned to the rows of chairs set up in the far corner of the massive garage. "You'd better head on over."

Tuck eyed both men. "You're the boss," he finally said, before turning and starting toward the meeting area.

"I *am* the boss," Clint said, turning to Vernon. "I own the race team. I'm the one responsible. You're a sponsor, Vernon. A silent sponsor who's here for exposure." Clint motioned to the newspaper. "Speaking of which, what's the circulation on that paper?"

Vernon shook his head. "What?"

"The circulation." Clint glanced at the top. "This is one of San Francisco's staples, which says the distribution is pretty large, which means a lot of people are seeing this."

"That's my point," Vernon went on. "This is bad publicity."

"You and I both know there's no such thing."

"Maybe not," Vernon consented, "but there is a thing called image. We're not interested in sponsoring some fly-by-the-seat-of-his-pants driver who makes mistakes on the track because he's too much of a hell-raiser in his personal life. We want a winner. That's why we backed your team in the first place, Clint. Because you're a winner."

"I am, and this team will have a Rookie of the Year. Trust me. Have I ever let you down?"

"You've given me all these gray hairs and nearly

caused a heart attack a time or two and you're definitely to blame for the onset of my ulcer back in '87 when those first pictures came out, but your word *has* always been right on the money."

"Which means you should relax and trust me when I tell you my team's going to bring home a championship this year."

"He's already wasted two races."

"But he's not far behind in total points. We'll make it up."

Vernon gave him a pointed stare. "I trust you, Clint. But you're not behind the wheel of that car this time."

"I might as well be. Tuck's just as good."

"He's stupid."

"He's just young, that's all, and that's no cause to boot his ass off this team. He deserves a chance."

"We're embarrassed, Clint," Vernon stressed. "Very embarrassed."

"More embarrassed than the time the press caught me doing donuts in the parking lot the night before the Bud Shootout back in '94?"

Vernon was silent for a long moment before he finally shrugged. "Maybe not that embarrassed. You were the one topless then. And bottomless."

"I was a little drunk."

"You were a lot drunk and you had good reason. You raced a helluva race. But Tuck isn't just celebrating after the big event. He's sowing his wild oats twenty-four-seven and it's affecting his racing."

"Last week didn't have anything to do with sowing his wild oats. He choked. It happens sometimes." Clint knew that firsthand. "He'll be back in form today."

"I hope so. I'm tired of the bad publicity."

Clint grinned and clapped him on the back. "How many times am I going to have to say it? There's no such thing, buddy. There's no such thing."

Lindy Beckendorf wasn't sure what infuriated her the most about Tuck Briggs. His total lack of respect for the sport of stock car driving itself—as clearly evidenced by the newspaper article now doubling as a drip pan beneath the front fender of Cowboy, Inc.'s #62 Chevrolet—or the way he grinned at her when he glanced up from his pow-wow with CI's crew chief, Jeep McGraw.

"Hey, there, Sis."

"I am not your sister."

"You look like my sister."

"She has red hair?"

"No, she's blond."

"She has brown eyes?"

"Blue as the sky on a hot summer day."

"Then how do I look like her?"

"You *look* like her. Like you're ready to skin somebody alive. She always looked at me like that."

"I can't imagine why."

He scratched his head and winked, his mouth curving into that all-too-familiar shape. "Me either."

Okay, forget his lack of regard for the sport. It was totally that grin punching her buttons.

"You act like her, too."

"Mature and responsible?"

"I was thinking bossy and pretentious. She never smiled either." Another grin. Lindy barely resisted the urge to reach out and grab a hunk of his muscular bicep and pinch for all she was worth.

"At the moment, I don't see anything to smile about. I

do see plenty to worry over, however. I even see a few things that make me want to frown, yell, and maybe do bodily harm. But smiling isn't anywhere on the list."

"Do you like barbecue?" Tuck wiggled his eyebrows, obviously oblivious to her outburst. "I know a place in Austin that makes the best barbecue."

"I know. They also serve up lap dances."

"That sauce can be mighty messy."

She was *not* going to pinch him. Or slap him. Or grab the nearest oil gun and nail him smack dab in the middle of his forehead. She drew in a deep breath and tried to focus on seeing the good rather than just the bad.

Okay, he was a smart aleck. But physically, he was male perfection. His overalls accented a toned, tanned, trim body that would have made her mouth water if she'd been interested in the reckless pretty boy type.

She wasn't, and so she didn't even feel the slight stirring in her middle or the heat creeping up her thighs, and she wasn't the least bit put off by the way her heart rate was speeding up.

"You're looking at me," Tuck said.

"It's a free country. I can look at anyone I want."

"But you're looking at me and you're not talking. That's a first for you."

"I was just thinking. That's a new thing, in case you haven't heard. It actually involves using your head for something other than wearing a bra."

He actually frowned at her then, a complete break from his typical it's-all-good-and-so-am-I expression that grated on her nerves. Lindy smiled.

He eyed her for a long moment before his expression slid back into place. "You really should lighten up," he drawled. "That's a new thing, in case you haven't heard.

It involves pulling the corn cob out of your ass and actually enjoying yourself once in a while."

Her smile disappeared. "It's not about enjoying myself. This is my job. I take it seriously."

"My point exactly. You take it too seriously. It's an adrenaline rush. Fast cars. Screaming fans. Lots of money. Hell, it's entertainment."

"This isn't WWE. This is a real sport."

He touched his hand over his heart. "On behalf of Stone Cold and the bunch, I'm mightily offended."

"You don't get offended. You're the offendee."

"What's that supposed to mean?"

"That you're irresponsible."

"It's called laid back."

"It's going to be called laid *off* if you screw up like you did in the Poconos. I told Clint we should have hired Linc Adams. He knows how to get the job done and he takes it seriously."

Tuck's grin widened, but something flashed on his face. Something deep and intense that told her she'd punched a few of his buttons.

As if he had any. He was a wind-up toy if she'd ever seen one. Simple. Silly.

"Stand back," he said. "You've got that look again. You're definitely thinking."

"You're right. I was thinking what a waste of an incredible set of buns."

Shock wiped the smile off his face and satisfaction rushed through Lindy. Temporary reprieve from the heat pulsing through her body. She turned, satisfied that she'd killed the strange feelings, and stomped away.

Let him think about *that*.

Chapter Eleven

"I *really* need a man," Skye said the minute she heard Xandra's "Hello?" on the other end of the phone line.

"That's why God invented the King Kong Deluxe with its ten different speeds, three variable heat settings and the ever-popular vibrating head."

"You're the one to blame for that, and I'm talking need from a completely different perspective."

"No hot and horny?"

"More like frustrated and fed up." She blew out an exasperated breath and hooked the phone between her head and shoulder and stared at the instructions spread out on the floor in front of her. "Thanks to a fifty-two-inch RCA big-screen television with dual picture control."

Xandra let loose a low whistle. "The lessons must be paying off. You're turning into a he-man's wet dream."

"I'm so confused I could scream. You would think that you could just pull off the cardboard box, plug it in and be good to go. But no. You have to unpack, then hook up the cable."

"Yep, you've got to have cable."

"Then you've got to program the blasted thing."

"Yep, you've got to program."

"*Then* you turn it on only to find out that it doesn't work." She shook her head and barely resisted the urge to hurl the remote control at the blank screen. "I knew there was a reason I never bought one of these things. I hate this." She pressed a few buttons and the screen turned a bright purple before she snatched up the directions and re-read steps one and two in the programming section. "I'm doing what it says." Another button press and the screen blazed neon green. "Mine *has* to be broken. They sold me a lemon. Either that or my brain's still recovering from Friday night's malfunction and I can't think straight."

"What happened Friday night?"

"I went over kiss specifics with Clint MacAllister."

"And this caused a brain fart in what way? You know that lecture like the back of your hand."

"It wasn't the lesson itself that caused the problem. It was the demonstration."

"You gave him a demonstration?"

"Actually, he initiated the demonstration and I reciprocated."

"Sounds delicious."

"It was." The kiss itself wasn't the problem. They had great chemistry and so a kiss had only seemed natural. It was everything leading up to the kiss that had her so freaked out.

When they'd been talking and he'd revealed his dyslexia she'd actually felt a kinship with him. A connection. Despite the fact that she'd had only one macho lesson and they had virtually nothing in common.

"Then was he a bad kisser?"

"Let me just put it this way. Skipper and I had a showdown over a leftover graham cracker after I got home, and it wasn't pretty."

"That still doesn't answer my question. Did you freak out because you expected it to be great and it wasn't so great and it threw you for a loop? You only freak out when something catches you off guard."

"It was as great as I expected."

"So what's the deal? You've been kissed by hot men before and not once has it scrambled your brain."

Because she'd never felt any sort of closeness before a kiss. It had always come after a kiss, and certainly not to the degree she'd felt it with Clint. As if she not only knew him, but she understood him.

"That's because they were available hot men," she blurted, grasping at an obvious explanation, unwilling to voice the truth to even Xandra. Just thinking it scared the bejeezus out of her. "Clint is not available. He has a significant other. I shouldn't be kissing him."

"You like him, don't you?" Xandra asked.

"I hardly know him."

"You're attracted to him."

"There's a difference between being attracted to someone and actually liking them. I don't know Clint well enough to like him and I don't plan on getting to know him that well." If only she didn't feel like she already did.

She forced away the thought. "Actually, I'm starting to hate him. He's the one who suggested I buy this damned TV in the first place." She slapped the remote control against the carpet several times and punched another button. Pink lit up the screen followed by an orange zigzag that worked its way down the middle. "I really suck at this guy stuff."

"You're making this harder than it is. We're talking about TV programming here, not rocket science."

"Easy for you to say. The delivery man did yours."

"True, but if I had to, I could have figured it out, and so can you. You're a smart, vivacious, successful woman who teaches sex for a living. You're rarely intimidated."

"True."

"You can do this and when you do I'll send you the King Kong Ultra Deluxe I'm working on."

"A second model?"

"This one's got fifteen speeds, a vibrating head, three variable heat settings *and* it talks to you."

"Mark's off on another business trip, isn't he?"

"He came home for two days, and then packed up and left for Paris this morning."

"Why didn't you go with him?"

"I have a business of my own to run. I can't just up and leave. I'm a busy woman."

"He didn't ask, did he?"

"He told me to be sure and feed the cat and then he left."

"I'm sorry."

"It's okay. I know he's really busy on these trips and he doesn't have much free time."

"You want a cigarette, don't you?"

"I'd give up my firstborn child and streak naked through the halls of Georgetown High for a teeny, tiny puff. I think about cigarettes. I dream about them. I even caught myself sniffing an old butt I found in the bottom of my purse and my mouth actually watered."

"It should get easier with each smoke-free day."

"It should, but it isn't. At the rate I'm going I'll be working on King Kong's tenth edition before I get the craving completely licked—hey, that's it!"

"What are you talking about?"

"I've done the chewing and the sucking until I'm blue in the face. It's time to pull out the big guns."

"I'm still not following you."

"A lollipop to replace the cigarettes. Lollipops have sticks, not to mention you don't have to lick them. You can suck. If I'm sucking—that's where the candy comes in— and have something to hold in my hand—a stick is nothing but a skinny version of a Marlboro Light—maybe I'll forget all about a cigarette."

"You think?"

"Not really, but at this point, I'm running out of ideas. If I don't do something soon, I'll be lighting up again and I promised my lungs I wouldn't give in."

"I promised my thighs the same thing." Skye wouldn't give in to her cookie craving, no matter how stressed she got, or how much she wanted Clint MacAllister to kiss her again.

He wouldn't and she wouldn't, and that was the end of it.

She hung up the phone and fixed her attention on the instructions and the remote control. She had bigger battles to fight.

"It's just you and me, buddy," she growled as she started programming the sequence for the third time. "And I'm taking no prisoners."

"It's about time you picked up the phone. I've let it ring ten times—are you watching a football game?"

Skye stabbed the Mute button on the remote control. The TV blared louder, proof that while she'd managed to get a picture and sound, she hadn't worked out all the programming bugs. She tried for a nonchalant laugh that came out more like a nervous giggle as she bolted for the TV. "What makes you say that?"

"I can hear the Hank Williams Jr. music."

Skye stabbed the Mute button once, twice and the screen finally fell silent.

"I don't hear any music." Not anymore, thankfully.

"Something is wrong, I just know it. First I can hardly get you on the phone and when I do you find some excuse to let me go and now you're watching a football game and no daughter of mine would ever watch such a violent, pointless, male-dominated sport—"

"I'm not watching a football game." She was watching football highlights. Big difference. Especially to a woman who'd never perfected the art of lying.

"I distinctly heard football," her mother said again.

"Maybe we've got a bad connection. Maybe we're picking up a country station. One of my clients can pick up a local weather station with her daughter's baby monitor. It's something about the signal for a cell phone being similar to the signal for other mobile devices—"

"I'm not on my cell phone and I didn't call you on your cell phone."

"Wow, you're right. Listen, Mom, I'm really busy right now. I've got to go over a new booking and give the hostess a call before dinner and—"

"Did I or did I not hear football?"

"You did not hear a football *game*," Skye said. Guilt snaked through her, settling in the pit of her stomach. Skye knew then that she was about to crack. One more question, and she was going to spill her guts about the whole Clint thing.

"Speaking of which," she rushed on before her mother had a chance to say anything, "how's the new book going?

Do you think it will do as well as this last one? Number eight on the *New York Times* will be tough to top, but I'm sure you can do it—"

"Slow down," her mother cut in and Skye prepared herself for the worst. Sure, Xandra got away with the whole avoidance thing, but she'd had more practice. Skye had been avoiding for all of five seconds. She was an amateur.

"Of course I can top number eight," her mother surprised her. "This book is sure to be even better. It's a detailed study of the male as a single parent. How men must then step into the female role and be the primary caregiver. An easy task financially, but a tough one as far as nurturing goes. Due to their biological makeup men simply can't nurture as well as women and, therefore, it has a negative effect on the rearing of healthy daughters."

"I see your point."

"Of course you do. It takes a female mind—"

"How's Dad?"

"—to truly nurture . . . What?"

"Dad. How is he? Where is he?"

"He's fine. He's in Brazil on an iguana retreat. I hate the things myself, but your father is committed, and that I can understand. Speaking of which, I hope you caught last night's episode of *Get Sexed Up* because I talked about the difference between a life partner and a sex partner. I used your father as an example of both, much to his relief . . ." Her mother went on, dropping the subject of male-dominated households and football faster than she would have gotten rid of a platinum engagement ring.

Skye smiled. She'd programmed the damned TV and avoided her mother's prying questions. Things were definitely looking up.

*   *   *

"What the hell is that?" Clint came up short in the doorway to Skye's living room later that afternoon, after a full half-hour phone call with her mother—her mother had done almost all of the talking—and another two hours working the kinks out of her programming.

She'd done it. Every button on the remote now worked and she smiled as satisfaction bubbled inside her. While she didn't get the whole electronic addiction that most men had, she had to admit that getting it all to work was somewhat of a rush.

She smiled. "It's a TV."

"It's not a TV. It's a big-screen TV."

"I bought it this weekend."

He stepped closer and eyed her new purchase before turning an accusing stare on her. "It's the same brand as mine."

"I know."

"I can't believe you even noticed the brand of my television."

"Not just the brand. There are seven different models. This one has advanced picture programming just like yours."

"This thing is a bitch to set up."

"Tell me about it. It took me all day."

"*You* hooked it up?"

"And programmed the remote. It took me awhile, but I finally got it to work so I didn't have to keep getting up to pause the game when I had to go to the bathroom."

"You watched a game?"

"After last night's taped episode of *Get Sexed Up.* I watched a DVD of the Super Bowl."

"A *football* game?"

"Last I heard that was the only sport that had a Super Bowl. It was pretty exciting once I got into it."

"Exciting?" He shook his head. "You really thought it was exciting."

"Crazy, huh? I just knew I was going to hate it. But it was great. That's why I checked out these at the video store." She held up a stack of DVDs. "Every Super Bowl game for the past five years and I'm not just watching the game either. I'm watching the commentary, too. Pre-game, post-game. I'm going the whole nine yards. I really do like it."

Sure, she liked it, Clint thought. It was easy to like something when you were watching from the comfort of your own home. You could kick back on the sofa, a drink in one hand and a sandwich in the other. Food made everything that much better.

During his lunch break, he'd been known to tune into *A Makeover Story* a time or two. But that didn't mean he would enjoy actually sitting down and letting some hairstylist whose name he couldn't pronounce foil and fry his hair before stuffing him into a black see-through mesh shirt and a pair of leather pants like on the last episode.

Clint dropped his own stack of DVDs—tonight's lesson—on her coffee table and said, "Let's go."

"But I thought we were going to have lesson number two."

"We are, but not here."

"I really need my comfort zone."

"It's not about comfort." It was one thing to watch from a distance. Getting up close and personal was the real test. "It's about two men, lots of muscle and a throng of screaming, bloodthirsty fans."

"Bloodthirsty?"

"The more blood the better." He took her hand and started for the door.

She tried to pull away. "I don't think that's such a good plan."

"It's the best one I've had in a long time."

"But I get really queasy at the sight of blood."

"That's what I'm counting on."

Otherwise, Clint would be forced to consider the fact that Skye Farrel was a lot more his type than he cared to admit.

"His boobs are bigger than hers," Skye stated as she stared at the wrestler who'd just entered the ring opposite the women's current champion.

"They're not boobs," Clint told her as he watched the man and woman face off in a battle of the sexes. Clint had seen to it that he and Skye were sitting ringside. "They're pecs."

"If I pointed to the exact same spot on her, you would call them boobs." She took a sip of her soda. "Why do men's pectoral muscles get an athletic-sounding name, while women are stuck with the synonym for several fools?"

"Your feminist roots are showing."

"I'm a womanist, and it's just plain unfair."

"Okay, look at the boobs on him."

"They're pecs."

"I know that, but I thought you wanted to be fair."

"If you want to be fair, then say something like 'hey, would you look at the pecs on her?' Women have pecs, too." She frowned as she watched the ring. The male wrestler picked up the woman and slammed her down on the mat. Skye cringed.

The move upset the woman's partner who'd accompanied her to the ring. He was a big, brawny, mouthy guy who grabbed a nearby chair, parted the ropes and jumped into the ring on her behalf. He slammed the chair over the guy's head.

"Oh, no." Skye covered her eyes. "Is he bleeding?"

"Everywhere." Actually, it was just a small cut on his forehead that sent him stumbling backwards.

She swallowed. "I think I'm going to be sick."

"We can always leave," Clint told her as the chair guy pulled the female wrestler to safety before jumping back into the ring, chair in hand, and going after the other wrestler a second time. "Just say the word and we're out of here. I know you don't like this."

"But men do. Macho men."

"But you don't," he pointed out again. "You don't, do you?"

"I . . ." She swallowed. "It's not that I don't like it. I tend to get nauseous at the sight of blood."

Clint barely resisted the urge to slide his arm around her shoulders and pull her close. She was cringing and he was glad and that was the end of it.

"Wow," he said, eager to press his advantage all the way home. She was this close to making a run for it. "It's smeared all over his forehead."

"A head wound?"

"A bad one. That guy really gave it to him good with that chair and—oh!" The crowd roared. "He hit him again."

"Again? Is it bad?" She was still covering her eyes, but she'd slid forward to the edge of her chair. "How bad?"

"He's stumbling around."

"I don't like this."

"He's barely conscious."

"I *really* don't like this."

"He's going down. He's going . . . There! He's down."

But she already knew because her fingers had parted and she was peeking between the space.

"Get up," she murmured as the referee started his count. *One . . .*

"Come on," she pleaded. "Get up."

Two . . .

Her hands fell away from her face. "*Come on*," she yelled out. "Get up!"

Three . . .

"That's the way to go!" She jumped to her feet along with the rest of the crowd as the wrestler struggled upright before the referee slapped the mat for the third time. "Get that guy for hurting your woman!"

Clint was on his feet next to her. "What are you doing?"

"Cheering." She clapped and whistled as the two men went at it again. "He's defending her honor."

"He's beating the guy to death with a chair."

"Yes, and on the woman's behalf. He's her hero. Atta way to go!" she yelled out.

Clint frowned. "What about the blood?"

"What about it?"

"It's all over him."

"He asked for it. He hit that guy's girl. Let's go!" she shouted out before letting loose a wolf whistle. "Give that jackass a taste of his own medicine. That'll teach him to hit a woman."

She looked so excited and eager and passionate, and it was all Clint could do to keep from tugging her into his arms and kissing her.

This was *not* good.

Chapter Twelve

Tonight was strictly sex.

Skye clung to the comforting thought as she pressed Clint's doorbell and waited. There would be no talking or sharing about anything other than hot, pleasurable S-E-X.

That had been her mistake on Friday night. All the conversation about his past and her past had derailed her thoughts and sent her careening off into the land of the ill-prepared. That's when she'd gotten nervous and that's why she'd responded to his impromptu kiss. She'd been anxious and desperate for a cookie and then he'd kissed her and he'd tasted just as sweet. And so she'd kissed him back.

She licked her lips and pushed aside the sudden image of Clint hovering over her, his eyes so dark and intense, his lips parted just enough to let her know that he intended to taste her . . .

Skye shook away the thought and reached into her bag for a SweetTart. She popped the candy into her mouth. She'd taken Xandra's advice and found a substitute. Kissing involved puckering and sour candy definitely delivered a pucker.

She wasn't going to fall victim to her craving tonight and she certainly wasn't going to act on her attraction to Clint. He was sort of taken and she didn't do sort of taken men.

Even if he were completely available, she wouldn't be doing him. Chemistry aside, they wanted different things out of life. She wanted long-term commitment minus the ball and chain, while he couldn't wait to snap on the shackles and throw away the key.

They were worlds apart, even if they did both enjoy a good wrestling match.

She still couldn't believe she'd actually enjoyed last night. She'd never really seen the appeal of wrestling before. The moves had always seemed so fake. But sitting ringside, she'd actually found herself caught up in the sport. However over-the-top, the wrestlers and the fans had been so enthusiastic. So passionate. And if there was one thing Skye could relate to, it was passion.

The sport, while theatrical, had oozed energy, from the oversized, loudmouthed wrestlers themselves, to the very vocal crowd of fans packed into the arena, Skye included.

Never in all her thirty-three years had she pictured herself ringside at WWE Monday night RAW, but that's exactly where she'd been, and she'd enjoyed every moment.

Okay, she hadn't enjoyed every single moment. At first, she'd been skeptical and sick to her stomach. But every match seemed to have its own theme and story—the arch rivals finally facing off with each other, the underdogs fighting for their pride and dignity, the bad boys everyone loved to hate getting away with being bad yet again.

She knew she wouldn't have been nearly as into it watching from the comfort of her own living room. Clint had known that and so he'd hauled her out to a live show. He was definitely fulfilling his end of the proposition, which meant she had to keep her mind on business and fulfill hers.

Strictly sex.

With that thought firmly in mind, she straightened her shoulders and pressed the doorbell again. Somewhere inside Jezebel started to bark. She glanced around while she waited. She'd noticed his home before, but only from the inside.

The truth of just how different they were surrounded her in the form of a huge yard with towering oak trees and neatly trimmed hedges. She stood on a big, sprawling front porch with a wooden swing just to her left. It was the sort of place just made for a handful of kids running here and there. The perfect place to raise a family.

Skye's high-rise apartment, in direct contrast, was barely fit to raise plants. Her teeny, tiny balcony could barely hold a small ivy and one lounge chair. Sure, her apartment was sizable, with a spacious living room, two roomy bedrooms and a large office area, but the place had been crafted more for looks than comfort.

Looks were important, of course, particularly if one were raising daughters. She'd loved her grandmother's treasured porcelain dolls and her china cabinet that housed antique crystal and a collection of glass frogs.

But boys? They definitely demanded comfort. Forget the miniature table and chairs, the mini china cabinet filled with tiny teacups and saucers and the frilly skirted vanity table—peach to match the bedspread and curtains—that had dominated Skye's room as a child. Boys needed beanbag chairs and big stuffed pillows shaped like footballs and shatter-proof furniture for WWE Raw imitations.

Clint was definitely preparing himself for boys.

She smiled as an image hit her of Clint running across the yard with a football in his hands, a half dozen little boys with his same dark hair and dancing blue eyes hot on his heels.

She frowned as the image shifted and she saw herself standing on the front porch, her belly overflowing with little Clint number seven, a smile on her face as she watched her man.

Bellies and babies and *Clint*?

Before she could dwell on the disturbing thought, the door creaked open and a frazzled-looking redhead appeared, her arms overflowing with files and newspapers.

"Can I help you?"

"I'm here to see Clint MacAllister. I'm Skye Farrel. He's expecting me."

"I remember you from the wedding. The owner of the sex company."

"Girl Talk and it's more like an educational company."

"That educates people about sex."

"Yes."

"Exactly. The sex company. Come on in." She opened the door and stepped back so that Skye could walk by her.

"Can I help carry anything?" Skye asked as the woman juggled the stack between her two arms and kicked the door shut with her foot.

"No thanks." She eyed Skye. "You don't really look like the type to teach sex for a living."

"No red velvet dress with a matching feather boa? I left that at home tonight."

The woman's stoic expression broke into a smile. "Actually, I was thinking black thigh boots and well-placed tassels."

"The boots are being oiled and the tassels are at the cleaners, so I got stuck wearing a suit."

Another smile and she motioned. "He's on a phone call right now, but you can wait in the den."

Skye followed Lindy down the now familiar hallway and into the paneled room lined with trophies. In the far corner, Jezebel the Blue Heeler sat on her doggie bed. She glanced up at Skye as if to say *I know you*, before nuzzling down and closing her eyes.

"So how long have you known Clint?" Skye asked as she placed her briefcase on the coffee table and sank down to the sofa.

"My entire life. Sort of." Lindy juggled her load to the opposite arm and used her free hand to shove her glasses back up her nose. "I lived just up the road from his folks and we used to walk the same route to school, but Clint always kept to himself. Until high school. Then he found shop class, joined the football team and became one of the beautiful people, and I wasn't."

Skye smiled and pointed at herself. "Glasses, skinny legs and a high IQ."

"Chubby, with braces and hair like Bozo the clown. I had the high IQ, too, which only made matters worse. Clint didn't even notice me until seventh grade when he saved me from a group of bullies."

"Did he beat them up?"

"He charmed them silly." At Skye's puzzled look, she added, "They were girls. The Wallace triplets. Fay, Kay and Wilda May. They were cute, blonde and brutal, at least to me. They used to give me hell every day after gym class. One day they were giving me their usual spiel about how I was the product of a mutant alien coupling and didn't deserve to share the same locker room with them. Clint came up to us and turned on the charm. In a matter of minutes, the girls had forgotten all about me and had eyes only for him. They never bothered me again after that."

"That was nice of him."

"I offered to pay him five bucks per triplet but he didn't want money. He wanted tutoring. I agreed and we've been working together ever since."

"She means she's been bossing me around ever since," Clint said as he walked in.

"Somebody around here has to do it." Lindy turned her attention to the stack in her hands. "Here's the contract I briefed you about. You need to sign it." She handed over a folded stack of blue-bound documents. "And here are the expenses for this past race and the projected expenses for next week." She handed him several folders, followed by a stack of various newspapers and magazines. "And here is all the press coverage for this past weekend."

Clint eyed the sizable stack. "Seems like they really like Tuck. Who won yesterday, in case you forgot."

"Who won despite the fact that he messed up on two turns and nearly took out another car during his last lap," she said pointedly. "Besides, most of their coverage is about you." She turned to Skye and smiled. "Nice to meet you." And then she left the room.

"She likes you," Clint told her once the door had closed behind Lindy.

"How can you tell?"

"She actually smiled. She's usually so uptight that any facial expression, even a pleasant one, looks more like a grimace. But I think I actually spotted dimples."

"We're alumnae for the same sorority."

"Lindy was in a sorority?"

Skye nodded. "Phi Kappa Geek."

He grinned. "You weren't a geek. You were a girlie girl."

"Same thing when you're always dolled up in a dress and all the other girls won't give you a chance."

"Why didn't you make your own chance? You should have proved them wrong."

"You like proving people wrong, don't you?"

"I like showing people that what they see isn't always what they get and that they shouldn't be too quick to judge. People judged me my whole life. They're still judging me."

At his comment, her gaze went to the newspaper and the headline Is THE WOLF PACK TURNING INTO THE WUSS PACK?

"They think you're afraid to get behind the wheel," she said as her gaze skimmed the first few lines of the article. "They really think you're afraid."

"They're trying to sell more newspapers." He shook his head. "It's not interesting that I'm ready to move on in my life, so they cook up something more juicy. It's more exciting to imagine I'm facing some awful fear that I might crash again. That I'm scared if there's a next time, *when* there's a next time, I won't be lucky enough to walk away with just a shoulder injury."

Silence fell between them for several long moments.

"So are you?" she finally said, suddenly eager to ease the tension in his expression. Despite her strictly sex vow.

The minute she voiced the question, something flashed in his eyes and she knew the answer even though he shook his head and gave her a *when the devil starts scooping up ice cream* look.

"Listen, Ruffles, I'm about as afraid of driving as you are of climbing onto the ropes and giving Stone Cold Steve Austin a piece of your mind."

Her cheeks heated at the memory. "I may have gotten a little carried away last night."

"A little?" He arched an eyebrow and grinned, obviously grateful to trade in the topic of his driving for another.

"Okay, maybe a lot but it was so much better than watching it on TV."

"Um, yeah," he said, his grin fading. "It's all right."

"Just all right? Are you kidding? It's a rush, like riding on the back of a motorcycle. I did that one time back in high school. I was a little afraid, but then I just climbed on and held tight."

The confession seemed to stop him cold. "*You've* been on the back of a motorcycle?" Before she could respond, he added, "I have a motorcycle. A souped-up 1973 Harley with fins."

"That's nice." As she continued, it was as if she were confessing to being a serial killer. "I don't really know much about motorcycles." Disappointment flared in his eyes and something tightened inside her. "I've seen a Harley before. I saw *Easy Rider* one night when I was up late working on one of my workshops."

Hello? What does riding a motorcycle have to do with sex?

Very little, unless one wanted to get really creative and a little daring. Position wise, it was perfect for lots of touching. If she were holding him around the waist, it would just be a matter of sliding her hand down and . . . She forced the thought away and retrieved a SweetTart from her pocket. She puckered and his attention fixated on her lips for a long, heart-pounding moment.

"We really should get started," she blurted before she drove them any further along the road to emotional involvement. "Tonight we're covering the sex act itself." She pulled out tonight's lesson plan. "Here are the high points." Handing him several sheets of paper stapled together, she fixed her attention on her own copy and tried to ignore the image of his tanned fingers against the stark white sheets that filled the corner of her eye.

He had exceptional hands, with strong fingers. They weren't too soft or too callused, but just rough enough to make her skin tingle if he touched her back and trailed up and down just so . . .

She shifted, suddenly warm and anxious and hot.

Hot was good. Familiar. Even if it didn't feel half as comforting as it usually did with him so close and the room so warm and her stomach growling for a lot more than a sour nickel-sized candy.

She drew in a deep breath, popped another candy and tried to ignore her craving.

"What's with the DVDs?" he said, eyeing the stack.

"My other sister is the owner and director of Sugar & Spice Sinema. They make how-to videos." She picked up the top DVD. "They have a wonderful three-disc series that covers various sexual positions." She stood, walked over to the DVD player and inserted the first disc.

"Sexual positions, huh?"

"Fifty-two of them."

"You have to be kidding."

"Actually, some theorize that there are fifty-four but Eve's a die-hard believer in the fifty-two theory, so I merely verbalize the last two suggestions."

A few seconds later, Skye sank down to the edge of the sofa, the remote control in her hand.

"Now," she said, punching the Play button. The DVD started and an attractive couple filled the screen. "This is a visual demonstration of the first twelve in order of popularity. The first is the most common and is widely known as the missionary position. This is a very intimate position because the man and woman are facing one another, which thereby facilitates eye contact—you're looking at me," she said, catching his stare.

"You're talking."

"I'm narrating. There's a big difference."

"Okay."

"This is the woman-on-top, a favorite of most men because men are very visual and this particular position provides an excellent view of a woman's face and breasts. This is one of the few positions that promotes—you're still looking at me."

"You're still talking."

"You should be looking at the video."

"They're not talking. They're grunting."

"It's sex. Grunting is allowed."

"No argument here." He shrugged, settled back into the cushioned sofa and glanced toward the big screen.

Her gaze hooked on his thighs outlined by a pair of tight, faded jeans that clung like a second skin. Denim cupped his crotch, revealing a substantial bulge that seemed even more substantial than when she'd stolen a glance at it a few minutes ago.

Not that she went around staring at men's bulges.

It was a matter of priorities. Sex topped her list and so when she veered off the safety of the subject into no man's emotional land, she could always treat herself to an eyeful to get back on track.

He was definitely an eyeful.

He lifted his legs, propped his feet on the coffee table and hooked his booted ankles, the motion drawing her attention back to his thighs. Muscles rippled, the denim pulling this way and that against the sinewy contents, and her mouth went dry.

"What are you thinking?" His deep, smooth voice slid into her ears and jarred her. She stiffened.

"What?"

"You're staring at me now. What are you thinking?"

"That you've got great legs for this next position." She turned her attention back to her note cards and flipped to the next one. "Strong legs, and strength is definitely a plus to insure a nice, deep stroke when it comes to what is commonly referred to as doggie style. The position entails the woman facing away from the man with the man directly behind her. This position is also a visual turn-on for most men as it provides an up-close view of a woman's backside—would you stop looking at *me* and watch the video?"

"You were looking at me a few seconds ago."

"In relation to the video. Are you looking at me in relation to the video?"

"Actually, I was trying to picture you on the back of that motorcycle. What were you wearing?"

"This has nothing to do with the video."

"I'm trying to get a visual," he persisted, punching the Pause button on the DVD player. "Tell me."

"It wasn't a pretty picture. Sundresses do not adapt well to the open road."

"You climbed on the back of a motorcycle wearing a dress?"

"I was always wearing dresses. I like dresses. I said I had fun. I didn't say it was easy. Now." She forced her attention back to the lesson plan. "After doggie there's the spoon position—"

"What did you like the most about it?"

"We really should get to tonight's lesson."

"Tell me what you liked the most."

She caught the determined glint in his gaze and shrugged. "The wind. I liked the feeling of the wind on my bare skin." At his knowing look, she added, "and underneath my dress." She eyed the television. "What I liked most was the way my heart pounded because I knew I wasn't supposed to be doing something so wild and reckless." She shook her head as the memory bubbled to the surface. A smile touched her lips. "My mother would have had a fit if she had known. Not about the actual riding, but about being on the back. *'No daughter of mine would ride behind a man. She would be the one driving, the one in control.'*" She glanced up. "I wasn't driving, but still felt in control. There was all this power beneath me and it made me feel like I was sitting on top of the world. I know that sounds crazy," she said, but one look into his eyes and she knew he didn't think it was so crazy, after all.

"I know what you mean. It's no different than driving a race car. There's all this power at your fingertips and you feel larger than life. Invincible," he said, voicing exactly what she was thinking. But even if he hadn't said the words, she knew that he knew. In the dark depths of his eyes, she saw the proof. The understanding. The kin-ship. The connection.

The realization sent a burst of panic through her and Skye did what any other sexpert would do in her predica-ment—faced with an ultra-hot, marriage-minded he-man who not only turned her on physically, but punched her emotional buttons, as well.

She leaned forward and kissed him.

Chapter Thirteen

Kissing Clint MacAllister was even better than being on the back of a motorcycle.

Skye admitted that to herself as his tongue delved into her mouth and her nerves started to buzz.

Kissing Clint felt more wild, more reckless, more heart pounding than anything she'd ever done before, including the midnight ride with the baddest and most chauvinistic boy in Georgetown, Texas.

She wasn't sure why. It certainly wasn't because she'd initiated the contact. She'd kissed many men, and many men had kissed her back, and not once had it ever felt so . . . *right*.

Right as in the way his mouth fit hers, the way his tongue dipped and tangled and danced with hers. The way his hands came around to pull her closer and initiate a more intimate contact. The way he guided her over and onto his lap. The way her thighs settled on either side of his. The way her breasts crushed against his chest. The way her pelvis straddled his growing erection.

She wrapped her arms around his neck, kissing him

with an intensity she often lectured about, but had rarely felt in her own relationships.

An intensity she'd never felt until that very first kiss last week.

The thought sent a thread of fear through her and she managed to pull back enough to catch her breath.

"I think we should get back to the lesson."

"I thought this was part of the lesson."

"No. I mean, yes. I just wanted . . ." To get off a very unsafe subject, onto something much safer.

Funny, but sitting astride him, staring into his eyes, she didn't feel as if she were wandering in safe territory. With his musky, intoxicating scent filling her nostrils and his gaze, dark and glittering with desire, holdings hers, she might well have been teetering on the edge of a cliff. All the more reason for her to pull back and stop right now.

But at the same time, there was something exhilarating about what had just happened. Something that went beyond a mere distraction.

It's called chemistry, girlfriend. Good, old-fashioned rip-off-your-clothes-because-I-have-to-have-you-now chemistry.

"You wanted to what?" he prodded, his gaze searching hers, his lips wet and parted and oh-so distracting.

"I, um, just wanted to make sure that you'd perfected the kissing before we moved on to the various positions. You," she drew in a much needed breath, "can't have a middle if there's no beginning."

"Did I ace the qualifier?"

Boy, did you ever.

"It was a little iffy." She licked her lips and tasted him—a combination of raspberry iced tea and warm, hungry male—and her stomach grumbled for more. "I think I need another demonstration to really be sure."

Before she could draw another much-needed breath, he grabbed the sides of her head and captured her lips in a hot, wet kiss that stole her breath and kicked up her heart another several beats. His tongue touched and mated with hers. Her arms curled around his neck and she tilted her head to give him better access.

The kiss went on for several fast, furious seconds before it slowed into something fierce and possessive and thorough. His hands closed over her shoulders before his arms slid around and he pulled her even closer. His palms slid down her back and underneath her skirt to cup her bare buttocks and heat fired between her legs. His fingers kneaded her flesh and his rock-hard groin rubbed her through the delicate satin of her panties, and instead of pulling away and giving him his well-deserved A+ for Kissing 101, she moaned and clutched him tighter.

She was only human, after all, and it had been over six months since a man had held her, touched her, stroked her. Her resolve melted like ice cream on a hot piece of apple pie and she forgot that her entire objective in kissing him in the first place had been to steer his attention away from their personal lives and back to the subject matter at hand—sexual positions.

Mission accomplished.

She'd never been a big fan of the lap dance—woman facing man, sitting on man's lap—until this moment. With this man. Her nipples throbbed, pressing against the lace of her bra. Heat flooded between her legs and desire curled through her. She was on fire. Aching and burning and ringing . . . *ringing?*

". . . can't take your call right now, but if you leave

your name and number, I'll get back to you . . ."
Beeeeeep.

"This is Donna Dee Lite, Mr. MacAllister. I know you don't know me, but I'm here at The Leap Frog with Tuck Briggs and there's a problem."

"*Shit!*" Clint swore as he tore his mouth from hers. His chest heaved and his eyes were glazed with passion as he glanced at the answering machine. "I'm sorry. I have to get this."

"I . . ." She nodded, scrambling off his lap as he got to his feet.

Her skirt was up around her waist and her blouse had ridden up under her breasts and she felt the same way she had the first time her grandmother had flicked on the porch light when she'd been kissing her prom date good night.

Nervous and uncertain and . . . *nervous?*

She killed the DVD and watched Clint cross the room and snatch up the phone. He swore a few more times as he listened to the person on the other end before hanging up and turning back to her.

"We'll have to do this later. I've got to go."

But Skye was way ahead of him. She'd already snatched up her briefcase and her educational materials and she was headed for the door.

"No problem. We'll do positions next time. You did really good on number six."

"Another test?"

"A demonstration."

A distraction, she told herself despite the niggling truth that followed her out the front door and to her car.

She climbed behind the wheel, grabbed her roll of SweetTarts and fed several into her mouth to kill the craving deep inside her and the taste of him that was still potent on her lips.

Her hands trembled as she grasped the steering wheel. She was nervous, uptight, stressed, despite the fact that they'd just had some really hot, mindless groping.

Because of it.

Because Cowboy MacAllister had not only punched her buttons physically, but he'd given her a charge emotionally, as well. Despite her best efforts, they were getting to know each other on a personal level.

"No," she groaned, swallowing the mouthful of candy and reaching for more. She wouldn't . . . She couldn't . . .

Oh, no. She was starting to actually *like* him.

Her stomach grumbled at the thought and Skye did the only thing a desperate, hungry woman could do—she stopped at the first convenience store and bought herself a bag of Chips Ahoy.

"I didn't know who else to call." The six-foot buxom blonde wearing red short-shorts and a now dry T-shirt that said THESE PUPPIES WERE MADE FOR SUCKING led him through a maze of tables, to the back of the small Austin nightclub where Tuck Briggs had hosted a wet T-shirt contest. Tuck sat at a small round table, his back to the wall, his head hanging as if he'd dozed off while sitting upright.

Donna Dee Lite, as she'd introduced herself a few moments before, handed Clint a black leather wallet adorned with a silver concho and embroidered with the initials T.B. "Your name and phone number were the only thing I found in his wallet. Except for a few condoms."

"He doesn't have a wife or a significant other." Or any

family to speak of. Clint had once heard him mention a mother in his childhood, but he'd rarely spoken of that part of his life. Clint had a feeling that Tuck had had his own hard time growing up. He saw it when he looked at the rebellious young man.

He saw himself.

"That's right," Tuck piped up as if Clint's words had penetrated the alcoholic haze surrounding him. A mountain of beer mugs were stacked pyramid style on his table, but the minute his gaze locked with Clint's, Clint couldn't help but get the feeling that the empty mugs didn't belong to Tuck.

"No wife," Tuck went on. "No girlfriend. No mother. No father. I'm twenty-two, driving solo and lovin' every minute of it."

Clint ignored him and pulled the blonde off to the side to speak to her privately. "Thanks for calling me instead of the newspapers."

"I doubt they would risk coming in here after he hit the photographer who tried to take his picture after the contest. He broke the guy's nose and knocked out a couple of teeth. The guy tried to hit back and accidentally hit one of the bystanders. That's when everybody just started swinging at everybody else."

She motioned to a young guy wiping down the bar. "Travis over there helped me persuade Mr. Briggs to hide out back until the ruckus died down and the police left with most of the troublemakers."

"I'll take things from here." Clint pulled a business card from his pocket and handed it to her. "Call my office and they'll hook you up with free tickets to any NASCAR race. Your choice."

"That's awesome." A smile lit her face. "My little boy

loves NASCAR." She turned toward Tuck. "That's why I was so excited about tonight's contest. But he's not at all what I would have expected."

"You and me both," Clint growled as the blonde walked away and he turned back to Tuck.

Clint's boots made quick work of the few feet separating them. He motioned to his driver. "Time to go home."

"But I'm still having a good time." He leaned back in his chair, a belligerent light in his eyes as he held up his glass. "Good enough for one more round."

"You've had enough." Clint grabbed the glass and set it on the table. He reached for Tuck's arm, but the young man shrugged him off.

"Hey, hey, watch the jacket, man. This is my lucky racing jacket."

Clint towered over Tuck, his hands on his hips as he stared at the smiling man. "Get your ass out of that chair right now and come with me." Clint's words were low and dangerous, fueled with the anger boiling inside him.

Tuck let loose a low whistle. "Looks like somebody's mad." He leaned back and squinted up, his gaze guarded. Sober. Despite how he seemed to try to act otherwise. "I don't think I've ever seen you mad."

"Well, take a good look because if that jacket is doing its job, you'll get lucky and this will be the last time. You're embarrassing this race team."

"I'm taking this race team to Victory Lane." He tapped his chest. "Me. I'm the one who just won at Sears Point. I racked up the points. *Me*."

"You, my car and an entire crew. We're a team. You're a driver. Just one of a dozen team members. No better. No worse. You need to keep your perspective."

Tuck frowned. "And you need to realize who you're

talking to. I'm Tuck Briggs. *The* Tuck Briggs. Nobody can beat me."

"You're good, but there's always somebody better, somebody right there dogging you, just waiting to pass. Forget that and you won't last too long in this business." He leaned down until they were nose to nose. "Keep fucking up and you won't last past New Hampshire next weekend."

Tuck sat silent for a long moment, as if weighing Clint's words and trying to figure out if his boss was as serious as he sounded.

Finally, his face split into a grin. "You wouldn't fire me. You need me. It's too late to find another driver who can gain enough points to win the championship. You won't break a seven-year winning streak. That's why you stepped aside and let me in. You want to win."

"Actually, I want to punch you in your face, but I won't. You're young and stupid, Tuck. You need to grow up."

A dark look passed over Tuck's face. "I don't need to do anything, and I sure as hell don't need anyone telling me what I need to do. You're not my daddy."

"I'm better. I'm your boss and I'm paying you a hell of a lot of money, and it isn't so that you can go around disrespecting women and punching out the press. You're a professional driver. Start acting like one."

The anger faded into that annoying grin. "Yessir, Mr. Cowboy, sir. You want fries with that load of bullshit? Because I seem to recall a certain driver way back when who raised a lot of hell every chance he got."

Clint passed a hand over his face. He was tired and frustrated and, worse, he was horny thanks to Skye and her demonstration, and the three didn't make for a pleasant mix. "Just get your ass out of that chair, go home and get to bed. You fly out to Dover Downs tomorrow for some test sessions for next month's race and I want it to go smooth." His voice lowered as he caught Tuck's stare. "And if it doesn't, you'll be back driving those dirt tracks out in the middle of Assbackwards, Texas, faster than you can blink. Is that clear?"

Tuck eyed Clint as if he were trying to make up his mind whether or not to tell him to get fucked. "You're the boss," the young man finally muttered. "I'm getting the hell out of here." He pushed to his feet and rummaged in his pocket for his keys.

"Forget it. I've got a cab outside. I'll drop you at your apartment on my way back to the airport."

"I can get home just fine."

"I'm sure you can because you're not near as shit-faced as you want me to think." At Clint's comment, Tuck's gaze narrowed. "But I'll rest easier tonight knowing that you're safe and sound and home, instead of out at some after-hours club doing more damage."

"I don't need a babysitter."

"And I don't need any more trouble. This is it. No more."

It was all about sex.

Clint admitted that to himself a good hour later as he watched the lights of Austin fade. He pulled back on the throttle and the plane gained altitude. The sky stretched in front of him like an endless black void and his hand adjusted the Cessna's controls.

He usually loved to fly. Like driving, flying gave him a sense of power. Control.

But tonight he didn't feel the typical rush of adrenaline, the bubble of satisfaction that overwhelmed him when he *was* in control, calling the shots, making things happen, *doing* something important when he'd been told his entire life that he could never do anything at all.

Instead, he felt hot. Frustrated. Desperate. Disappointed.

It was definitely all about the sex.

Skye Farrel wasn't even remotely interested in *him*. She'd proven as much tonight when she'd been much more eager to kiss him than talk to him.

He'd given her the benefit of the doubt. He'd tried to start up a conversation, to get to know her, but she'd killed his attempt with one helluva kiss.

As much as he'd started to think that maybe, just maybe they connected on more than a physical level, he'd been wrong. She probably hadn't even really liked the football and the wrestling. It had been an act to get close to him.

He'd suspected as much. Women like Skye Farrel didn't go for men like Clint MacAllister. Not in a forever kind of way. They got close because they wanted something.

Obviously, it wasn't because he was all that in the sack. Darla had opened his eyes to that all-important fact, though he'd been somewhat disillusioned about it during his teen years.

He realized now that the attraction back then had been because he was the most popular boy at his high school. He'd excelled at sports and raced in his spare time. In a sense, he'd been a celebrity. An amateur stock car driver with a future. Then he'd turned professional and his appeal had grown. Women had been wowed by the image, attracted to the fast and furious persona of a successful race-car driver. They craved a brush with greatness. They didn't want the reality of the man. They wanted a fantasy, and sleeping with him fulfilled that fantasy. No matter how mediocre the sex.

Skye was obviously no different from all the women in his past. Women who'd pretended interest in him merely to get close, to get what they wanted.

In tonight's case, a kiss and possibly more if they hadn't been interrupted.

You poor thing, a voice whispered. *You're such a victim.*

Okay, so he'd kissed her back and he'd wanted more, too, but it was understandable. He hadn't had sex for nearly five months, and he'd obviously never had the good, quality, state-of-the-art sex that Skye lectured about. With all that moaning and groaning in the background and the fact that Skye was so skilled at her job, he hadn't been able to resist.

She'd wanted him and he'd wanted her, and so things had heated up.

His groin twitched. Things were still *up*.

For now.

Because Clint was attracted to her. But that attraction would fade the more he saw her true colors and realized she wasn't half as interested in all the guy stuff—his stuff—as she pretended to be. It was merely an act to get close to him because of his fame. She didn't want *him*.

Women like Skye Farrel—the high-brow, sophisticated, feminist types didn't go for simple, down-to-earth, macho men like Clint MacAllister. They liked to go slumming once in a while for a charge of excitement and a change of pace, but they didn't want to live there.

He knew that firsthand.

*   *   *

Sue Anne Randolph had been the head cheerleader, president of the National Honor Society and the mayor's daughter, and his first lesson in uppity-up women. They'd gone out a few times. She would sneak out and meet him at the racetrack on Saturday nights to watch him compete. She would get up close and personal in the front seat of his car, and the backseat, too. But she wouldn't go to the prom with him.

Clint and Sue Anne had had fun together, but they were going different places. While she liked him, she didn't *like* him. That's what she'd told him. What he'd heard thereafter in his head every time he spotted a classy woman and even thought about getting close to her for more than just sex.

It simply wasn't going to happen. Women like Sue Anne and Skye and the entire uppity-up population were too refined for him. Too complicated. Too smart.

He pushed aside the last thought.

It was all about the infamous Holy Commitment Trinity that Skye preached with so much fervor. Shared interests? Nada. Mutual respect? A definite nada. Great sex? A nada on her part.

Clint thought back to the previous evening. He could hear her labored breaths and see the desire flaring in her eyes and feel the frenzied desperation in her fingertips as she'd clasped at his neck. She'd seemed so genuine.

So real.

But all it was, he told himself, was a carefully played out act to seduce him and gain bragging rights. No way did she *really* like all this guy stuff, any more than she *really* liked him.

And Clint knew just how to prove it.

Chapter Fourteen

"This certainly looks interesting." Skye stood in the open doorway of room number twelve of the Catfish Castle on Ocean Front Road and stared at the ancient furnishings. She wrinkled her nose. "It smells interesting, too."

Clint grinned. "That's not the room. It's the guys two doors down. They're cleaning the day's catch."

The Catfish Castle could have doubled for the one-story motel featured in the Hitchcock classic *Psycho*, with its side-by-side rooms that extended down and around, and its wooden walkway running the perimeter. She glanced down to see three guys several doors away. They hunkered near an open ice chest. The hum of an electric knife filled the air, mingling with a slow Dolly Parton tune that whined from a portable radio. "They're chopping up Nemo on the front porch."

"They're not chopping. They're fileting, and it's not Nemo. It's a pretty decent-sized redfish, and being able to filet on the front porch is one of the motel's amenities. You don't have to find a place to freeze and store your catch while you're here. You can take care of the nasty stuff right away. That way it goes home ready to eat. Each kitchenette is also fully stocked with freezer wrap and masking tape for packaging, and equipped with a small freezer for storage."

Her gaze shifted from the double bed covered in a polka-dot lime green and red bedspread, past a small TV with rabbit ears, to the opposite side of the room that served as a kitchen. A mustard yellow refrigerator hummed in the corner. Cracked Formica covered the countertop next to a large sink. There was no microwave or hand towels or even an ice bucket. An orange plastic Tupperware glass sat on the sink's edge.

"You okay?" Clint asked from behind her. "You seem a little shell-shocked."

And how.

She ignored the thought, turned toward him and forced a smile. "I wouldn't say shocked. I'm just surprised." She tugged at the collar of her new bright yellow, short-sleeved, button-up shirt with its fishnet lining—for breathability, the clerk at the sporting goods store had assured her.

She looked at Clint, who wore an old white T-shirt with the words FISH TEXAS in cracked red and blue letters on the front. Worn denim shorts frayed at the edges and flip-flops completed the ensemble. A direct contrast to the crisp tan shorts and boat shoes she'd also purchased in preparation for lesson number three.

She could still hear Clint's instructions when he'd called on Tuesday—the day after her personal demonstration of the lap dance and the hottest kissing of her life.

"Pack your bags. We're going on a fishing trip."

She'd spent the rest of the morning clearing her schedule for the following two days—Wednesday and Thursday since Clint had to be at Dover Downs on Friday—and watching the Outdoor Channel so that she wouldn't seem totally clueless about the sport itself.

She'd watched six thirty-minute fishing episodes back to back, and all of them had featured breathtaking scenery, comfortable lodging and state-of-the-art equipment.

Not one had mentioned anything about front-porch fileting or fish stench or the all-important fact that she could have worn comfortable flip-flops rather than the blinding white canvas shoes that made her average size eights look and feel like size twelves.

She looked stiff and new and totally out of place, while he looked comfortable and in his element. Especially when the fish-gutting guys down the walk lifted a hand and said hello.

Hello? They're guys and he's Cowboy MacAllister. Of course they know him. He's been on every major sports show. He's been on the news. He's been on the front of a Wheaties box. Everybody knows him.

She prepared herself for the typical hoorah that usually followed the initial recognition. The charging fans. The plea for a picture and an autograph. The gushing and panting.

But the men simply turned back to their catch, testimony to the fact that men were, indeed, a different breed from women. A trio of females would have been on them in a matter of seconds, begging for everything from free tickets to the chance to have Clint's baby.

The thought brought her up short and killed her smile. Not that she was jealous, mind you. She didn't have enough invested in Clint to be jealous.

You like him, a voice whispered.

True, but she didn't *want* to like him, which meant she wasn't a complete goner. There was hope for her as long as she kept things physical and not personal.

No talking about the past, the present or the future, unless it directly involved sex.

Or fishing.

"The rooms also offer a live well to keep bait—"

"Let me guess," she cut in. "Alive and well?" He nodded and she tried for another smile. She could do this. Already she was starting to think like a man.

It wasn't that bad. It wasn't that smelly. It *wasn't*.

"It's really not that bad," Clint said as if reading her mind.

"No, no, it's great. Sure it's not the fully stocked mini-bar and complimentary bathrobe great, but still pretty awesome in its own way. A definite break from the normal routine. I can see why you guys love it."

"This is a fishing trip, not a luxury retreat."

"A mini-bar isn't a luxury. For some, it's a necessity. Not for me, mind you. I go with the flow." She cleared her throat. "But I'm sure there are a few fishermen out there who would appreciate a free, fluffy bathrobe."

"Most of the men I know barely shower on these trips." At her raised eyebrows, he added, "It's like this. Men come to Rockport to fish. To catch the Big One. To get away from the trappings of civilization and enjoy the great outdoors. Besides," he shrugged, "the fish smell is so strong it masks everything else."

"So if you can't smell it, it doesn't exist?"

"You're starting to catch on."

Unfortunately. "These rooms do have bathrooms, don't they?" At his odd look she added, "Since you guys don't shower, you probably just hang it over the side of the boat if you have to pee or out the window when you're here. So it seems like a bathroom would be wasted space."

"Now you're starting to think like a guy."

"It was a joke." He didn't crack a smile. Instead, he walked past her and set one of her suitcases down on the bed.

She followed him inside, panic rising with each step across the lime green shag carpet. "There *is* a bathroom, isn't there?"

He didn't reply right away, which sent her anxiety through the roof. "Sure there is," he finally said. "A guy comes here to get away for a little while. Not go completely AWOL. A man's still got to have his daily Sports section."

His meaning hit her, almost as hard as the smell when she crossed the room to the one doorway. Hinges creaked as she pushed the door open and flipped on the light. Lime green tile covered the floor and crept halfway up the walls of the small bathroom. A bright yellow toilet sat off to the side, a sink perched on the wall next to it. Water drip-dropped from the faucet head, adding to the rusty round water stain near the drain. A dingy yellow shower curtain covered a small shower stall that looked barely big enough to accommodate her, much less any of the bulky men perched on the front porch next door. Then again, according to Clint, showering wasn't a top priority.

Her gaze shifted to the small magazine rack wedged between the toilet and the wall. Old newspapers overflowed the small space.

"All the bare necessities." Clint's voice rang out and she turned to find him standing behind her, watching her, as if he was searching for some clue as to what she was thinking.

"All the comforts of home."

"You have to look at it from a guy's point of view."

Unfortunately, she hadn't had the prerequisite six-pack to do that yet, and without a mini-bar, she stood little chance unless she intended to walk up the road to Barnacle Bob's, a nightclub that was little more than an awning over a bunch of lawn chairs.

Getting drunk wasn't the answer.

Another whiff of the room and her nose wrinkled again. Okay, maybe getting drunk was an answer, but it wasn't a solution. Once the effects of the alcohol faded, she would be back in motel hell.

She had to look at the situation through fresh eyes, through a man's eyes. "Men really find all this relaxing?"

"It is relaxing."

"A hot bubble bath is relaxing. This is more like survival training."

"When a man is fishing, he's thinking about fishing. It's the focus that's relaxing. That and the challenge. Men love challenges, and there's nothing more challenging than catching a thirty-five-inch trout."

"The state record is thirty-three inches." She'd also purchased *Fishing for Dummies* when she'd bought her new clothes. During the eight-hour drive, she'd crammed as much knowledge as she could, determined to get a head start on the topic.

"That's why a thirty-five incher would be a definite challenge. It's a dream fish."

"I've dreamed about a lot of things, but a fish has never been one of them."

"You're not a man," he pointed out, his gaze skimming

her, pausing at several distinct parts that made her different. Her lips. Her breasts. And lower . . .

With him so close, so observant, she actually forgot her primitive surroundings.

Heat flooded between her legs and sent electricity pulsing to her nipples. They hardened, pressing against the lace of her bra. She took a deep breath and the ripe tips rubbed and throbbed.

"So all men dream about fish, huh?"

"Among other things."

"And the other things?"

You. Me. Naked. Panting. The answers flared in the glittering blue depths of his eyes.

She licked her lips and he stepped closer, as if he wanted to show her rather than verbalize his answers.

Fine with Skye. After a sleepless, frustrated night thinking and re-thinking about their kisses and what could have happened, she was ready for more.

His arms came up on either side of her, his palms flat against the wall as he pinned her in place and leaned in, so close she could feel the warm rush of his breath against her lips.

Her mouth tingled.

"Men don't just dream about fish in general. They dream about *the* fish. The Big One."

A smile tugged at her lips. "Women dream about the Big One, too."

"I thought size wasn't important."

"It isn't, but we're talking dreams. Fantasies. You wouldn't fantasize about an unattractive woman, would you? Of course you wouldn't. You would give her breasts out to there and legs up to here."

"And long blond hair," he added, fingering a tendril that had come loose from her ponytail. "Soft blond hair."

"Exactly," she managed, despite her pounding heart. He was so close and he smelled so good and she wanted a kiss.

So kiss him.

She wanted to, but something held her back. Crazy because Skye Farrel had never let anything keep her from acting when it came to sex. She'd never been intimidated or hesitant or scared. Sex was her game and she could play better than anyone.

Clint wanted to play with her. She saw the desire burning in his eyes, heard the deep, rasping breaths sawing past his lips, felt the need in the hot heat of his body.

She sensed his lust, but she didn't *know*. She wanted proof that he wanted her. That he was just as hot and bothered as she was. As eager. She wanted him to kiss her of his own free will, which meant she wasn't going to bait him.

The next move would be his.

"It's a fantasy," she went on, eager to keep her cool despite the hot body in front of her, surrounding her. "And, um, fantasies tend to be unrealistic. Hence, the Big One."

"Do you dream about the Big One?"

"All night last night." The words were out before she could stop them. So much for not baiting him. "But mine was a thirty-six incher," she rushed on.

"Thirty-six inches?"

"Maybe thirty-seven. If you're going to dream, you might as well dream big."

"The fish," he said as reality seemed to hit him. "You're talking about the fish."

"Specifically a trout. A thirty-seven-inch redfish

wouldn't be all that unheard of. We are going after trout, too, aren't we?"

He eyed her for a long moment, as if he was trying to decide what to do. Or what *not* to do.

He stiffened and pulled back. "I need to check on our charter for tomorrow morning. You'd better get settled and get to bed. We've got an early day." He turned and left her plastered to the wall in the bathroom.

"How early?" she called after him.

He paused in the doorway and glanced back at her, his eyes glittering with an emotion she couldn't quite read. "Let's just say a man's idea of relaxing isn't sleeping until nine. It's—"

"—getting up at five A.M. to catch a thirty-five-inch trout," she cut in, a smile curving her lips. The more she smiled, the easier it came, specifically if she focused on him and not all the lime surrounding her.

He frowned. "Three-thirty. We have to get our bait and be on the water by five."

Her smile died a quick death. "Three-thirty? Three-thirty in the morning? Three-thirty as in four hours from now?"

"That would be the one." He grinned. "Unless you're too tired and want to call it quits on the fishing. You've been a good sport so far with the football and the wrestling, but I know you're not really into all of this."

"Yes, I am."

"You're giving it a good try. I admire you. But you're not cut out for it all."

There it was. What every man in her past had ever thought about her. The killer for all her relationships.

But it wasn't true. Not completely. Not anymore, thanks to Clint and his lessons.

"I liked the football and the wrestling. I really did. And I'm going to like this just as much. I just know it."

His grin disappeared. "This is a lot different. This isn't a spectator sport. You can't just watch a man fish. You have to get in there."

"I know that. I didn't buy these clothes because of the way they looked." Obviously.

"You don't have to pretend. If you want to go home, I'll understand."

"I don't want to go home." What was she saying? She wanted to run home. She also wanted to jump his bones, but she wasn't about to do that either. She'd made up her mind to stick this out, and to stick him out.

She was fishing and she was leaving the first move to him.

"Don't worry about losing face. You don't have to do this. Just say the word and it's over."

"I'll see you at three-thirty."

He eyed her, his lips thinning into a frown, almost as if he wanted her to chicken out.

Crazy. What did he care if she fished or not?

He didn't care, because there was no caring involved. No personal emotions at stake. No actual *like*.

"Sleep tight," he finally said. The click of the door punctuated his sentence and Skye found herself alone.

Sort of.

She walked into the bedroom and peered up at the small silvery spiderweb that dangled from the corner near the bed. No sign of its owner, but she had no doubt he was around somewhere.

The urge to snatch up her suitcase and bolt hit her hard and fast. She'd seen a Holiday Inn back off the highway. Sure, it wasn't across the street from the coast, but it was undoubtedly spider free. There would be no lime green shag carpet. No drip stains from an ancient faucet. No blinding lime green and red polka-dot bedspread. No freezer wrap or masking tape. No fish smell. No . . .

No.

Okay, so it wasn't exactly what she would have picked for a weekend getaway. That was the point. She knew what she liked. She needed to see how the other sex lived. To learn their likes and dislikes. To learn to like those likes. To really develop some common interests, rather than just paying lip service to the whole thing.

Besides, the room wasn't *that* bad. There was a bathroom, however small and primitive. And the sheets looked clean. Worn, but clean. And the air conditioner worked even if it chugged louder than a passing freight train. And she *could* use the masking tape to remove the white fuzzies from the black Capri pants she'd packed—part of her just-in-case outfit—along with a red blouse and black open-toed slingbacks.

Not that she would be going anywhere except out on one of the huge boats she'd seen on any number of the fishing shows she'd tuned in to. But one never really knew and Skye was always prepared.

Her nipples tingled and her stomach hollowed and she retrieved her overnight case from the floor. She rummaged inside and pulled out several rolls of SweetTarts. They hadn't worked last night to relieve her stress, but she wasn't one to give up without really trying.

Besides, since he hadn't kissed her, her mouth needed something to do and the candy was the only relief inside.

Skye popped a few candies into her mouth and sucked for all she was worth.

She could do this.

*   *   *

There was *no way* she could do this.

Gravel crunched beneath Clint's feet as he stepped down off the porch and crossed the parking lot, the sound mixing with the chirp of crickets, the distant crash of water hitting the pier across the street and the whine of an old country song drifting from a nearby radio.

He headed for the small building near the road. The word OFFICE blinked in pink neon from the window. June bugs buzzed and bumped into the bare bulb that glowed from the front porch. The smell of fish hung in the air, mingling with the faint aroma of boat oil and salt water.

His nose twitched, but he didn't grimace. These were familiar scents to him. He loved to fish. He'd been down to this neck of the woods every year for the past ten for a week-long trip with Jeep and a few other guys from his race team. They drank beer, caught fish and talked cars. It was always great. Relaxing. Invigorating.

Certainly not stressful.

But then he'd never had a woman in tow before.

He forced aside the thought and concentrated on his steps to the office. He'd stayed at this exact motel a time or two, and a dozen others just like it scattered up and down Ocean Front Road. Sure, there were a few newer versions up the road that accommodated families. They were nicer, cleaner, more modernized to appeal to not only the serious fisherman but also to his better half. A few had cable TV and one even offered room service.

Skye's shocked expression flashed in his mind and guilt niggled at him. He could have taken her someplace more her speed. But that would have defeated the purpose.

She was here to beef up her guy knowledge. There was

more to fishing, real fishing, than deciding what sunscreen factor to wear. Fishing was an art. A way of life. Skye Farrel didn't have a clue, even if she had impressed him with her knowledge of trout. And redfish.

So what if she'd read up on the subject. That didn't mean she could actually go out there and catch a fish. Knowing and doing were two different things. And liking what she was doing? There was no possible way. She was way out of her element and this weekend would finally prove it. By the time Friday morning rolled around, Skye would be begging to go home and Clint would see firsthand that they had nothing in common other than some really great chemistry.

And chemistry wasn't enough.

Clint wanted a woman for more than sex. He wanted companionship, encouragement. He wanted a woman who really and truly understood him, and liked him anyway.

He and Skye had nothing in common. They lived in two different worlds. While he admired her tenacity when it came to the guy lessons, he knew she wasn't learning nearly enough to really share a common interest. She was learning enough to get by, to give her an arsenal of knowledge that would help her catch some poor macho schmuck and keep him a little longer than usual. But enough to really make a connection and form a common, *lasting* bond? Maybe with a guy who was more refined than macho. An uppity-up type who wore boat shoes when he fished and hired an assistant to bait his hooks so he wouldn't have to get his hands dirty.

That was more Skye's speed. Slow. Safe. Definitely within the speed limits. Meanwhile, Clint put the accelerator to the floor and hauled ass wide open through life.

He always had. Except when it came to lust. He'd made the necessary pit stops to refuel, but then he always pulled back onto the track and gunned it again.

He and Skye raced at two different speeds in life. He knew that, he just wasn't seeing it right now. Her excited gazes and her gung-ho attitude when it came to the football and the wrestling had colored his opinion of her and made him think that maybe, just maybe she really related to him.

That's what stirred his lust. What had always stirred him up in the past. Her enthusiasm for the guy activities in their lessons portrayed a certain image—a sports-loving, down-to-earth image—that was far removed from the real woman. That's what had him so hot and bothered. Not Skye herself, but his image of her.

While he'd known many women like her—pretty, successful and smart—he'd never really liked them. Early on, he'd come to realize that what he really liked was the idea that a pretty, successful and smart woman could like him.

Skye was putting on an act, all right. A really good one judging by the size of the erection throbbing in his pants, but an act nonetheless.

And like every time in his past with every woman like her, Clint had no doubt that his attraction and said erection would take a nose dive the moment Skye Farrel showed her true colors.

"I'm turning into a lobster." Skye stared at her arms the next day and damned herself for not buying the SPF 45 instead of the 15 before she'd come on this godforsaken trip. But she'd just figured that if she started to get too pink, she would take a breather inside the boat's cabin.

Her gaze swept from one end of the small fishing boat to the other, a total of fifteen feet, and its contents—an ice chest topped with a cushion for her to sit on, a rod holder, a center console with a steering wheel and gauges, and a small fifty-horsepower Mercury motor on the back. It was ancient and barely big enough to accommodate two people.

She hadn't batted an eye that morning when they'd crossed the street to the docking area and found the decrepit bay boat waiting for them. Then again, she'd barely been able to open her eyes, batting had definitely been out of the question.

With only the stars overhead and a bare lightbulb hanging from the corner of the shack that served as a marina, the boat hadn't looked all that bad. But when the sun came up and she was sitting on the small seat with little to protect her from the blistering heat, she'd realized that this wasn't football or wrestling and there would be no surprise excitement in it.

Misery. Pure, sweltering misery.

She plucked at her shirt. She could barely draw air herself, so it didn't surprise her that the sixty-dollar breathable material had morphed into a sweat-soaked second skin.

"I definitely want my money back," she grumbled.

"What did you say?" Clint cut her a gaze from his position at the front of the boat.

"I definitely think we're getting our money's worth." She forced a smile.

He studied her a long moment before turning back to his fishing and giving her his profile. He stared out at the water, polarized sunglasses covering his blue eyes, a Big Tex Motor Oil cap turned backwards on his head, a fishing rod in his hands. He still wore the FISH TEXAS shirt he'd worn last night, along with the same shorts and flip-flops, testimony to the fact that he hadn't changed, much less showered.

Not that he smelled bad. She'd caught a whiff of him when he'd stepped past her to retrieve a shrimp from the portable five-gallon bucket-sized live well humming near the ice chest. Her nostrils had flared at the familiar scent of warm male and testosterone and her nipples had ripened.

He'd noticed her response, too, judging by his double take, those dark lenses directed at her for a long, drawn-out moment. Not that he'd thought anything about it.

They were fishing, after all. Which meant the fish and nothing but the fish, so help him God.

She knew based on her extensive research that men didn't multi-task very well and so it shouldn't hurt her feelings that he didn't take the initiative when she was burning for him.

It didn't hurt her feelings, because feelings were not involved. It was strictly sex.

She stared at the red cork that had been bobbing on top of the water in the same spot for the last forty-five minutes. Without so much as a dunk beneath the glass-like green surface.

Okay, so not only was she not sexually stimulating enough to take his mind off a thirty-five-inch trout, she sucked at catching her own.

You can do this. It's all in the mind. If you want to like it, if you tell yourself you do like it, you will like it. You're strong. You're invincible. You're a fearless Farrel.

"If you're ready to call it quits for today, just say the word." His deep voice drew her from her thoughts.

"Are you kidding?" She glanced at her watch and squinted against the glare. "It's only two o'clock. We've only been at it for . . ." Her mind did a quick calculation. ". . . a little over ten hours." *Ten* hours? No wonder her arms ached and her back hurt and her skin burned and her stomach grumbled for sustenance. "I can go a full twelve easy." Of course, she might pass out from hunger and exposure. "Maybe thirteen."

"If you're sure?"

"One hundred percent. I love this." She eyed the bobber thing. "It's the most fun I've ever had in my entire life—whoa!" The red dipped below the water. The line jerked. The rod bowed. And Skye quickly found herself fighting what had to be Jaws himself. "I got one!" She jumped to her feet and the boat wobbled. "I got one." Excitement raced through her as she struggled for her balance.

Like an ant on a sweet apple pie, Clint appeared behind her. Large hands steadied her waist. His arms came around and his hand closed over hers.

"Easy," he murmured. "Reel in slowly, slowly until you get it close to the boat." He guided her, spinning the reel and drawing in the line.

"There it is," she shrieked, seeing the slick body fighting just below the surface. "Ohmigod, it's a fish. A real fish. Probably thirty inches easy."

"A little more," he murmured, guiding her, helping her draw in the fish. "And then you reel up." He jerked up. The rod bent in the opposite direction and the line pulled, tighter, tighter . . . *pop!*

The rod straightened, the tension eased and the fish disappeared. Skye shook her head. "What happened?"

"The line snapped." He released her and turned to eye his own rod he'd left in the holder a few feet away.

"What do you mean?" She reeled the rest of her line all the way up and stared at the dangling line.

"The fish popped your line."

"But I had it."

"That's the way it goes."

"But it was right there. I could see it just beneath the water. It was my fish. My first fish. It was a big fish, too. A good thirty-five inches."

"I thought you said thirty."

"Maybe thirty-six."

"It happens sometimes. They can be tricky little things. If you're a little slow—"

"I am not slow. I *had* it." Until those strong arms had closed around her and he'd taken control. "You messed me up."

"Me? I was showing you how to do it."

"Do what? Lose my fish? I could have done that by myself." She turned toward the live well, flipped open the lid and ducked her hand in the water, mindless of the small net Clint had used to catch the bait. She grabbed one of the slippery fish.

"You can't bait your own hook."

"I can, too." She struggled for a few moments and jabbed herself more than the fish, but finally she managed. Much to Clint's surprise. "See? I can do fine without you."

"You can't cast the line."

"I most certainly can." She glared at him, daring him to say anything more.

Finally, he shrugged and turned back to his own rod. "Fine, but I didn't mess you up. You're no good at this. Just admit it."

"No good?" Okay, so she wasn't good. The fish had been luck, pure luck, and she really sucked. But thinking it herself and hearing him say it out loud were two very different things. "At least I can latch onto something bigger than a piggy perch. I don't see you hauling in a giant redfish."

"It wasn't giant, and it wasn't a redfish. It was an average-sized sheepshead. Nothing special."

"It was, too, special. I saw it. It didn't look anything like a sheepshead. It was definitely a redfish. A big one. An easy thirty-seven inches."

"In your dreams."

"You're just afraid I might be better at it than you."

"I might be afraid that you like it as much as me, but I sure as hell am not afraid you'll be better at it."

"What's that supposed to mean?"

He shook his head, as if he'd said more than he meant to. He glared at her. "Just shut up and fish. *If* you can manage to cast the line."

"I can cast just fine." She'd read about line-casting yesterday, and she'd watched him all day. She could do it. "Better than fine. Step back and prepare to be humiliated."

"This is ridiculous." Another head shake and he turned and stared off in the opposite direction. "Just fish."

"I will," she huffed, and scooted toward her end of the boat. She reared back, opened the reel and threw her arm behind her. So far so good. Now all she had to do was bring it forward like this and . . . *splat!*

The fish hit the back side of the boat before flying forward into Skye's line of vision.

"Clint," she said after several long, thoughtful moments. "I think I have a problem."

"Now we get to the truth," he said. "It's about time you stopped being so stubborn and started using your head—"

"I've got no head," she cut in. At his sharp glance, she held up her bait. "I decapitated my fish."

Clint had seen a lot of things in the years he'd been fishing, but never had he ever seen someone cast a line and rip the head clean off a croaker.

Guilt carved her expression, her gaze distraught, as if she'd kicked a puppy instead of ruining a measly piece of bait. Something shifted inside him and he had the sudden urge to reach out.

She stared at the fish and then at him, and then she said the words he'd been waiting to hear since he'd ushered her onto the boat that morning.

"I can't do this. I don't want to do this. I'm hot and miserable and this boat is even worse than my room at the Catfish Castle." The brave, interested front she'd been putting on fell away and in a rush of words, Skye Farrel revealed her true feelings. "I hate fishing. I hate the rods and the reels and all this water and all the heat and the smell. I hate it all."

Clint stared at her and watched as her eyes welled with tears. She despised the fishing. She really and truly *despised* it. The truth sank in for a long, heart-pounding moment, and then he did the only thing he could now that he saw the real woman beneath the facade.

He stepped forward and kissed her.

Because, despite the truth, Clint still wanted her.

Now more than ever.

Chapter Fifteen

He wanted her more than a thirty-five-inch trout.

The realization found its way into her head as Clint's tongue found its way into her mouth. Her lips parted, giving him better access as he tasted and stroked and delved.

She forgot all about her decapitated bait, her sunburn, her empty, deprived stomach and the fact that she was having the most miserable time of her life. Things had suddenly taken a turn for the better. So much so that perhaps she didn't despise fishing nearly as much as she'd originally thought. Particularly with Clint as her personal guide.

His large hands found their way beneath her fishing shirt and his fingers burned into the bare flesh of her back. His touch trailed up and around the sides of her breasts and heat pooled between her thighs.

A heat that had nothing to do with the one hundred degree temperature and the scorching sun and everything to do with the man himself and the way he affected her.

Her blood pounded. Her heart raced. Her knees buckled. Her body swayed—*whoaaaaaaaa*!

The boat tipped from all the added weight on one side. Skye opened her eyes just as her balance failed and she teetered sideways. Clint tried to save them both, but it was no use. Gravity fought against them as the boat rocked and dipped and tossed them overboard.

The water sucked her under and she flailed, kicking her arms and legs and fighting for air. She reached the surface and gasped for air just as Clint's head bobbed up several feet away from her.

She coughed up a mouthful of water and sputtered, "Did I mention that I really hate this boat, too?"

"You and me both." He sliced his arms the small distance to the boat, grasped the edge with one powerful arm and hauled himself over the side while she treaded water. Grabbing the oar, he kept one hand firmly on the steering wheel as he leaned out to offer her a lifeline.

She grasped the edge and he pulled her the short distance to the boat. Reaching down, he clasped her hand and pulled her in. The fiberglass edge scraped her sunburned legs as she climbed over and collapsed in the two inches of water that swished in and out through the water vent holes in the bottom of the boat. The boat rocked this way and the water went that way. Her forgotten croaker floated past her head and she closed her eyes. Her lips parted and her chest heaved as she drank in some much-needed oxygen and tried to slow her pounding heart.

"We actually fell overboard," she grumbled when she managed to catch her breath. "And not because of a storm or bad weather or anything normal. Because of a kiss."

"One helluva kiss." His deep voice sounded a split second before the engine cranked to life. Skye opened her eyes to find him standing at the console. "You'd better get in your seat. We're getting out of here."

Skye scrambled onto the cushion-topped ice chest and braced herself. *God is definitely a woman and all is right with the world once again.*

Almost.

Despite the fact that she was safely in the boat, her heart was still pounding. She still felt nervous. Light-headed. Anxious. More so now because of the deep timbre of his voice and the admission that he'd liked the kiss.

Even the sudden gust of air that surrounded her as they headed into the marina did nothing to cool her flushed skin or the desire blazing deep in the pit of her belly.

There was only one thing that could do that.

She half turned, her gaze hooked on Clint as he stood behind the driver's console and steered. Large hands clasped the wheel, his fingers long and purposeful as they curled around the black plastic. She'd never actually seen him race, but she could picture him in his car, gripping the steering wheel as he maneuvered around a track at a dangerous speed. He looked focused, intent.

A man with a purpose.

In this case the purpose wasn't to win a race, even though they made it back to the dock in record time. No, he obviously wanted her.

A truth that hit home when he docked the boat, grabbed their stuff and ushered her back across the street to the Catfish Castle with an urgency that made her pulse quicken and her insides coil in anticipation.

The minute Skye was inside her room, she dropped her stuff and turned toward him. He was already halfway out the door.

"If we're going to do this, we're going to do it right. Pack your stuff. I'll be back in ten minutes."

Nine minutes later, they left the lime green room and

the smell behind as they climbed into the car and headed back up the highway.

Fifteen minutes after that, they pulled up to the Holiday Inn that had haunted Skye's dreams during her scant four hours of sleep the night before. Clint checked them in and hustled her into the elevator along with their luggage. Soon he unlocked a door and led her inside what looked like heaven compared to the room she'd just vacated.

Tasteful beige carpeting.

A real TV with a remote control.

A mini-bar.

And one king-sized bed.

The lock clicked, he stepped up behind her, and something strange happened to Skye Farrel. Panic welled inside her and she did what she'd never done in her entire life when it came to a sexual situation. She bolted for the bathroom.

"I'm sticky and salty and I really need a shower," she blurted as she made the four strides to safety. "Just give me a minute." The slam of the door punctuated her sentence and cut off any response he might have had. She drew a shaky breath, collapsed onto the toilet seat and tried to understand what the hell had just happened.

She'd chickened out. For all her bravado when it came to sex, Skye had never actually checked into a hotel with a man for the sole purpose of having it.

It seemed so tawdry. So cheap. So . . . *strictly sex.*

So?

That's what she wanted. What she'd wanted since the moment she'd first met him.

At least that's what she'd thought. But sitting in the bathroom with her skin itching from the sunburn and the saltwater and her heart pounding from much, much more, she wasn't so sure.

This felt like something altogether different from anything she'd felt in the past. Hotter. More intense. Dangerous.

Dangerous? She'd never been threatened by sex. It was her comfort zone. Her area of expertise. She *knew* sex.

But it wasn't the idea of sex that had her acting so freaky. It was the idea of sex with Clint MacAllister.

As if her thoughts had conjured him, she heard a tap on the door.

"Are you okay?" His deep voice slid past the door and into her ears, skimming her nerve endings and bringing them to full awareness.

She stiffened. "I'm taking a shower."

"I don't hear any water running."

"I'm about to take a shower." She jumped up, reached into the tub area and turned on the faucet. Water streamed from the shower head.

Skye peeled off her clothes and stepped under the spray. The water sluiced over her, washing away the salt, but it didn't ease her panic.

Not that the feeling had anything to do with the fact that she liked him. Sex had nothing to do with like. Sex was about pleasure. Pure and simple. Unfettered and uncomplicated. Physical.

Like was a different story, and it was completely out of the question. While she wanted him and she respected him, they didn't have any common interests. Sure, she liked football and wrestling. But she hated fishing—an obvious passion of his—and she hated marriage, a subject which topped his list at the moment. Genuine like simply wasn't possible without all three points of the Holy Commitment Trinity. Skye had learned that very early on when her mother had caught her baking the cookies for her seventh-grade Valentine. It hadn't just been the cookies that had sent her mom into a tailspin. It had been the Valentine she'd made, complete with a heart and the words "This Valentine Entitles the Bearer to Free Fraction Worksheets 'til School Do Us Part" written in red crayon.

"But he has trouble with his fraction sheets and I want to help him. I love him, Mom. I really do."

"Nonsense. You're thirteen and your hormones are starting to rage. He's a boy and he's cute and you're physically aware of him. That's not love, Skye. If you're attracted to someone, fine. You can act on that attraction, but don't mistake it for more. You can care for someone. You can even care about them to the point that you would do a great many things for them. But you should never choose that someone based on a physical attraction. No daughter of mine would ever make such a decision without taking into account all three points of the Holy Commitment Trinity."

Her mother had been right. She and the seventh-grade heartthrob had had nothing in common except the fact that they'd shared a desk. Once the semester ended, their seating assignments had been changed and he'd immediately started talking to his new deskmate—a cute redhead named Trisha—and had forgotten all about her.

She was too smart to make the same mistake again. She was Jacqueline Farrel's daughter and she knew the score when it came to sex and relationships.

So her hesitation was simply because her conscience was getting to her. Clint was spoken for, and so Skye would be doing a great injustice to the future Mrs. MacAllister. Not to mention, she would be flagrantly violating the student/teacher relationship. She was his instructor.

Then again, the subject *was* sex. While she could give him the information, there was no way she could be absolutely certain he understood what she was saying, or that he could take the knowledge and adapt it to his own life, incorporating her techniques with his own.

And it wasn't as if Clint had definite wedding plans. The woman had turned him down, and while he intended to go back and pop the question again, there was no guarantee she would say yes. Then again, if Skye did her job correctly and lived up to her company's reputation, the young woman would be foolish not to say yes.

But that was the future, and this was now.

Right now, Clint was free and single. And Skye was free and single.

He was a mature, consenting adult. And she was a mature and consenting adult.

He was desperately turned on by her. And she was desperately turned on by him, so much so that she didn't even hear him enter the bathroom. Instead, she saw his shadow on the other side of the shower curtain.

The shower curtain slid to the side and he stood before her, naked and fully aroused.

Skye swallowed as her gaze swept the length of him. His broad shoulders framed a wide chest sprinkled with crisp, dark hair. The dark brown silk stretched from nipple to nipple in a V-shape that narrowed and funneled down his abdomen and pelvis to disappear in the dark hair that surrounded a very impressive erection. His legs were braced apart, his thigh muscles taut, sprinkled with the same dark hair that covered his chest.

If she'd ever doubted that race-car driving was, indeed, a sport, she had no doubts now. He had an athlete's body, all hard muscle and powerful grace. And he had an athlete's look, his blue eyes dark and intense as he stared at her.

"What are you doing?" she blurted, a crazy question because they were both naked and very much aroused.

"Your minute's up." He stepped in, his big, powerful form filling up the narrow space and blocking the spray of water. Water hammered the back of his head, running in tiny rivulets over his shoulders, down his chest and abdomen, to drip-drop off his swollen testicles.

"What are you doing?"

"Taking a shower." He stared at her, but he didn't touch her. True to his word, he reached for the soap and rubbed it between his large hands. Lather squeezed between his fingers, trailing down his powerful forearms. He soaped his shoulders, his chest, his abdomen. He spread the lather under and around his penis, clasping the thick length and stroking up and around the plump head.

She watched for several long seconds, her nipples tightening and heat coiling in her belly. When she finally looked up, she found him watching her, his gaze dark and even more intense, and expectant.

She realized then that where she'd left the first move in the boat up to him, he was leaving this one up to her. She'd retreated the moment they'd reached the hotel, and so they were at an impasse. Time to either get busy or throw in the towel.

"I've been thinking," she said.

"Yeah?" He arched an eyebrow and kept soaping.

She cleared her throat. "In order to really be good at pleasuring a woman, you should probably practice."

"I've thought the same thing myself."

"And since I'm your teacher, I would be the obvious one to practice with. I can tell you when you're doing something wrong. And when you're doing it right."

"Am I doing it right so far?"

"Most definitely. But if you weren't, I would be the first to tell you and steer you on the right path. After all, Girl Talk usually offers a money-back guarantee. Since you're not paying me—you're giving me lessons instead—this is the next best way to insure customer satisfaction."

"Satisfaction, huh?"

"Most definitely, so I would be glad to help out in any way possible. Just so long as we're both clear about what's going on."

"Sex," he said.

"Strictly sex."

"Now," she said as she reached down and took the soap from his hands. "We really should start at the beginning."

"I already know all I want to about Dinah the Vagina."

"Dinah was just a model. Today you'll be meeting the real thing." She lathered her hands, slid the soap in the dish and touched her own flesh.

"Let me," Clint started, but she shook her head.

He'd made her watch and stirred her up, and now it was his turn.

"This isn't an interactive lesson." Her palms slicked over her skin, starting at her neck and moving lower, over her collarbone, off to one shoulder then the other in a slow, gentle massage. "Not yet."

She wasn't sure he would oblige her. His gaze was too dark, too hungry as he stared her down.

She paused her ministrations and watched him swallow. A heart-pounding moment later, he nodded and raised his arms. One hand gripped the shower curtain rod while the other flattened against the opposite wall. His biceps bulged and his penis jutted forward and suddenly Skye couldn't seem to catch her breath.

There was just something about watching all those muscles ripple that stole the air from her lungs.

She enjoyed the view for a few more heartbeats before drawing a deep breath and turning her attention back to the soapy hands paused on the slopes of her breasts. She slicked the lather down, around, under. Her nipples ripened even more as she touched them with her palms and massaged them for a stirring moment that made his gaze darken to a smoldering blue as hot and iridescent as the center of a flame.

She let her touch slide lower, down her quivering abdomen to the vee between her legs. Her fingers slicked through the hot flesh between her legs. Her lips parted in a gasp at the sudden contact and his knuckles went white, as if he was fighting very hard to keep from touching her.

Not nearly as hard as she was fighting, but she wanted to make sure she turned him on as much as he'd turned her on with his slow, thorough strokes.

Her fingers slid back and forth, spreading the lather and making her entire body tremble. She'd touched herself intimately before. Masturbation was a normal expression of sexuality, but there was just something about doing it in front of him that made it feel that much more pleasurable.

At the same time, it wasn't nearly enough.

A few more strokes and she knew she'd reached her limit. She took his hand from its place on the wall, his flesh warm against hers, and pressed his palm against her lower abdomen. His touch burned into her, sending flurries of heat dancing along her nerve endings. She moved his fingers lower, guiding him to the spot that ached for him the most.

At the first moment of contact, she jumped. His thumb brushed over her throbbing clitoris and intense pleasure rushed through her.

"Now this," she said breathlessly, "is Dinah's real-life counterpart."

"Pleased to meet you," he murmured, his fingers stroking back and forth in a tantalizing motion.

Her teeth sank into her bottom lip. "That's good."

"Just good?" He slid a finger just a fraction inside her slit and a moan rumbled up her throat.

"Great," she said once she found her voice. She braced her hands against his hard chest and wiggled just enough to pull him a little deeper. "Better than great."

"And how about this?" He pushed deeper and she thought she would orgasm right then and there. She could have. If he pulled back and plunged deep just once more, she would be a goner.

But she didn't want that. She wanted him. Inside her. With her.

"Stop," she gasped, grabbing his wrist. "Not yet. Not without you."

The last word faded into a gasp as he kissed her. His mouth was hot, determined and there was no doubt that he scored an A+ in the kissing department. His tongue delved deep, stroking and stirring in a hungry exploration. Then he pulled back, leaving her to take the lead, to chase his tongue back into his mouth and coax him back into action. Fast and slow. Aggressive and shy. He teased her, then retreated in a maddening cat-and-mouse game that drew her entire body to full, throbbing awareness.

Until she wanted him so much she had to touch him.

Her hands were on him then. She touched everywhere she could reach, slicking her palms up and down his hard shoulders and hair-roughened chest. His arms went around her, his hands sliding down her back to pull her flush against him. His hard length pressed into her stomach and he rubbed himself, his mouth devouring her in a long, wet kiss that made her knees tremble.

He cupped her buttocks, kneading her bottom for a long moment as he drew her closer. Then he lifted her and she wrapped her legs around his waist, her arms around his neck.

His hard, throbbing flesh grazed the sensitive area between her legs, the length rubbing against her slick folds as he turned and stepped out of the tub. He kissed her hungrily as he walked the few feet from the bathroom to the bed and eased her down.

Light filtered around the closed drapes, pushing back the shadows just enough to give her a good view of Clint as he rounded the end of the bed to grasp the shorts he'd shed. His arms flexed as he leaned down and retrieved a small foil packet from his pocket.

A few seconds later, he stood beside her, towering over her as he rolled the condom down his thick length.

She opened her legs and he settled between them.

"I see you remember the missionary position," she gasped as she felt the tip of his erection slide just a fraction inside her.

"You're tight."

"I have a confession. I know a lot about sex, but I don't do it a lot. Not as often as people might think." She wasn't sure why she told him except that she was hot and bothered and totally unprepared for the mix of feelings that assaulted her as his body pressed into hers: excitement, vulnerability, hunger, desperation. And Skye Farrel did crazy things when she was unprepared. "I mean, I've had lovers, just not that many, and not here lately. Unless you count the King Kong Ultra my sister Xandra gave me last Christmas, but that's only once in a while and I primarily use it for clitoral stimulation—"

"You talk a lot during sex."

"Talk can be stimulating." She clasped his jaw, his stubble rough against her palms as she drew him down for a quick, deep kiss before she slid her mouth across his cheek to his ear. "Sexy talk can be *very* stimulating."

"Sexy as in?"

"I can feel you, so hot and hard, and I want you inside me so much I don't think I can stand it anymore."

At her words, he retreated the inch he'd penetrated. His hands slid under her, cupping her bottom and tilting her to take all of him as he plunged deep.

A shudder ripped through him and she touched him, feeling his body quake as she trailed the length of his back and touched his hard buttocks, pulling him even deeper.

He stared down at her. "I must be doing it right."

"You get an A+ for effort. But I have to see the full technique before I can give you any real feedback."

He grinned, withdrawing and sliding deep again, and again.

Her body clasped him and he pounded into her, harder

and faster, grinding her into the mattress and making the bed shake. The headboard slammed against the wall.

She barely heard the noise, however. She was too focused on her own pounding heart and his deep, raspy breaths as he pushed her higher and higher toward the edge. Another thrust and she went flying over into the Land of the Sexually Satisfied.

A tremor worked its way through her body, starting between her legs and spreading outward, gripping every nerve in her body until she felt like a live, pulsing wire. Exquisite sensation followed, sweeping through her and drenching her senses. Her inner muscles clasped at him, reluctant to let go and lose the delicious orgasm pulsing through her. She held him tight, drawing him deeper, again and again, until he followed her over the edge.

A curse tore from his lips as his back arched, the cords in his neck drew tight and he climaxed.

He collapsed on top of her for several fast, furious heartbeats before rolling over and pulling her on top of him.

She rested her head in the curve of his shoulder and concentrated on trying to catch her breath.

His hands slid up and down her back, soothing and calming for a long while, until their breath slowed and their heartbeats slowed and the air grew cool around them.

"I guess I aced the test."

She lifted her head and stared down into his eyes. Amusement danced in the deep depths, along with something deeper. Something fierce and possessive that sent a tiny thrill through her, quickly followed by a rush of panic.

She frowned. "I wouldn't get too smug yet. This was

just a pop quiz." Surprise filtered across his face and anger gleamed in his eyes.

"This is just one of the top ten most popular positions every man should know if he really wants to pleasure a woman. Which means the jury's still out. Not to mention there's at least another ten Kama Sutra positions I personally recommend to lift the average lover to a higher level of performance."

"Is that so?" He flipped her on her back in one quick motion that caught her off guard.

Uh, oh. Sure, she'd been trying to push his buttons, to push him away so that she could think, but maybe she'd pushed him too far. Men were much more delicate than women realized. At least, when it came to their egos.

Clint smiled and hot challenge gleamed in his eyes. "I guess I'd better get started then. One down and nineteen more to go." He dipped his head and drew her nipple into his mouth. He suckled her, his tongue licking and teasing the tip.

Mmm . . . Maybe she'd punched the right button after all.

Chapter Sixteen

"Looks like I'm not the only one who's been having really good sex." Jenny stood in the doorway of Skye's office Sunday morning and eyed her boss.

"That's ridiculous." Skye glanced up from her laptop and the new handout she was reworking for tomorrow night's Girl Talk party. She smiled. "I have not been having really good sex."

She'd been having really *great* sex.

Not for the past few days, mind you. They'd driven back late Thursday afternoon. Clint had dropped her at her high-rise and headed for the airport to fly out for practice and qualifying for this afternoon's race. She hadn't seen him since. But in the twenty-four hours before they'd parted ways, he'd made quite an impression as they went over nine more positions to complete the Most Popular Top Ten.

Ten more to go to make the recommended twenty.

Heat rushed through her body and made a permanent pit stop between her still tender thighs. Where he'd claimed to have been a poor student back in school, he shot the notion completely to hell and back in the bedroom. And the bathroom. And the small elevator of the hotel. And the tiny alcove near the ice machine.

He'd kept up his A+ through each and every encounter, and even earned a few bonus points with a very creative move Skye had since dubbed *Ice, ice, baby!*

The old Jenny would have demanded to know everything from kisses to positions to the number of orgasms, and Skye would have filled her in willingly. What good was sex if you couldn't share the details with your best girlfriend?

But the woman standing in her doorway simply watched her for a long, silent moment, before giving a shrug.

The apprehension Skye had felt in the two months leading up to the wedding returned full force and her mother's words echoed in her ears.

"Once a woman gets married, she loses the woman she once was. She loses her spark. Her fire. Her freedom. She becomes just a shell. She looks the same, but there's nothing inside. No more substance."

"I'm so glad to be back." Jenny dropped a bright pink wicker satchel on her desk before collapsing into her chair. "I've got so much to do."

"I didn't expect you until tomorrow. You're technically still on vacation."

"I knew you would be working on Sunday—you're always working—and my vacation ended the moment I stepped off the plane yesterday. Thankfully. A woman can drink just so many margaritas and watch just so many romantic sunsets. I mean, it's great for a little while but I'm used to being busy. I could hardly sleep last night thinking about everything I needed to do today."

Okay, so maybe Skye was wrong. Just because Jenny had handcuffed herself to Duke, didn't mean she'd morphed into the poster girl for wedded bliss.

"It *is* going to be a busy week," Skye said. "We've got eight bookings and we need to make an emergency run to the printers for more workshop brochures. I meant to go last week, but I got caught up in something." Or rather someone. A certain someone by the name of Clint.

Her thighs gave an answering ache and she smiled.

And then she frowned.

She was too busy to sit around thinking about Clint. Sex was fine, but it had its place and time. And it wasn't here or now.

Despite the very large bright orange rubber penis sitting on top of her TO DO tray.

Skye grabbed the rubber penis and tossed it into her top desk drawer before heading back to the tray for the half-inch stack of stapled questionnaires she'd collected from this week's hostesses. "I'm so glad you're back. I was just about to dive into these and the thought of going it alone wasn't the least bit appealing."

"I'm right here with the supportive vibes." Jenny winked. "So you get to it and I'll tackle these." She unearthed a pile of opened gift cards. "I've got at least two hundred thank-you notes to write. And once that's done, I've got to fill out a new checking account application—Duke and I are going joint now, not to mention I have to change my name and then there's the whole social security thing to go through, and the driver's license forms, and I'll have to request new credit cards . . ."

Bye, bye dear friend. Hello Mrs. Duke the Dietician.

Skye's stomach grumbled and her mouth watered as she thought of the gourmet cookies just waiting for her at the deli around the corner. Fifteen minutes away at the most. Ten if there was no line at the register.

She forced the thought away, reached for her roll of SweetTarts and popped several into her mouth.

Skye spent the rest of the afternoon organizing the questionnaires and compiling a list of answers to the most frequently asked questions. She paused only to offer a few variations on Jenny's standard "Thank you for the Fry Daddy."

There was the obvious "We really appreciate the Fry Daddy," to the "We loved the Fry Daddy," to Skye's stroke of standard wedding gift genius, "Fire up the vegetable oil, we can't wait to fry instead of boil!"

"All done," Jenny finally declared after Skye had sucked her way through three rolls of candy. "How about you?"

"Right with you." Skye filed the questionnaires and logged off her laptop before closing the lid.

Jenny glanced at her watch. "Duke's probably still at the hospital." At Skye's raised eyebrows, she added, "He was just as eager to get back to work. Say, why don't we head over to Potent Produce. I haven't had a really good salad since I left for Jamaica."

If she'd said cookies, they would be in business. As it was, Skye was depressed enough without adding a very healthy salad to the mix. "You go on ahead. I've still got a lot of work to do for tomorrow night's workshop."

"See you in the morning then." She gathered up her stuff. "Oh, I almost forgot." She reached into her purse and smiled. "I brought you a souvenier."

Shock rolled through Skye as Jenny pulled out a hand-carved piece of wood.

"It's a penis," she said when Skye remained silent.

"I can see that."

"A wooden penis."

"I can see that too."

"A wooden vibrator. Not that it vibrates. The natives don't have access to batteries. But it has these smooth little ridges and when you twist it, it's better than a vibrator. I found it in this quaint little village when Duke and I went on a safari inland. The woman said it was originally crafted to keep the women happy while the men were away on hunts."

"You brought me a wooden vibrator," Skye said as the meaning of the souvenir sank in.

Jenny frowned. "You don't like it, do you? Duke told me to get you a T-shirt, but that's so impersonal. I wanted to get you something I knew you would love and this is a one-of-a-kind. They're all individually crafted, so that no two penises are alike. I thought you could work it into one of the workshops when you give a brief history of masturbation and its universal appeal. It's educational."

"It's great."

A look of relief passed across Jenny's face. "I'm so glad you like it. You were so nice about all the crazy wedding nonsense and I wanted to get you something extra special."

"It's the best thing anyone's ever—what did you say?"

"You were so nice."

"You said crazy wedding nonsense. I heard it. You said it. Crazy as in wedding as in nonsense."

Jenny gave a sheepish smile. "I did get a little crazy. I actually hyperventilated because the caterer cut the carrots lengthwise instead of across for the vegetable trays." She shook her head. "I was just under a lot of pressure and people do crazy things under pressure."

Skye eyed the SweetTart wrappers piled on the corner of her desk. "You're not kidding."

"Anyhow, I know that I'm married now and things are a little different."

But *she* wasn't. She was still the same Jenny at heart. The fun-loving, intuitive, thoughtful woman who knew a wooden dildo was a hundred times better than a T-shirt, at least to her sexpert boss.

Relief rushed through Skye and she smiled. "I don't really understand the whole wedding thing, but if you're happy, I'm happy."

"I'm very happy, and I may be part of a couple now, but I'm still here for you. And so is Little Duke."

"*Little* Duke?" Skye eyed the enormous penis before shifting her attention to Jenny.

Her assistant smiled and shrugged. "You didn't think I married him just because he makes a mean Caesar salad, did you?" Without waiting for a response, Jenny ran a red-tipped fingernail down the length of wood. "Not that Duke and I actually had sex before the wedding. But we did fool around in other ways and I knew what to expect. Little Duke definitely fits, but you can change his name." She gave Skye a quick hug.

"Not that you'll be getting to know him on a first-name basis right now," she said as she started for the door. "You've got the glow."

"I do not."

"You do, and it says you're getting the real thing, even if you don't want to admit it."

Jenny was right. Skye definitely had the sex glow going on. She was also right when she'd said that Skye wasn't ready to admit it.

Admission meant that it was worth talking about. And if something was worth talking about, that meant it was important. And if sex with Clint was important, it meant that Clint was important, and Clint MacAllister was *not* important.

Even if Skye did make sure she was planted in front of her big-screen TV just as the sports announcer said the four most famous words in racing—at least according to the *NASCAR for Dummies* book she'd picked up at the bookstore.

"Gentlemen, start your engines!"

She watched as the red, white and blue Chevrolet painted like a Texas flag roared past the starting line and zoomed onto the track with the other cars. The Chevy settled into the front pack of the four leading cars as they went into the second lap.

Skye sank down onto her sofa, her book on her lap and Earl Grey tea steaming in her favorite pale pink teacup, and her attention fixed on the screen.

Research, she told herself. She wanted to get a jump on the last and final lesson coming up.

Of course, she caught a few glimpses of Clint, too. Naturally, the race coverage consisted of more than just the cars driving lap after endless lap. There were cameras in the pit area with the racing teams, including one focused on Clint and his crew. He wore a royal blue racing jacket with MACALLISTER MAGIC printed in big bold red letters. Sponsor emblems lined the arms and blazed across both sides of the front. He paced the sidelines, a headset firmly in place. While members of the other teams would pause to offer a few words to the press, Clint didn't so much as glance toward the cameras.

She'd never seen him completely shun any sort of attention before. He looked so serious, so focused, so *un*-like the half-naked cowboy who'd grinned and hammed it up for the cameras in those notorious pictures. It had been well over fifteen years—she'd been seventeen and he'd been twenty—and he'd undoubtedly grown up since then. At the same time, he still smiled and flirted and soaked up the attention.

Up close and personal attention. The one-on-one kind like the meet and greet at Jenny and Duke's wedding reception.

This, however, was the media and Clint seemed determined to keep his distance from the reporters and even the sports announcer who called out, "There's the leader of the Wolf Pack himself. Hey, Clint! Come on over and tell the folks at home how you feel about number sixty-two's showing today."

"We'll talk later," Clint called out, smiling and waving.

But Skye knew from the determined light in his eyes that there would be no later. Despite his easygoing I'm-the-greatest-and-everybody-knows-it expression, there was an air of caution about him that made her think he wasn't near as comfortable being in the spotlight as he pretended to be.

Not anymore.

The thought struck her as #62 roared into lap fifty and the camera shifted to the track. She watched the car take a turn and she wondered about Clint's accident. A good thing, or so he kept saying, since it had opened his eyes and made him realize how empty his life was without a Mrs. Clint and a bunch of little Clints. But Skye couldn't help but wonder how she would feel if, during one of her workshops, she were to suddenly drop Dinah or forget her handouts or something equally disastrous. Her confidence would certainly be shaken. Of course, she wouldn't call it quits and give up her business just because of a little upset. But Clint had actually suffered an injury. Climbing behind the wheel didn't just mean his livelihood. It meant his life.

Or his death.

The notion stayed with her as she watched cars roar around the track at breakneck speed. She was just searching in her book for the number of casualties the race world had suffered when she heard the commentator mention Clint's car.

"There goes MacAllister's infamous number sixty-two Chevy out of the second turn and straight into a pass. And he's doing it folks! He's passing Jeff Burton and edging up on number eight. He's out front now and he's wide open, folks! Tuck Briggs is in the lead and he's—holy Toledo, he's buckling on the third turn!"

Her head snapped up in time to see the car swerve and spin.

"He cut it too short and—oh, no, he's lost it, folks! Tuck Briggs has lost it and he's out of control and—oh, no, he's grazed number 8! The impact is sending him toward the center and—he's stopped, folks! Number sixty-two is stopped!"

Skye watched as smoke poured from under the hood and the driver crawled out. He hauled off his helmet and stumbled away from the car just as a small crowd of officials and fellow team members descended on him.

"Looks like Tuck Briggs can kiss Loudon goodbye. There'll be another winner today at New Hampshire International Speedway. Is it going to be Burton or Dale Jr.'s number eight? Stay tuned to find out . . ."

A wave of disappointment welled inside Skye, particularly when she caught a glimpse of Clint as the camera panned in for a close-up of Tuck and his team's owner near the smoking car. He looked angry and upset and sad—all at the same time—and Skye had the incredible urge to reach out and comfort him.

Thankfully it was a television in front of her and not the real man, because comforting was not on her agenda when it came to Clint MacAllister.

The phone rang and Skye reached toward the coffee table, her gaze fixed on the Caller ID on the display. She punched the Mute button just before she said hello.

"Hey, Sis, what's up—"

"This is your mother," Jacqueline Farrel's voice floated over the line. "I knew you were checking the Caller ID, that's why you haven't been answering your phone when I call."

Skye punched the Off button and the TV went blank.

"I do look at the Caller ID, but I can't help it. It's right there when I reach for the phone, and I have been answering when it rings—"

"Really?" her mother cut her short. "I've been calling you for the past three days and the only thing I get is your voice mail after at least a dozen rings."

"I haven't had a chance to call you back. I was out of town for Girl Talk business. What are you doing in Houston? I thought you were in California."

"That was last week. I'm en route to Harvard for an alumnae luncheon. I hopped a plane after I taped the show this morning—a segment called *The Man Who Gives Me My Orgasms*. It's about men who are life mates who come to expect more from a woman than just sex. They get comfortable in the relationship and bam, they start acting like actual *husbands*. The problem is rampant and must be nipped in the bud before it starts. Why, when your father starts being the least bit possessive, I completely cut him off from sex so that it shifts his focus back to what's really important. If he isn't getting any, then he starts to think about it more and more. Believe you me, he stops wanting me to rub his feet in hopes that I'll rub his—"

"Mom, I really don't want to hear this."

"Nonsense. This is informative. I didn't raise you to bury your head in the sand when it comes to such an important issue. Why, no daughter of mine would ever turn the other cheek while a man took advantage of her and—"

"How long is your layover?" Skye blurted, eager to get them onto a safer subject.

"Five hours, three and a half of which I spent on what should have been a twenty minute cab ride here to your sister's. I visited for a half hour and my cab should be arriving any minute to go back to the airport. But that's neither here nor there. The point is, I'm *here*, but you haven't been *there*."

"I bet Xandra's thrilled that you're in town, even if it is just a short visit." She was going for the old avoidance technique.

Hey, it worked the last time.

"Of course she is. She answers her phone when her mother calls."

"When she's home," Skye pointed out. Okay, so she got lucky last time and her mother wasn't falling for it again. "I told you I've been out of town and since I've come back, I've been really busy with work."

"Busy," Jacqueline snorted. "That's a fine how-do-you-do. Was I too busy to endure thirty-seven hours of stage two labor pains? Was I too busy to push for forty-five minutes straight during stage three? Was I too busy to change diapers and do midnight feedings and . . ."

Skye wanted to tell her that her grandmother and her father had helped with everything after the pushing.

". . . too busy to gut every magazine in the house—even though drawing would have been much better for the eco-system—for your papier-maché project in the first grade? Was I too busy—"

"I saw an advertisement for your next book in *People*," Skye blurted. "It was full color with a write-up about the importance of female empowerment." Hey, if at first you don't succeed, try, try again. "And how you've revolutionized the entire movement by giving all females a voice."

"I wouldn't say I revolutionized it, but I do pride myself on helping those less fortunate women who are still imprisoned by society and its social constraints . . ." Jacqueline's voice went on while Skye closed her NASCAR book, reached for her cup of tea and wondered how far the reception on her cordless would reach if she opted to head downstairs and around the corner for a cookie.

Or two. Or three.

She'd fantasized about a full dozen by the time her mother finished her ten-minute womanist sermon and said a hurried goodbye because her cab had arrived.

Skye made a mental note to send a donation to the cab driver's union this Christmas and punched the On button on the remote control. The screen lit up and a close-up of Clint's car filled the screen.

"Why did you let her call?" Skye asked when Xandra took the phone.

"As if I could stop her. Besides, I endured thirty minutes of preaching about everything from Mark to strange sperm to babies to Blow Pops. You're the oldest. It's only fair that you share in the misery."

"I'm the oldest which means I've been miserable a lot longer."

"Hey, I held her off for a full half hour. I could have made the suggestion sooner than I did."

"A-ha. You did get her to call me."

"I just suggested it."

"Traitor."

"Liar."

"Kiss-up."

"Bitch."

"Okay," Skye said. "Bitch outdoes kiss-up. You win. I'm not upset."

"That makes one of us."

"Mark and sperm and babies, I understand," Skye told her sister. "But Blow Pops?"

"Remember my brainstorm about the lollipops in place of smoking? Well, I tried Dum Dums first, but they were too little. Not enough candy to get any real sucking action going, but the sticks did give my hand something to do. So instead of tossing in the idea, I figured I'd give my craving a little more to sate it. I switched to a bigger lollipop and then a gum-filled one. It's a triple whammy. First sucking, then chewing and some hand action."

"Is it working?"

"Before Mom arrived. Now my nerves are shot and I'm a woman on the edge and I'm ready to get myself a pack."

"You'll hate yourself tomorrow."

"I hate myself right now. Mom actually spotted the three pounds I put on since I started trying to quit. I mean, I knew they were there, but I didn't think anyone else could see them."

"It's definite. Mom's the original Big Brother. She knows all. Sees all."

"Mom's a preachy, womanist nut."

"She's passionate," Skye said, always the first to jump to her mother's defense. "But that's no reason to call her names."

"She took my Blow Pops."

"She what?"

"She told me I was obviously eating too much sugar and she took my Blow Pops. Stuffed them all into her purse and marched out to the cab."

"Okay, so maybe she's a little nutty."

"She's a lot nutty. She defines the word." Silence ensued before Xandra's voice came over the line again. "Then again, maybe she's just looking out for my best interests. Maybe I should just give up trying to give up. I don't want to smoke, but I certainly don't want to be fat again. Mark hates cigarette smoke, but he *really* hates frumpy, fat women."

"You are not frumpy or fat and you're not giving up. To hell with Mom and Mark. You're quitting for you, remember?"

"Yes."

"So stop doubting yourself, march down to the store, stock up on Blow Pops and lick that craving."

"Easy for you to say. You don't know how it is to want something so bad you can hardly stand it."

Skye's gaze shifted to the big screen and the coverage

of the damaged race car now sitting off to the sidelines of the New Hampshire track. Dozens of people surrounded the car, but there was no mistaking Clint's familiar form. He stood near the front, hands on hips, as he surveyed the damage to his #62 Chevy.

Her mouth watered and her stomach grumbled, but the sudden hunger had nothing to do with a cookie and everything to do with Clint.

She wanted him.

She wanted to take him into her arms and hold him until the distraught look on his face disappeared.

"Actually, I know just how you feel," she told her sister.

But not for long, she promised herself as she wished her sister good luck, hung up the phone and snatched up her purse.

The SweetTarts hadn't suppressed the cookie craving, so Skye had little faith that they would help the Clint addiction.

She would have to find something bigger and more powerful to do that.

"For the last time, it wasn't me."

Tuck's voice echoed in Lindy's ears as she stood off to the side of the garage and watched the hotshot driver face off with Clint.

A very unpleasant Clint, judging by the dark look on his face. He was oblivious to the reporters who stood just outside the doorway snapping picture after picture past the burly looking engineer who kept them from gaining entrance.

Lindy had seen Clint mindless of the media only once since she'd come on as his personal assistant, and that had been when he'd given an interview to the editor of their hometown paper. The woman had brought up his less than stellar academic record. He'd been polite at first, steering her questions toward his success and how he'd risen above his handicap. But the old biddy had been hell-bent on making an issue of the fact that, however far he'd come, he still had a learning disability. Clint had finally cut her off, excusing himself and leaving the living room of his parents' house where they'd been conducting the interview. He'd left in a flurry of clicks and flashes, and he hadn't stopped once. He'd headed out the door, into his Hummer and down the road before he'd done something disrespectful, like tell the old woman where to get off.

Lindy had done that for him, in that tasteful, academic, over-the-head sort of way that left someone wondering whether they'd been flattered or insulted. Needless to say, the article had been mixed.

He was just as mad as he'd been that day. But he wasn't holding back now. He was about to unleash on Tuck and for a crazy second, Lindy almost stepped in.

Almost, but she'd known Clint too long, not to mention this is what she'd been waiting for—to finally see someone put Tuck Briggs in his place.

"The car wasn't stable," Tuck went on. "It wobbled coming out of the turn."

"Because you were following too close to the lead car," Clint said. "You were disturbing the air flow off the car in front of you and you were hung out to dry all by yourself. You were out of the draft. There was no way you had enough force to pass."

"I could have made it. The car slipped."

"You shouldn't have made the move without another

car in back of you. That's why you have to listen to the spotter. He can see what you can't. Like the fact that you were too far out of the line of cars. You need the draft for speed if you want to pass."

"Look, I don't need a lesson in passing," Tuck said.

Lindy had to hand it to him. Tuck had as much nerve as he had good looks. Clint had presence. Talent and power and confidence, and the three made for a very intimidating mix to other men. To females, it was a definite chick magnet. But men either wanted to buddy up to him, or stay out of his way. Tuck was doing neither.

"It was the car," Tuck said again. "How many times do I have to say it?"

"Until I believe it, which isn't likely to be anytime soon. If the car slipped, it would have been slipping during practice. You didn't say a word."

Tuck looked as if he were about to say something, but then he clamped his mouth shut, his lips thinning into a line and he shrugged. "What's the big deal? We fix the car and we're good to go."

"It slipped, but you didn't notice it, did you?"

"Whatever. Look, are we done yet because I've got pictures to take."

"I'm sure the press got plenty of you spinning out. I would think you'd had enough pictures today."

"Shit happens, man."

"Shit happens, or you made it happen?"

"What's that supposed to mean?"

"Where were you Friday night?"

Tuck eyed Clint for a long time before shrugging. "You tell me. You obviously already know."

"Damned right I know. You were dancing it up at some

bar in town. You, a few of your MTV buddies, a few women, and a lot of beer."

"It wasn't that much. It was no big deal."

"We're talking Winston Cup," Clint exploded. "Everything is a big deal, particularly when you're driving the next day. But then you won't have to worry about that if you keep this up."

"What's that supposed to mean?"

"That you forget test laps in Atlanta and take the next three days off. You're suspended. I'd suggest you use the time to think about where you're going and what you're doing, and get yourself into an AA program by Friday."

"Or what?"

"Or you're fired."

"This isn't fair. You can't dictate my personal life."

"I can when it affects your job."

"I don't drink before I get behind the wheel. I'm stone-cold sober."

"And dog tired, and hungover after partying it up all night and making the headlines."

"I'm just blowing off steam. You need to lighten up."

"You're blowing this season, is what you're doing. Lindy's got a number for you to call." He turned to her and motioned her forward.

She stepped to attention and avoided any comment. Clint eyed her a moment, as if surprised that she kept quiet. Of course, he figured she'd be ready with an "I told you so".

She should have been ready, but for some reason she wasn't. She was tired herself and for some reason, gloating seemed like too much work. Instead, she produced one of her business cards, looked up the number in question on her Palm Pilot and scribbled it on the back while Clint turned to Tuck.

"Call it and get your shit straight, or don't come back."

"You won't fire me," Tuck said as Clint turned toward the door.

"I hope I won't have to," his boss called over his shoulder before he disappeared through the door that led to the garage area where #62 had been towed after the race.

"Nice working for you," Tuck called after him. "Thanks for being such an understanding guy."

"You're a jackass, do you know that?" Lindy asked as she turned toward him.

"I sure do, darlin'. You see fit to inform me every chance you get."

"Obviously, it hasn't sunk in. What are you doing? Why are you pushing him?"

"What do you care? You ought to be happy he wants to fire me. You can't stand me."

"Whether or not I like you has nothing to do with your driving ability or today's disaster. You're still in a good position. Your points are solid. You'd be stupid to blow it because you can't control your wild side." She handed him the card. "Get smart."

"Thanks for the advice, but no thanks. It wasn't me." Even so, he stuffed the card into his pocket instead of tossing it back at her. His gaze met hers and there was something about the look in his eyes that told her he was telling the truth. "I had that pass. I know I was out of the line, I heard the spotter. But I was still in the draft."

The draft was when cars raced single file down the track and shared airflow. It was a factor of aerodynamics that became even more important when drivers raced the larger tracks. The basic theory was that cars go faster when they race in line because the lead car punches an imaginary hole in the air and the cars behind it slip more easily through that hole. Out of line, the engine had to work harder, therefore slowing down the car.

"You were out of line," she told him.

"Not when the car slipped," he growled, his temper rising.

"You were out of line and you slipped."

"I was in line and *then* the car slipped, just like it slipped during practice."

"It did slip," she said accusingly. "Why didn't you *say* something?"

He shrugged, his gaze guarded once again. "I thought I could handle it myself."

"You don't have to handle it yourself. There's a whole team here to help you. Geez, you have such an advantage over all these other drivers. Your owner is one of the best. If you think that he's never had a car slip on him, think again. Why didn't you just tell him?"

"It's too late now."

She shook her head before leveling a stare at him. "I was wrong about you."

"I'm not a jackass?"

"Yes, you're a jackass, but now I realize it's not just an act. The whole time I thought you were just pretending to get media attention."

"I never pretend."

"Exactly." She indicated his pocket. "Just don't be an unemployed jackass."

"And forfeit the chance to add another adjective to the title?"

"Trust me, it's worth the risk." She turned and did her

damndest to ignore the prickle of awareness that shot through her and told her he was watching her.

"Don't be shy, darlin'. Tell me how you really feel."

"I think you've had enough bad news for one day," she called out over her shoulder. "I wouldn't want to add to the list by telling you how much you get on my nerves."

"You want me," he called after her.

"You're crazy."

"Crazy over the way you're swinging your hips. Anybody ever tell you you've got a really hot walk?"

"All the time," she said, blowing off his comment as she pushed through the door and walked out into the pit area. She didn't have a hot anything, and Tuck Briggs knew it. He was just flirting with her like he did all women. No way did he actually mean what he'd said.

Guys like Tuck didn't mean anything when they flirted with women like Lindy, and they certainly didn't lust after them. She wasn't pretty enough or big-breasted enough or blond enough for a man like Tuck, who cared more about looking cool than actually being cool.

Now if she could just remember that when he trained those deep brown eyes on her and made her feel like the last petit four at one of her mother's infamous Ladies of Town luncheons.

Tuck Briggs did not want her, and she didn't want him, and that was that. No matter how much her hormones screamed otherwise.

After an exhausting plane ride, Clint should have headed straight home to bed. He'd had a shitty day and the sooner it ended the better. He knew that, but he found himself on Skye's doorstep later that night anyway.

He liked her. He really liked her.

He'd admitted that to himself when she'd admitted the truth to him—that she hated fishing. He'd expected to be turned off, but damned if he hadn't been all the more turned on. He'd still wanted to kiss her. More than ever, in fact, because she'd looked so miserable standing there and he'd wanted to make her feel better.

But while he liked her, he wasn't positive she felt the same way. He had a sneaking suspicion, though, and it drove him. He passed a hand over his face and punched the doorbell.

"What are you doing here?" Skye asked around a mouthful of Tootsie Pop.

"I thought we could talk."

She pulled the candy from her mouth, her gaze widening. "You want to talk?"

"I need to talk. Things didn't go so well."

"I saw." For a split second, warmth flashed in her gaze, feeding his suspicion about her true feelings. He actually thought she might reach out, but then something seemed to snap and she stiffened. "That was a tough break."

"I gave him an ultimatum."

"Who—" she started, but then she seemed to catch herself. "I mean, I would love to hear the rest, but I'm really busy right now."

"Doing what?"

"Working."

"With a handful of Tootsie Pops?"

"I know they look like candy, but they're for work. Research," she blurted. "I'm developing a new foreplay technique and it uses Tootsie Pops. Yeah," she smiled, as if pleased with herself at the explanation. "That's it. The candy is for a new technique that's sure to revolutionize the female orgasm."

She was feeding him a load of bunk. He knew it even before she licked her lips and averted her gaze. She obviously didn't want to talk to him, but he wasn't so sure why. Because she really didn't like him, or because she didn't want to like him?

He could press her for answers, but that would only make her that much more nervous, and that much more determined to change the subject. Or he could go along for the ride and see what happened . . .

She licked her lips again and his groin tightened and he knew instantly which route he was going to take.

A new technique to revolutionize the female orgasm?
The words echoed in Skye's head as she stared up at Clint. Okay, so it was a little out there as far as concept, but she'd never been one to think fast on her feet. Her nerves were jumping and her heart was pounding and she was desperate. And surprised.

She hadn't expected Clint to show up on her doorstep.

And she certainly hadn't expected him to show up wanting to talk.

Nor had she expected him to show up looking so tired and worn and defeated.

His hair was disheveled. Exhaustion rimmed his eyes. His shoulders didn't seem as broad as usual. He looked nothing like the cocky, self-assured Cowboy who made it his business to win, and everything like a man who was fast learning what it was like to lose.

And damned if she didn't feel the familiar stirring in her belly. And something else . . . something softer.

Holy Mother of God, he wanted to *talk* to her.

No way, no how. It wasn't happening. Their relationship was all about sex, and so Skye did the one thing she felt certain would keep them on the straight and narrow.

She kissed him.

He didn't respond at first, but then she swept her tongue across his bottom lip and his mouth opened. He returned her kiss with a fierceness that took her breath away and eased the panic beating in her chest.

"That was nice, but what I really want is—"

She pressed her fingertips to his lips and said, "Positions eleven through twenty."

He gripped her wrist and pulled her hand away and she braced herself for what would come next.

"Actually, I really want a demonstration of this new technique. The positions can wait." He backed her into the foyer and closed the door behind him.

A determined light gleamed in his eyes, as if he'd decided to let her change the subject and steer them onto safer ground.

Let her, as in he still meant to stay in control. To keep her on the defensive.

But Skye didn't play defense. She was all about offense, even if she had no clue as to what her next move would be.

"So?" He arched a dubious brow at her.

"So . . ." She licked her lips and shoved a pop into her mouth. "First you have to suck on the candy."

"And then?"

"Well, you keep sucking until your mouth fills with flavor and the pop is thoroughly wet. In the meantime . . ."

Her mind riffled through a variety of possibilities before settling on one in particular. One guaranteed to not only put him on the defensive, but keep him there for a very long time.

"In the meantime," she said around the candy, "you have to take off your clothes." She sucked on the pop and slowly unbuttoned her blouse.

With every button, his gaze darkened to reach a deep, dark flame blue when she finally let the silk blouse slide from her shoulders. Her bra quickly followed until she was naked from the waist up, and his gaze practically smoldered.

But there was something else in the dark depths when he looked at her. Something that sent a wave of self consciousness through her and scrambled her thoughts.

"After the clothes," she started, desperate to push aside the strange thoughts. This was sex and she was reading too much into the situation. "After the clothes," she said again, "you have to—"

"You've still got clothes on," he cut in.

I knew that, she told herself as she glanced down and saw her slacks still firmly in place. She'd just been trying to build anticipation. Prolong the excitement.

She reached for the button on her slacks. The opening slid free and she pushed the pants down and shoved them aside. Her fingers hesitated on the edge of her thong, but then she braced her shoulders and shoved the lace all the way down until she stood completely naked and vulnerable.

Vulnerable?

She most certainly was not vulnerable. She was au naturel, that was all. He was looking at her body, not beneath. Even if she did get the sudden feeling that he saw a lot more than she wanted him to.

Crazy. This was sex.

She held tight to the thought and reached for the Tootsie Pop in her mouth.

"Once you're completely naked," she touched the pop to her bottom lip and rubbed it back and forth, "it's time to really have some fun. Tootsie Pops are all about sucking, so the first thing you do is flavor things up so that the sucking is tasty."

He swallowed and she knew her words had sparked all sorts of ideas. Then his gaze darkened and she knew his thoughts had shifted to what she was about to do, rather than why she was doing it.

The realization fed her courage and she licked the lollipop again before touching it to the tip of her nipple. She swirled the candy around the tip and it ripened, pressing against the hardness, absorbing its flavor. She delivered the same treatment to her other breast and a moan worked its way up her throat.

Maybe she was really onto something after all.

"This feels really good," she murmured. But it was nothing compared to the feel of his mouth closing over her bare breast and sucking her grape-flavored nipple.

Her knees buckled and she slumped against him as he suckled, drawing on her so hard that she felt the pull between her legs.

Another moan and he lifted her, carrying her into the bedroom and easing her down onto her comforter.

"Pretty interesting technique so far," he said as he leaned back to stare down at her. He pulled his T-shirt up over his head and tossed it to the side.

He had such a great chest, dusted with that silky dark hair. Her gaze touched on his nipples and an idea struck.

"Your turn." She climbed up onto her knees and

touched the lollipop to the tip of one dark nipple. He didn't take his eyes off her, his gaze dark and smoldering.

She leaned forward and drew the small nub into her mouth. He tasted sweet and fruity and heat flooded between her legs. She sucked harder, devouring him until his hand closed around the back of her head and he pulled her away from him.

"What's wrong?" she asked.

"This is all about the female orgasm, remember?" He pushed her back, took the Tootsie Pop and slid down her body. He parted her thighs and settled himself between them.

Before she could draw her next breath, he trailed the pop along her slick folds and sensation bolted through her. The candy was slick and hard and she closed her eyes, her fingers digging into the soft mattress. A flush crept over her skin, spreading like wild fire.

But while the candy itself felt pretty pleasurable, sliding back and forth along her flesh, it was nothing compared to the bolt of heat that rushed through her when he slid the pop a fraction inside and twirled the stick.

A moan burst past her lips and she arched, so close to going over the edge. Just a little more. Just . . .

He pulled back and left her hanging long enough to take a quick deep breath. And then his mouth was on her. He stroked and licked and sucked, and she came in a blur of dizzying sensation that swept over her like a huge wave and tossed her to and fro. And as she lay there, heart pounding, her body alive and pulsing, she realized she had, indeed, revolutionized the female orgasm.

Her own, anyhow.

Thanks to Clint and his Tootsie Pop Twist.

Chapter Seventeen

"This guy must really be something," Jenny said on Wednesday evening as she gathered up rubber penises.

"What are you talking about?" Skye packed up her workshop materials while the hostess and few remaining guests stood near the dining room table devouring the last of the refreshments. The proverbial after-sex munching. Or in this case, after-talking-about-sex munching.

"You," Jenny said. "I've never seen you like this."

"Am I glowing again?" Skye reached into her briefcase and pulled out a compact.

"As a matter of fact, yes, but that's not what I'm talking about. I'm talking the inner you, not the outer you." When Skye gave her a puzzled look, she added, "You answered five questions from the floor tonight that weren't on the note cards."

Skye's mind riffled back through the past hour. "They were easy questions."

"Easy has never figured in before, not to mention there's an entire plate of Famous Amos sitting over there and you haven't so much as glanced in that direction."

"I've kicked the habit." Thanks to Clint. Since he'd shown up at her house on Sunday night and helped her with her new sex technique—number twenty-one of the recommended top twenty—she'd been cookie free and loving it. Of course, she still had a thing for the Tootsie Pops but they were a lot less calories, not to mention a lot more fun.

In fact, the past two days had been the most fun she'd had in a very long time. After her initial freak-out about his talking comment and the great sex that had followed, she'd opened her eyes several hours later and realized what an idiot she'd been. As if not talking to him could help keep things in the proper perspective between them.

They were so very different that talking to him wasn't about to bridge the gap. In fact, talking was just what she needed.

Purely research, she'd told herself. She'd never had such a macho man at her disposal and it would be a grave injustice to her own education not to gather as much information as possible.

It certainly had nothing to do with the fact that she *wanted* to get to know him.

So in between finishing off the remaining ten positions, they spent the downtime talking about everything from NASCAR—her next and final lesson—to Skye's family—he'd spotted her photo box in the corner of her bedroom—to his family. Of course, he wouldn't let her pick his brain without doing a little picking of his own and so they'd both done an equal amount of talking.

He'd told her about Tuck and the ultimatum, and she'd assured him that his driver would smarten up and take the deal in time for that weekend's Pepsi 400. He'd gone on to talk about his career with NASCAR and how everything had come to a head during the Daytona 500. How he'd realized then and there that he wasn't invincible. He'd suffered only a minor shoulder injury, thankfully, but the next time? He'd made up his mind never to find out. He still had goals in his life, namely to settle down and raise a family of his own. After all, what was a man without a good woman and a half-dozen kids behind him?

Skye gave him a womanist earful on the proverbial good woman behind the good man theory, or as Clint had said, she'd chewed him a new asshole, before going on to tell him about her own hope of finding a long-term relationship.

They'd shared tips on what it was like to be the oldest child—namely that it sucked most of the time because of the added pressure of younger siblings. He'd told her what it was like to grow up in a family of mostly boys and she'd filled him in on the danger associated with having one bathroom in an all-girl household.

The conversation had continued, along with the sex, until they'd parted ways early that morning. Clint had several PR things to do before the Pepsi 400 that weekend which, he'd told her, would be her final lesson—an up-close look at the sport of racing.

Likewise, they had now completed three parts of her four-part workshop—the body, foreplay, sex play and after-sex play. He was due for the after-sex lesson which Skye intended to give him in the plane ride over. It was primarily just a summary of past points and a list of appropriate things to say and do in order to keep your lover coming back for more.

Of course, Clint was sure to ace the subject. He'd left

her with a hot, deep kiss and a promise to see her soon, and she definitely wanted more.

"You like him," Jenny said, her voice pulling Skye from her thoughts.

"I do not."

"Yes, you do. You really like him."

Jenny's words followed Skye home after the workshop, crawled into bed with her and kept her tossing and turning all night long.

She climbed out of bed the next morning even more confused than she'd been the night before.

Like? Real, true, genuine *like?*

It was impossible. She couldn't really *like* him. Not without totally upending her entire belief system. *Like* came after the Holy Commitment Trinity, not in spite of. It was a direct result of all three points. Without the Trinity, there could be no real like.

True, they had great sex.

Ditto for the mutual respect.

But common interests? While she'd beefed up her macho knowledge, she was still way out of his league. She didn't just dislike fishing, she hated it and Clint was a man who prided himself on mounting his catches and putting them on his wall.

Forget any sort of like.

That's what she told herself until she opened the door to find Clint on the other side. She took one look at him standing on her doorstep with his dark good looks and his intense eyes and something shifted inside her.

We're worlds apart, she kept telling herself as she gathered up her suitcase and headed out the door for Florida. Even if they had seemed pretty darn close with all that talking. And sex. And more talking. And more sex.

This was it. The end of the line. The last lesson for him, and the last lesson for her. The future with a yet-to-be discovered macho man waited for her, while Darla waited for him in Florida.

It was the first time she'd really let herself think about the other woman. A surge of jealousy went through her, followed by anxiety because she had no right to be jealous. Unless . . .

"What's up with you?" he asked as they headed toward the airport.

"Nothing." Except for the fact that she needed to think. To clear her head. To find her perspective and get her priorities back in order and remember that Clint MacAllister was *not* one of them.

And there was only one way for a thirty-three-year-old sexpert to do that.

"Do we have time to make a stop? It's an emergency."

"A shoe emergency," Clint said a half hour later as he sprawled in a chair at Anne Kleins, in the heart of downtown Dallas.

Skye slid on her tenth pair and eyeballed her feet in the mirror. "I need something comfortable for Florida."

"Those look painful, not comfortable."

Skye wiggled her toes in the three-inch-red sandals and winced. "You're right. Let me try that other pair." She spent the next ten minutes trying and re-trying at least a dozen different styles of sandal, but she kept coming back to the painful red ones.

Definite Barbie shoes.

"Why don't you just get those?"

"I can't get these."

"Why not?"

"Because they're not practical. You said it yourself. They look painful."

"But you still like them."

"So?"

"So if you like them, get them."

"I can't get these," she said again, eyeing the shoes.

"Do you like the damned shoes or not?"

"Yes."

"Then that's all that matters."

But it wasn't, Skye realized in a startling instant as she watched Clint toss the red stilettos into the box and hand it to the sales clerk with a deep, final, "We'll take them."

Panic welled inside her and fear rushed, cold and gripping, through every inch of her body. The same fear she'd felt when her mother had caught her baking the cookies for her seventh-grade Valentine, and staring at the Princess Barbie in the toy store window, and riding on the back of the motorcycle that time in high school.

Not the fear of being caught, but the fear of disapproval. Of seeing the disappointment in her mother's eyes.

It wasn't about whether Skye liked the shoes or not, because her own likes and dislikes had never mattered. It was about what she was expected to like because of who she was, because of who her mother was.

"No daughter of mine would ever wear shoes created by a man purely for a man's enjoyment, at the woman's expense. Men are visual. High heels slim the calves and make the female legs more visually appealing, all the while doing irreparable damage to the feet. Why, no daughter of mine would ever condone, let alone finan-

cially support, such an invention. She might as well stab me in the back and put me out of my misery right now."

She being Skye.

Skye had heard the preaching her entire life, so much so that she'd embraced it as her own. It was easier to go along than stand up for herself, particularly since she'd grown up as the proverbial outsider. She'd never been accepted by the other kids, never included in their activities or their social circles. She'd had only her mother's acceptance, and so she'd held onto it for all she was worth. She'd learned early on that the more she appeared to be the model daughter, the more her mother seemed to like her.

To love her.

To accept her.

And so Skye had spent her entire life trying to please her mother. She was still trying, and still falling short, because she wasn't her mother and Jacqueline Farrel would be satisfied with nothing less. The woman didn't want a daughter. She wanted a miniature copy of herself to preach her womanist doctrine and further her precious movement. Even more, she wanted affirmation. Seeing her daughters live and breathe and succeed as modern womanists merely confirmed her beliefs and gave proof that her time and energy had been well spent.

But Skye wasn't a carbon copy of her mother. She admitted that to herself as she stood at the sales counter and watched them bag her shoes. A thrill of anticipation raced through her, and nothing else. No hesitation. No fear.

She wasn't her mother. She never would be.

She had her own identity now. She wasn't just Jacqueline Farrel's daughter. She was the successful owner of a growing company. She had her own home, her own career, her own friends. She didn't measure her self-worth by what other people thought of her.

She was all grown up now, and that was okay.

She didn't live and breathe for her mother's approval. She could have her own likes and dislikes.

And she liked the red Barbie shoes.

Almost as much as she liked Clint MacAllister.

"This isn't the Daytona International Speedway," Lindy said as she walked up to the small jail cell and stared past the bars to the man sitting inside.

"Nah, really? I never would have guessed." Tuck sat on the small bunk situated against the far wall. He wore only jeans, boots and that irritating grin that made her want to slap him. Or kiss him.

Instead, she frowned. "I can see why they arrested you." She could see a lot more, as well. His broad shoulders and bare chest dusted with golden hair. He was really gorgeous, and much too big for his britches, judging by the sarcastic tone of his voice.

"They don't arrest you for being a wiseass," he told her.

"So why did they arrest you?"

"Disorderly conduct. I sort of got into a fight."

"Did this sort of fight hurt anyone?"

"No. It just pissed off the reporter from *Car & Driver*. He wanted a picture and I wasn't in a picture-taking mood. I was trying to relax."

"At a shot contest at a bar. Downing tequila isn't relaxing."

"I didn't do any shots. I had one beer. I'm not an alcoholic like Clint thinks and I don't need an AA program. I drink to unwind and have a little fun."

"Alcohol impairs. How do you know what you need?"

"Because I watch myself. I have a three-beer limit and I never pass it."

"You never drink more than three beers?"

"I may act a little drunk, but that's all it is. My old man was a social drinker. He hated drinking alone and so he was always after me to join him. But I knew while I might want to tie one on just to forget him and my shitty life, I couldn't. Because somebody had to pick him up and take him home, and that somebody was me. Since I was twelve years old and my mom walked out, it was always me."

As Lindy stood there gazing at Tuck, she got more than just a good look at his bare chest. She got a good look at what was beneath.

Fear and desperation and sheer loneliness flashed in his gaze. Lindy couldn't help but remember her own childhood, and her own loneliness.

"The night before my high-school graduation," he went on, "he tied one on so bad that he actually stopped breathing. I had been out at a party and I remember when I came home, I found him on the sofa. Unconscious. I called an ambulance and they rushed him to the hospital. They were able to revive him and he was all right, but I've never been so scared in my whole life. He was all I had after my mom left. I couldn't imagine losing him, too. I realized then that I had to get myself together and get out of there." His gaze met hers. "I left the next day and I haven't seen him since."

"So you ran away."

"I didn't run away. I needed some distance and my dad needed to realize that there wasn't always going to be someone there to pick him back up." He shook his head.

"It doesn't matter. What does matter is that Clint was wrong. I'm not an alcoholic."

"No, you're just an idiot."

"What's that supposed to mean?"

"If you had an ounce of gray matter, you would have told Clint what you just told me and then he would have realized that the only reason you act like a jackass is because you don't want people to get too close to you. Because then you might get too close, and then you would be right back where you were before you ran away. Needing someone."

"My past is my business."

"If it affects his race team, then it is Clint's business. He likes you, but if you don't trust him enough to talk to him, you can't blame him for thinking the worst. You should have called the number anyway to satisfy him and keep your job."

"I don't need this job. I don't need Clint. And I sure as hell don't need all your advice." He shrugged. "All I need is to be left alone."

"Is that so? Then I guess it was someone else by the name of Tuck Briggs who called me on my cell phone and asked me to come down here and bail him out."

"I'll give you the money back just as soon as I get out of here and get to an ATM."

"I don't care about the money. You need me. Admit it."

"You don't know what I need."

"I know how you feel. You're not the only who's ever been scared or disappointed or lonely. Try having a socialite mother who wanted her only daughter to follow in her cheerleading, homecoming queen footsteps. Needless to say, I was a big disappointment. I could get straight A's but not a date to the prom. I didn't even go to the right college. I won a scholarship to the University of Texas when my parents were Aggies through and through and got a geeky accounting degree."

"But you're not an accountant."

"Not technically, but I do keep Clint's books."

"Why didn't you join some fancy accounting firm? You're smart enough."

A zing of warmth rushed through her at the sincere compliment and stopped her from telling him to mind his own business. Instead, she shrugged and said, "Because Clint needed me as his personal assistant. No one had ever really needed me before. My parents just ignored me. Clint was different. He didn't care what I looked like or how popular I was. He was the first pretty boy who ever really liked me. The first one that I ever really liked. He was never mean like the other boys."

"And that's why you hate those pretty boy types. Because they're mean?"

"Actually, I hate them because they're self-centered and too stubborn to ask for help."

"Not all pretty boys are self-centered and stubborn."

"No, just you. Speaking of which," she glanced at her watch, "it's been nice talking to you, but I've got a qualifier to catch. Take care and good luck." She turned and managed two steps.

"Wait."

She stopped, but she didn't turn around.

"I need you, Lindy. That's why I called you. Because I need you."

She turned back to him and the light blazing in his eyes stopped her cold. He was sincere and desperate and he didn't try to hide it behind his usual irritating grin. He grasped the bars, his face serious, his eyes slightly narrowed as he eyed her and waited for her response.

She smiled. "Maybe you're not an idiot, after all."

The expectant look on his face eased into a crooked grin that made her heart pound and her palms sweat. "And maybe you like me a lot more than you let on."

"Maybe. Now put on your shirt and let's get out of here."

"Most women would rather have me take my clothes off."

"I'm not most women. I have priorities. We have a race to get to." Her smile widened. "Then we'll worry about taking off the clothes."

"A woman after my own heart."

"Maybe."

"He'll be here," Clint told himself for the umpteenth time as he paced the garage late Saturday afternoon. He glanced at his watch yet again. Only five minutes later than the last time he'd looked. Only ten minutes shy of three P.M. and the second round of qualifying for those drivers who weren't among the twenty-five fastest during the first day. Or, in this case, for drivers who didn't bother to even show up on Friday.

He still couldn't believe it. He'd flown in with Skye early Friday morning. After dropping her off at the hotel, he'd headed out to the track to check out the car and give Tuck a few words of warning about communication with the spotter and the car chief.

The entire crew had been hard at work. Everyone, but Tuck. No one had seen or heard from him.

Clint hadn't panicked. He'd been sure the man would

show up. No one would be stupid enough to throw away a championship.

That's what he'd told himself all day yesterday and all morning. Tuck was mad because Clint had dealt him an ultimatum, and so he was trying to make Clint sweat.

He was doing a damned good job.

"He'll be here," Clint told Jeep, the only other person who knew Tuck still hadn't shown up. "What about Lindy? Is she here yet?" He and Lindy usually flew in together, but since he'd had Skye with him, Lindy had opted to hop a commercial flight. She hadn't said anything, but Clint had the feeling she thought he was sweet on Skye. "I tried her cell phone but it just went to voice mail."

"I haven't seen her, boss. You think she's with Tuck?"

"Hardly, but she still might know where he is."

Jeep shook his head and eyed the rest of the crew, who went about their business as if nothing were amiss.

Clint's gaze went to Skye, who followed his car chief around with pen and notebook in hand, taking notes for her NASCAR lesson. One he had intended to give her himself, before his life had turned into a big pile of crapola.

"You want me to tell everybody the bad news?" Jeep asked.

"He's still got five minutes."

"I knew this was going to happen," Vernon said when he arrived a few minutes later and saw #62 still sitting in the garage. "I told you that boy was unreliable. We can kiss the Pepsi 400 goodbye, not to mention our winning streak." Vernon eyed Clint. "Unless you get your ass out there and get us into this race."

"I don't drive anymore."

"You don't, or you can't? I never thought I'd say this, Cowboy, but maybe the press ain't all that far off with all that stuff they're saying."

"I'm tired, Vernon. That's all. Can't a man get tired?"

"Well, maybe this team isn't worth our money anymore."

"This team is worth more than your money. This team is a part of your image."

Clint leveled a stare at his old friend. "You're a sponsor, Vernon. A good one and a good friend, but still a sponsor. I own the team. I hire and fire the crew, and I decide who drives. I appreciate your input, but that's the reality of it. If you want to continue to be a part of this team, then you need to let me do my job and you do yours. Get on up to the sponsor's suite and cool down and I'll handle this."

Vernon looked as if he wanted to argue, but then he clamped his mouth shut. He walked away red-faced and angry, but definitely in his place.

"That was a good speech and all," Jeep said after the door rocked shut on Vernon's heels. "But how are you going to handle this?"

"We've still got two minutes." He knew it was useless to keep hoping. "Shit." Clint passed a hand over his face and damned himself for thinking that Tuck Briggs could ever really amount to anything.

He'd thought he knew Tuck. When he watched the young man race, he saw the raw talent. He'd remembered the beginning of his own career, the way he'd had to prove himself to everyone. He'd seen Tuck and he'd remembered and he'd hoped to give someone like himself the chance he'd had.

But while Tuck had the talent, he obviously didn't

have the drive or determination to be anything other than the hellraiser who'd gotten fired from every race team he'd ever driven for.

Jeep herded the crew out into the pit area to break the news about Tuck. The garage was empty now, except for Skye and Clint and the #62 Chevy. "What's going on?" Skye asked as she came up to him. "One of the mechanics said that you don't have a driver."

"Tuck's still not here."

"Why don't you just drive? I mean, you can do that, can't you?"

"I'm a licensed NASCAR driver, and NASCAR does allow for a relief to step in in emergency situations. I *can* drive. But I don't drive anymore. I'm an owner. I've got different priorities now. You know that."

"The wife and kids?"

"I've spent fifteen years working my ass off and for what? So I can wake up alone every morning?" He shook his head. "No more. I won't do it."

Skye eyed him, a curious glint in her eyes. "You won't, or you can't?"

He frowned. "What's that supposed to mean?"

"That maybe you're not half as scared of ending up old and alone and past your prime without having fathered even one of the half dozen, as you are of finding out that you can't do it anymore."

"I can drive. I'm one of the best drivers this sport has ever seen."

"That's not what the press is saying."

"Fuck the press. They don't know anything." He ran a hand over his face. "You would think that after fifteen years they would know that I can do anything I damn well put my mind to." He shook his head. "My whole life it's been this way. I've had to listen to the garbage and then jump right in and prove everybody wrong. Well, you know what? I'm tired of it. I have other things to worry about. I'm not getting any younger. Hell, you know what I'm talking about. You want a man in your life. You're tired of waking up alone every morning."

"True. I know exactly how you feel. *If* that's how you feel. But I can't help but think that maybe you're blowing all of this off not because you don't care about it, but because you care too much."

"I think you've been inhaling too much exhaust." He said the words, but he wasn't so sure he meant them.

Because Skye was a lot more right than he wanted her to believe.

"You're looking for an excuse not to get behind the wheel," she went on, "because you're afraid that what everybody is saying is really true."

"Like hell I am," Clint growled, his tone low and threatening, warning her to shut up.

"You're afraid that you've reached the limit," she persisted, stirring his respect as much as his temper. "That your heyday really *is* over."

"It's not over unless I say it's over."

"So say it." She rounded him and touched the hood of the car, challenge gleaming in her eyes. Along with a warm, understanding light that eased the sudden pounding of his heart as he stared through the open window at the familiar interior. "*You* say it. Don't let anybody else say it for you."

"I don't know if I can," he said, his voice low, filled with the fear he'd felt for so long. "I just don't know. I've crashed before. Things have malfunctioned. One time the carburetor blew and I suffered a broken leg and several broken ribs, but those things weren't me. They were the car. When I crashed during the 500, it was my fault," he said, admitting the truth out loud for the very first time. "My hand slipped on the wheel. My hand has *never* slipped."

"Then you're entitled." Her voice softened. "You're only human, Clint. And humans make mistakes. We're not invincible."

He shook his head, wanting to believe her. But Cowboy MacAllister had been building himself up, feeding his own ego for so long to keep himself focused and determined, that a small part had actually started to believe the hype. "Mistakes like that don't belong on the track. I'm dangerous, to myself and other drivers. I shouldn't be behind the wheel."

"Racing is dangerous, period. And you belong behind the wheel."

"How would you know?"

"I read *NASCAR for Dummies*." When she saw that the admission didn't impress him, she added, "In which you were mentioned two-hundred and seventy-six times. *And* I've watched TNN the past few Sundays since I met you. I've seen two races from beginning to end, including pre and post commentary. Not to mention the Winner's Circle show hosted by that sports guy—what's his name, Waltrip?"

"Darrell Waltrip. He used to be a driver. His brother drives."

"I thought the name sounded familiar. Anyhow, I lost count on how many times you were mentioned during all that coverage. You're a legend. The press has been speculating, true, but the real reporters, the ones that count, know how good you are and how important you are to the sport."

"And you know this based on two races?"

"And my reading, and I've learned enough to know that the sport wouldn't be near the phenomenon it is without you and drivers like you. If you want to retire, fine. You're entitled to that, as well. But don't do it because you feel like you have to. Because you're afraid not to." She held his gaze, her green eyes warm and compassionate. "Do it because you want to. Because it's time. Because you know you're the best and you've reached the pinnacle and there's nowhere else to go." When he didn't say anything, she added, "If you really want to get on with your life, you have to start fresh. Right now you've still got something to prove to yourself." She touched him then. Her soft, warm fingertips trailed down the side of his face in a feather-like caress that might not have meant anything were it not for the emotion bright in her eyes.

Skye believed in him.

It was the first time anyone had ever looked at him that way. Suddenly, it didn't matter that his own confidence had been shattered. Skye had faith in him and the realization was enough to feed his own faith, and urge him back behind the wheel.

Clint knew then that he'd been wrong about her. Skye Farrel wasn't every woman in his past. She was the one woman in his future, even if she didn't realize it.

Yet.

He planted a hot, hungry kiss on her lips before going to tell his crew and get suited up. A few minutes later, he climbed into the car, gunned the engine and spent the next few laps showing everyone, especially himself, that Clint MacAllister hadn't lost his touch, after all.

Chapter Eighteen

A cheer went up in the pit box when Clint raced past the green flag at the finish line and NASCAR officials announced the qualifying results.

Number 62 slowed and swerved onto pit road and pulled to a stop several feet past the pit box where Skye waited by herself. Clint climbed through the window and hauled himself out, pulling off his helmet. Their gazes locked and before she could draw another breath, he grabbed her around the waist and lifted her into his arms.

"I did it. I won pole position!"

"That's great." She hugged him back, relishing the feel of his strong arms. "It's better than great. It's wonderful. Pole position," she exclaimed. "Wow!"

He gave her a quick, intense kiss before easing her to her feet in a slow glide down his hard body. He stared down at her, a smile curving his lips. "You don't have a clue what pole position is, do you?"

"No. I don't mean to take away from the moment, but I'm totally lost."

"Pole position is a racing term that refers to the car who

starts the race on the inside of the front row. Pole position goes to the car with the fastest qualifying time."

"You had the fastest qualifying time."

"Bingo."

Skye beamed. "That's great!"

He stared down at her, his blue eyes twinkling. "It is great, but you know what's better?" Before she could answer, he went on, "You didn't have a clue and I *still* have a woody."

Her smile faded into a confused look. "What's that supposed—" she started, but the rest of her question was lost as the excited crew quickly caught up and surrounded them.

"Dammit, boy, I knew you could do it," Jeep said, slapping Clint on the back.

"That was beautiful!"

"Just like old times!"

Skye stepped back as the racing team congratulated their boss. Then it seemed as if the flood gates opened. Media joined the crowd and the number of people grew. Skye quickly found herself pushed to the outer edge.

But she didn't feel like the odd man out. She felt happier than she'd felt in a long, long time.

Because Clint was so happy, and she'd had a small part in that.

"Clint, Clint!" A tall brunette called out as she scooted up next to Skye and tried to wedge into the crowd. She was tall, a good head over Skye, her long dark hair pulled back into a simple ponytail. She was pretty in a quiet, unassuming sort of way. She wore a red Daytona Beach International Speedway T-shirt tucked into blue jeans. A handful of tags hung from a rope around her neck—everything from a pit pass to a Raceway nametag with the name DARLA in big black block letters—*Darla.*

Reality smacked Skye upside the head and she knew in an instant that this was *the* Darla. The woman who'd turned down Clint's marriage proposal. The woman Clint had been so eager to impress that he'd actually swallowed his male pride to take sex lessons.

"Clint!" she called out again, waving the clipboard in her hand. "We need you in Victory Lane."

"You're Darla," Skye blurted.

The woman turned on her. Big, brown eyes locked with Skye's. "Pardon me?"

"You're the Darla that works here at the racetrack. You're a friend of Clint's."

The woman smiled, a warm, genuine smile that sent a rush of dread through Skye.

This *was* Darla, and tomorrow was the Pepsi 400, and this weekend was Clint's big chance to show off his stuff.

Funny, but all of that had slipped to the farthest corner of her mind over the past few days as she and Clint had gotten closer with all the sex and the talking. Skye had gotten so caught up in fighting her own feelings, that she'd completely forgotten that their relationship wasn't about what she did or did not feel.

Their relationship was strictly a business deal. A means to an end, and for Clint the end was Darla.

Even if he did look at her with those deep blue eyes that whispered more. Much, much more.

He'd never once said that he felt anything for her. That he actually *liked* her. He hadn't said anything, except a heartfelt thank-you a few moments ago. And something about a woody.

Skye pushed the strange thought aside and focused on the moment and the woman standing next to her.

Darla seemed nice with her easy smile and naturally pretty without so much as a stitch of makeup and sincere with her big, warm brown eyes. Judging by the excitement in her gaze as she stared over the sea of heads at the man who dominated the middle, there was no doubt that she knew exactly what pole position meant.

Skye hated her instantly, and then she hated herself for having such feelings. She should be happy for Clint.

This was the woman he wanted, and if his performance over the past few days was any prediction of success, Clint was going to totally wow her.

This was it. The end of the line. School was out.

Time for Skye to step aside.

While she had, indeed, come to the startling conclusion that she liked him, her feelings didn't change anything.

Clint wanted more than a woman who liked him. He wanted a wife. Marriage.

Together, they'd gone as far as they could. Clint's next step was toward the altar.

While Skye was tempted to stay through the next day and draw out what little time she had left with him, she wouldn't. She already knew as much as she needed to about macho man Clint—namely that he was one of a kind and chances were she would never find another who made her feel half as wonderful. And he knew as much as he needed to about sex.

There was no sense prolonging the inevitable, not to mention the last thing he probably needed, let alone wanted, was to have Skye hanging around. This was his chance with Darla and Skye wasn't about to stand in his way.

If anything, she was going to help him.

Because as much as Skye liked Clint, she loved him even more.

She blinked back her own tears, tapped Darla on the shoulder and said, "Can I talk to you for a second?"

Clint was going to skin her alive.

He stomped up to the desk at the hotel where they were staying after a thorough search at the racetrack, prompted by a very enlightening conversation with Darla.

First he was going to kiss her, then he was definitely going to skin her alive.

Christ, Skye had actually *talked* to Darla about him, about the sex, about how great he was in bed. While Darla hadn't been half as excited about his new level of expertise, she had been touched that he would go to so much trouble just to make her happy.

Though she had no intention of reconsidering his proposal based on the new facts, she was willing to go out on a few dates and see where things might lead. Her words should have been music to his ears except for the all-important fact that he hadn't been able to get past the initial, "Skye told me what you did."

Where did Skye get off telling anyone anything? He didn't need Skye to talk him up. Hell, he didn't want her to talk him up, because Clint MacAllister had had a change of heart.

He no longer cared what Darla thought, which he'd quickly told her in a nice, polite way, before he'd said that he wanted to remain friends. Of course, she'd been agreeable. While they'd made terrible bed partners during their two quick encounters, they did make good comrades.

After all, they had a lot in common.

A definite plus between friends.

It didn't mean diddly between lovers.

Clint had realized that when Skye confessed her hatred for fishing and he'd still been as turned on as ever. He'd realized then that the Holy Commitment Trinity her mom was so passionate about didn't mean jack shit with his heart pounding so fast. In theory, it made sense. But to a man in love, it was just a bunch of bunk.

Christ, he *loved* her.

The realization hit him as he stood at the desk and listened to the clerk tell him that she'd checked out.

"She what?"

"She left in a cab about an hour ago and headed for the airport." The clerk searched behind the desk. "But she did leave you this." The man handed Clint a Tootsie Pop. "She said if all else fails, you should try this."

He was definitely going to skin her alive.

That desire faded as Clint walked out of the hotel and climbed into a cab. Doubt settled in and he considered for the first time that he might not get the chance to skin her alive. That for all his determination, this might be one race he couldn't win.

While he wanted Skye Farrel, she might not want him. Not in a forever kind of way.

The urge to turn the cab around and head back to the speedway hit him hard and fast. Two days ago, he might have done just that. After his mess-up at the Daytona 500, he'd let his fear cripple him. Not the fear of what everyone had thought about him because of the crash, but the fear of what he'd thought about himself. That he was dangerous. A loser. A has-been.

But he'd faced that fear today, thanks to Skye, and he would face his fear now.

Chances were she would tell him to take a walk on a short bridge. Regardless of his feelings and the undeniable connection between them, they *were* different.

The question was, were they too different?

Maybe. Maybe not.

Either way, he needed to know.

Skye finished unpacking and had just settled on her sofa to watch the replay of the race when her doorbell rang. Punching the Mute button and silencing the commentary, she wiped the tears from her eyes, walked over and gazed through the peephole.

Her heart jammed in her throat when she found Clint MacAllister staring back at her. Her hands trembled as she hurriedly wiped her face and opened the door.

"What are you doing here?"

He stared at her, his gaze unreadable. "Your last and final lesson."

"But you have to race tomorrow."

"Tuck showed up. It seems that he and Lindy had a meeting of the minds and, while I was tempted to boot his ass off the team, she talked me into keeping him. And then he talked me into keeping him. A first because Tuck never does much talking. But that's going to change. At least that's what he told me, and I believe him enough to give him a chance."

"Oh."

"But even if he hadn't shown up, I would still be here. Actually, I was halfway here before I even got Lindy's call."

"You could have blown your chances tomorrow by coming here tonight."

"Tomorrow doesn't matter. This matters." He handed her several handwritten sheets of paper. "Here."

"What's this?" Her mind raced and her heart pounded as she glanced down at the nearly illegible scrawl that covered line after line.

"A handout. You told me that things stick better when you see them on paper."

"You made me a NASCAR handout," she said, the words barely making it past the sudden lump in her throat.

"Actually, it's about me. My past. My present. Our future." At her sharp glance, he added, "I love you, Skye."

Her gaze scanned the words and the meaning of what he'd done and said crystallized.

She shook her head. "I'm really touched, but I can't . . ." She hadn't thought she had any more tears to shed, that she'd cried them all during the trip home, but she was wrong. "We don't have a future. We can't have a future. You want to get married and I don't."

"Then that's that."

His words hurt a lot more than they should have considering she was the one who'd turned him down. "I'm really sorry," she started, but he didn't give her a chance to say more.

"We don't get married. We live together."

"What?"

"I want to be with you regardless of the situation." He stepped toward her.

He looked so handsome wearing a plain red T-shirt with the team's racing logo on the front. The soft cotton outlined his broad shoulders and molded to his biceps and heat zipped along her nerve endings.

But he didn't just stir her physically.

It was the way he looked at her, his blue eyes so dark

and intense and purposeful, as if the entire world revolved around her and only her.

For the first time, Skye felt truly special. Precious. Worshipped. *Loved.*

His strong fingers lifted her chin and his gaze locked with hers. "It's your call," he told her. "I want to marry you, but if you don't want to marry me, that's okay. As long as you want to be with me, because I want to be with you. I want to make love to you every night and wake up to you every morning. Granted, I would rather have a ring on my finger and a piece of paper that tells the world I'm your one and only, but if you're not ready for that, it's okay. I'll take what I can get. *If* you love me. Do you?" A worried light filled his blue eyes and tugged at her heart.

"Yes," she said, suddenly eager to ease his mind. "I love you. I really do."

He grinned, his lips parting, revealing his straight white teeth. "Then that's all that matters."

Skye stared deep into his eyes. The intensity of his feelings for her mirrored what she felt inside, and suddenly it was all that mattered.

She loved him and he loved her and things would work out between them. With or without marriage. Because they would make it work. Together.

"So you would forget all about marriage just for me?"

His grin widened and he shrugged. "I can't promise I wouldn't bug you about it every now and then. Call me old-fashioned, but I'd really like to be married to the mother of my half-dozen children."

"Half of a half-dozen," she cut in, a smile tugging at the corner of her mouth. "Three is a good number."

"Five."

"Four."

He slid his arms around her and pulled her close. "See there? We're already starting to see eye-to-eye. Before long, we'll be finishing each other's sentences and you'll be begging me to walk down the aisle."

"I don't beg."

"I definitely remember some begging. Of course, I think it was in regards to me licking candy off a certain part of your anatomy."

"That wasn't begging. That was forceful instruction."

"Ah," he said, dipping his head to deliver a warm kiss to her waiting lips. "Married or not," he told her when he finally pulled back, "I want to spend the rest of my life with you. I love you," he said again. "*I love you.*"

The words slid into her ears and filled her with a joy unlike anything she'd ever felt before. A feeling that would have sent her running for a cookie and her sanity not very long ago because Skye Farrel didn't believe in love or like or 'til death do us part.

But then Clint MacAllister had upended her life and turned her belief system inside and out, and now she not only believed in those things, she lived and breathed them.

She also had a new craving that had nothing to do with food and everything to do with the dark, delicious man standing in front of her.

"What are you thinking?" he asked.

She smiled. "I'm wondering if that's a Tootsie Pop in your pocket, or if you're just glad to see me?"

He grinned. "I ate the Tootsie Pop on the plane."

"That's what I was hoping you would say."

And then she kissed him.

Epilogue

"I can't believe I'm actually doing this." Skye stood in a makeshift dressing area in one of the enormous garages behind pit road at Daytona International Speedway. Her fingers clenched and unclenched around a stack of engraved place cards.

"Stop worrying," Xandra said as she slid on the three-inch Prada pumps Skye had chosen for her bridesmaids. "You look great."

Skye turned toward the floor-length mirror that had been brought in and eyed her reflection. She wore a traditional A-line strapless satin wedding gown with a pearl-encrusted bodice. The result of a month-long trek through every bridal shop in Dallas and Houston *and* Austin after she'd asked Clint to marry him.

It had taken her six months of living and loving together, but she'd finally come to the realization that she wanted to marry him not because it meant something to him, but because it meant something to her. Because joining forces with him wasn't about giving up her sense of self, but adding another dimension to her personality.

Being with Clint didn't make her feel oppressed. Rather, she felt empowered. Smarter. Sexier. Stronger.

Skye wanted to need him, and she wanted him to need her, and she was no longer afraid of a little piece of paper that confirmed as much.

But while Skye had opened her heart to marriage, the wedding itself was an entirely different story. Especially since she was about to do something so traditional in a very untraditional setting—Victory Lane following the Daytona 500.

The race had ended a half hour ago, with last season's rookie of the year, Tuck Briggs, taking first place in Clint's #62 Chevy. Clint had overcome his fear by getting back behind the wheel for the qualifier of the Pespi 400, but he hadn't changed his mind about retiring. He'd had his heyday as NASCAR's hottest driver, and he was ready to pass the title to his protégé, and concentrate on making the three children he and Skye had agreed upon.

"I know you're out of your element, but the dress really *is* beautiful," Xandra said, drawing Skye's thoughts back to the moment.

"It's not very fancy," Skye said, remembering the numerous dresses she'd tried on. No hoop skirt or layers of tulle or rows of sequins and rhinestones. Just satin and pearls. "But it's floor length and white and it *is* a bona fide wedding dress, and I'm actually wearing it."

Even more, she *liked* it.

She even liked the way the hairdresser had swept her blond hair up into a cascade of curls and secured it with several pearl-encrusted hair pins.

"I wasn't talking about the dress when I said I can't believe I'm doing this," Skye told her youngest sister. "I was talking the reception and these." She held up the place cards before handing them over to a very impatient Jiles, who'd flown in that morning to oversee the ceremony and the traditional sit-down reception being held at a nearby hotel. "I sat Mom between Clint's Aunt Myrtle and Uncle Travis."

"And the problem is?"

"They've been happily married for sixty-eight years."

Xandra let loose a low whistle as she swiped on cherry red lipdick from the previous night's bachelorette party. The color matched her fitted strapless, floor-length red dress. "That must be some sort of record." She licked her lips. "The happily married is definitely a strike, but maybe it's not a total loss. Did Aunt Myrtle have a career?"

"Never worked a day in her life."

"Strike two."

"She was too busy cooking for Uncle Travis. She makes the best homemade biscuits this side of the Rio Grande."

"Strike three." Xandra smeared her lips together before wiping the corners. "The reception should be even more interesting than the ceremony. I still can't believe you're getting married at a racetrack."

"My fiancé owns the hottest racing team in the country. It's only fitting that we get married in Victory Lane." Besides, Daytona was where Skye had first realized her love for Clint. "Then again, maybe we should have done something more traditional. I wouldn't want to jinx this."

"Calm down." Xandra eyed her. "If I didn't know better, I would say all this wedding stuff is getting to you."

"Are you crazy? It's just a wedding, and I am not getting crazy over a wedding."

Even one that included a sit-down dinner and an orchestra and dancing and two ice sculptures—one shaped like the infamous #62 in honor of Clint, and one that looked suspiciously like Skye's good buddy Dinah the Vagina, though they'd told the guests it was a replica of Natural Bridge Caverns, which they'd visited on their first official date.

The sound of cheering and clapping drifted from outside, followed by an announcement telling the drivers to start their engines in salute to the bride-to-be. Skye knew then that it was almost time. Her nerves jumped and she drew in a deep breath.

"I'm calm. I'm cool. And I am *not* crazy."

"No, I am," Eve declared as she entered from an adjoining bathroom and held out her arms. "I can't believe I'm wearing this. I don't do red."

"It's cherry," Xandra told her. "And you look good. You need a break from the whole *Queen of the Damned* thing."

Skye was the oldest, obedient, conservative child, Xandra the young, do-no-wrong tomboy, and Eve the middle switched-at-birth daughter.

Eve was artsy with her grunge clothes and multiple piercings, and downright scary with her heavy makeup.

"Don't tell me they don't have French manicures in the Underworld," Xandra told her older sister.

Eve held out her fingers, adorned with tons of rings, and revealed two inch long talons painted as pitch black as her hair.

Black nails?

"I wanted everyone to have nice, pretty white nails. Maybe a little clear polish, but no color. Jiles said colored nails clash with the dresses."

Eve shrugged. "Black goes with everything, and at

least I have nails." She stared pointedly at her youngest sister.

Skye followed Eve's stare to the tips of Xandra's fingers. "You don't have any nails," she blurted, her heart pounding. "What happened to yesterday's manicure?"

Xandra curled her fingers, hiding the chewed-down nubs. "When Mom took my Blow Pops again, I got really desperate. I haven't rationalized how the substitution theory supports nail-biting, but I've been smoke-free for two months now."

"But you don't have nails," Skye said again, her panic rising.

Xandra smiled. "Eve has enough for both of us."

"But hers are black. *Black.*" She heard the rising pitch in her voice, but she couldn't stop it.

Months of planning and worrying and damning herself for doing either, caught up to her in one frantic moment where the fate of her marriage rested solely on her sisters' nails.

"This is my wedding, not my funeral," she shrieked.

"I know at least one person who would argue that," Eve told her.

"Yeah, and you know how much Mom likes to argue the point," Xandra added.

"Girls, girls." A man's deep voice sounded and Skye glanced up to see her father standing in the doorway.

Gone was the quiet, inconsequential academic who'd raised her. No neutral pants or matching sweater or round eyeglasses. Donovan Martin wore a black tuxedo that accented his broad shoulders and made him look taller. His salt and pepper hair had been slicked back. He'd left his reading glasses at home and his green eyes twinkled. Even better, he had nice, blunt-tipped, *un*painted nails.

"Peace, Pops," Eve said while Xandra whistled softly.

Donovan smiled before giving both women a stern look. "Stop upsetting the bride." His gaze shifted to his eldest daughter and a warm light filled his gaze. "Are you okay, dear?"

"I was, but now one doesn't have nails and one has black nails and we have to take pictures and Jiles is sure to freak and I don't know if I can handle a bona fide death threat right now and—"

Her words stalled as he pressed two fingertips to her lips. "Jiles is too busy to worry about something so minor. We're about to start." He glanced at Xandra and Eve. "You two had better get going. And keep your hands tucked under the bouquet."

"If it's any consolation," he said to Skye once her two sisters had left to join the rest of the wedding party, "I saw the other two bridesmaids, Jenny and Lindy, over in the groom's garage helping their husbands—Duke and Tuck, I think their names were—get dressed." He smiled. "Their nails looked perfect."

The comment eased Skye's nerves a little and she drew a deep breath.

"I guess this is it," she said as an acoustic guitar version of "Wind Beneath My Wings" drifted over Daytona's PA system, signaling that the ceremony was about to start.

"I never thought I would see the day when my little girl would worry over nail color and wedding pictures." Her father's green eyes grew bright.

Skye smiled. "If I didn't know better, I'd say you were touched by all of this."

He winked. "I have an image to protect, so don't tell your mother. And speaking of your mother, she's here and she's calm. She only hyperventilated once and that was when we drove up outside and she saw the getaway car.

"She didn't like Clint's Hummer?"

"She didn't like the words SHACKLED FOR LIFE painted in white shoe polish on the back window." He patted her hand. "But she ate two of your grandmother's chocolate-chip cookies and she's fine now."

Skye gave her father a serious look. "I've totally disappointed her, haven't I?"

"You're beautiful and healthy and happy. That's not a disappointment. It's a blessing. Your mother just has trouble accepting change. Her entire life has been about *not* getting married." He gave her an encouraging smile. "She'll come around. Just give her time. That's what I do."

"What you've been doing your entire life. You and Mom have been together a long time." Skye stared into his eyes and asked the one question that had always haunted her. "Why?"

"According to your mother and her Holy Commitment Trinity, we're a perfect match. We belong together."

"And according to you?"

"I love her. I always have." He winked again. "But don't tell her that either."

Skye slid her arms around his neck and gave him a hug. "Thank you, Daddy. For telling me the truth and for being here to give me away."

"Are you kidding?" He hugged her back. "I wouldn't have missed it for all the iguanas in South America." He set her away from him and stared down at her. "But I do have one favor to ask."

"Anything."

"When you toss the bouquet," he indicated the giant bunch of multi-colored Tootsie Pops sitting nearby, the sticks wrapped together with flowing white ribbon, "Toss it your mother's way."

Skye's eyes widened. "You don't mean—"

"No, no," he cut in. "At least not anytime soon. It's taken me thirty-eight years to get her to finally refer to me as her life partner rather than the man who shares her orgasms. It'll take a lot longer to warm her up to '*I Do*'." He patted her hand. "But if, when the day ever comes, I'm sure to need all the help I can get."

"I'll do my best," Skye promised as she reached for her bouquet.

"Are you ready?" he asked as he held out his arm.

"Ready," she said and meant it.

She slid her hand through the crook of his elbow and let him lead her toward Victory Lane and the rest of her life with the man she loved.

About the Author

Award-wining author Kimberly Raye lives deep in the heart of Texas with her very own cowboy, Curt, and her young children. She's an incurable romantic who loves Sugar Babies, Toby Keith and dancing to Barney videos with her toddler. You can reach Kimberly on-line at www.kimberlyraye.com, or write to her c/o Warner Books, 1271 Avenue of the Americas, New York, NY 10020.

growing company. She had her own home, her own ca-

Chapter One

This was *not* happening.

She was an attractive, sexy, vibrant, sensual woman in the prime of her life. Not to mention she was the owner and head designer for Wild Woman, Inc., the leading manufacturer of erotic toys and sensual enhancement products for women. Sexy, vibrant women who made their living by selling a sexy, vibrant image to other women didn't have gray hair.

Not *down there*.

That's what she told herself as she set aside the King Kong Ultra Deluxe Number Five vibrator she'd been trying out—she always tested her own products during the developmental phase and perfected every flaw before handing a prototype over to her manufacturing division.

Her hands trembled as she closed her eyes and tried to calm her pounding heart.

Maybe it wasn't really gray at all. Maybe it was a very light, silvery, blond hair that just happened to spring up among its very dark counterparts. A fluke, like the one hard, dark, skinny French fry always found at the bottom of a hot, piping order.

Or maybe it was the fact that it was ten o'clock on a Wednesday night—the Wednesday night following the Wednesday morning when her live-in boyfriend of eight years walked out on her—and she was still working, thanks to the King Kong Five which went into production first thing in the morning. The new version of a tried and true product would, hopefully, bring back the dozen or so accounts Wild Woman had lost in the past few months to Lust, Lust, Baby!, a competitive company that had recently been attracting a lot of attention with a new line of multi-colored, multi-speed, musical vibrators.

At five that afternoon, she'd noticed that the King Kong head wobbled more than it rotated. After six hours of going back and forth with the engineering department, she'd managed to perfect the movement. Trying it out had been the last step before calling it quits. She was tired. Mentally and physically worn out. No wonder her mind was playing tricks on her.

Then again, it could just be the poor lighting in her office, where she designed and tested her latest products. There were no fluorescent squares overhead like the ones lighting the rest of the suite that housed Wild Woman, Inc. Rather, she'd traded the bright fixtures for several small lamps strategically placed throughout the large room. The light played off the dark mahogany paneled walls, and rich, lush, pink carpeting to create an overall effect that was soft, subtle, *sensual*. The perfect atmosphere to relax and tune in to her body, and unleash the wild woman within.

Usually.

She forced her eyes open, eased her reclining leather

chair upright and smoothed her skirt back down. She double-pressed the button that controlled the red privacy light above her door to make sure that it blinked. It was one thing to be disturbed during a trial test, and quite another to face the world when she was *this close* to a major life crisis.

Close, but not quite there. Not yet.

Pushing to her feet, she rounded the desk. She was not going to panic. Or kick. Or scream. Or cry. She was going to get a better look.

Fifteen minutes later, she sat on the thick carpet, her skirt hiked up to her waist, her lace thong pushed aside and her legs parted in a vee. She adjusted the neck of the desk lamp she'd pulled to the floor with her. A pencil cup toppled over as the cord stretched tight and she went in for a close-up view.

Please, she prayed to the Big Lady Upstairs. *Don't do this to me. Not now. I'll change my ways. I'll smile at that snotty lady up on the tenth floor who spilled cappucino on me last week. I'll even stop scowling at that guy down on the second who wears the blue leisure suit every Thursday and offers to bend me over like a shotgun. I'll give up my pot of coffee every morning and stop eating those Snickers bars for lunch and I will never, ever tell the salesclerk at Saks that I found something on the sales rack when I really didn't.*

Hope renewed, she gathered her courage and drew in a deep breath. Sixty watts of light illuminated the area in question. Her gaze zeroed in on the hair and a lump formed in her throat.

It was there and it was gray, and it was now officially the worst day of Xandra Farrel's life.

*   *   *

"Knock-knock!" The deep voice rang out as the door to Xandra's office opened.

Xandra lifted her head from the desk where she'd collapsed after hauling herself off the floor ten minutes earlier. Her gaze went to the man who stood in the doorway.

Albert Sinclair was the head engineer for Wild Woman, Inc, and a bonafide walking, talking Ken doll. He was tall, tanned and blond, with sparkling blue eyes and a white smile and an athletic body honed from hours of racquetball.

He'd beaten her more times than she could count. Then again, she'd never really played to win. Just to talk. Albert could talk and listen even better than he could play thanks to hours of sensitivity training courtesy of his gay parents. He was kind and compassionate, and he was the closest person to her besides her two older sisters.

"Your light was off, so I figured you'd finished the test run. How did it go?"

"Fine."

"We still don't think the rotating head is smooth enough and so a few of us are working late on a new coggle. Not to mention, we're brainstorming ideas for the Sextravaganza next month. Have you come up with anything?"

"Not yet." How could she focus on the biggest marketing convention of the year when all she wanted to do was crawl into a hole and hibernate?

"I'm making a midnight food run. Can I bring you anything while I'm out?"

"A gun. Or a noose."

"I was thinking more like Chinese or Thai."

"Only if it's loaded with rat poison and guaranteed to

put me out of my misery." She reached for a tissue and swiped at the traitorous tear that slid down her cheek.

Albert's smile faded into a concerned frown. "Oh, honey, what is it? What's wrong? You're not upset about the Sextravaganza are you? You'll come up with something. You always do."

"I . . ." She shook her head and blinked. "No, no. I mean, I'm concerned, but I've already started my brainstorming list for the product." She eyed the familiar notebook where she kept her prized lists. She penned them for everything, from WHAT TO DO TODAY to CREATIVE WAYS TO KILL THE COMPETITION to NEW CONDOM COLORS. "Not that I can really think about the convention right now. Or a new product. Or that I'll be able to think about either of them tomorrow. Or ever. I might be all washed up professionally as well as personally. I might as well call it quits and go file unemployment. I'll lose my house and my car and end up bagging it on some street corner, my face all wrinkled from the elements." At Albert's puzzled stare, she added, "I'm just having a moment, that's all."

"One of those *Life is passing me by and I'm cooped up watching from the inside out moments*?" He nodded. "I know the feeling. I had one of those myself not more than a few hours ago when I watched the marketing girls head off to one of those dance clubs, while I stayed here with the rest of my team to work."

"Not that kind. This one's more of a *Wait! This is going too fast!* moment. Like when you ride a bike for the first time without the training wheels. Or when you slip behind the wheel of your first car. Or when you climb into the backseat with the hottest guy in high school who turns out to be a total dud in the sack. Or when you find your first gray hair."

"A gray hair?" He walked in and perched on the corner of her desk. "Is that what this is all about? Relax, honey. That's why God invented Bjorn over at Bolo's. That man works wonder with bleach and foil. He'll blend it in so you don't even notice."

"I seriously doubt that."

"He did mine and I've got *seventeen* of the stubborn little sons-of-bitches." He pointed near his temple. "Right here. And here. But you can't see a one of them thanks to Bjorn."

"I'm not doubting his ability. I just don't think the hair in question is long enough to foil."

He gave her a *get real* look. "Why, it's way below your shoulders."

"Boy, is it ever."

"Then stop worrying. All you need is a little careful bleaching and your problem is solved."

Another tear slid free and then another. "It's not exactly on my head."

"Let me get this straight. You've got a gray hair and it's not exactly on your . . ." Albert's words trailed off as the truth seemed to strike him. "Oh."

She bit her lip and blinked, trying to hold back a new flood of tears. "Not that it's the end of the world, mind you."

"That's the spirit."

She blinked frantically. "It's all in the way you look at it."

"Exactly."

"Gray doesn't have to mean old, right?"

"Right."

"It can mean mature. Experienced."

"Seasoned," Albert offered, handing her another tissue. "Weathered." At the last word, she threw him a watery stare and he shrugged. "Sorry. Poor word choice. How about . . . knowledgeable?"

She nodded. "Knowledgeable. That's good." She dabbed at her eyes and sniffled. "I'm not losing my youth. I'm merely starting a whole new phase of life."

"You're evolving."

"Right. This isn't the end. My life isn't over just because of a silly gray hair."

"Who cares about a couple of gray hairs?"

"It's just one. At least, I think it's just one." Panic rushed through her and her gaze caught his. "What if it's more?"

"I'm sure it's just one."

"But you said a couple."

"It was a figure of speech. I really meant one. Honest."

She nodded and tried to calm her churning stomach. "It's not the end of the world," she said again. "It's not like I'm going to shrivel up and die just because I have a gray hair and I'm alone for the first time in eight years. Alone doesn't necessarily mean lonely. It can mean free. Untethered. Ripe for the picking."

Albert nodded. "You're so ripe, you're about to burst—hey, what do you mean, *alone*?"

"I'm in my prime," she rushed on, eager to focus on the positive. "I'm enlightened. I'm mature and knowledgeable and weathered." As soon as the word popped out, a tear squeezed past her lashes. She shook her head. "Geez, who am I kidding? I'm past ripe. I'm *this close* to my expiration date. No wonder Mark packed up his laptop and walked out."

"He really left you?"

She nodded and whacked her forehead on the desktop. "Right after he told me I didn't do it for him anymore."

"He *didn't*!"

"What does that mean anyway? I don't *do it* for him? If he's talking sex, it's his own fault. He works more than I do, even with the Sextravaganza only a month away. When I initiate, he's always too tired. And when he initiates . . ." She shook her head. "Come to think of it, I can't remember the last time he initiated." She slumped back in her chair. "It's me. I'm old and unattractive and dried up. No one wants to have sex with a prune."

"You're not a prune. Mark is an idiot."

"Mark is perfect. We're perfect. We both like the same things, we both respect each other and we have great sex. Or we *had* great sex. In the beginning. In between his meetings and business trips." Her gaze met Albert's. "It's not supposed to happen like this. We had it all."

"Maybe you just thought you had it all."

She eyed Albert. "What's that supposed to mean?"

"That you love Mexican food and Thai and any and everything spicy, and Mark lived for tofu."

"I eat tofu, too."

"But it doesn't make your mouth water. Deep down in your soul," he tapped his chest, "you don't lust after tofu."

"You're right," she blurted after a long, contemplative moment. "It's me. I tried to hide it, but Mark finally saw past the front to the spicy food junkie who dwells inside." She shook her head. "I'm a fake. And I'm getting old."

"You're not a fake."

"But I *am* getting old."

"You're only twenty-nine."

"I'm this close to being thirty. Two months and bam. I'm there."

"It's just another year."

"It's *the* year. Do you know that a woman's number of fertile eggs decreases by fifty percent when she hits thirty? That's half."

"So that's what this is all about. You want a baby."

"Of course I do. I mean, not *now*, at this very moment. But I definitely want one before I hit thirty-five. Or I at least want to be pregnant by then."

"What catastrophic event happens at thirty-five?"

"The measly fifty percent of fertile eggs I have left decreases by *another* fifty percent. Each year thereafter, it's downhill. Fast." She shook her head. "I invested eight years. Mark and I were stable. Comfortable. We'd actually reached the no makeup phase of our relationship. I could walk around the house in nothing but my ratty warm-ups and sparkling personality."

"Maybe that's what scared him off." When she cut him a glance, Albert grinned, "I'm trying to make you laugh."

"We were so close to the next step in our relationship," she went on.

"Marriage?"

"Are you kidding? You know how I feel about marriage. It's the most archaic form of oppression," Xandra repeated the words that had been drilled into her as a child. Her mother, a widely popular Harvard-trained sexologist and host of Lifetime's *Get Sexed Up*, and her quiet, conservative conservationist father had been together for over thirty-seven years now without benefit of a formal license, their longevity due to her mother's infamous Holy Commitment Trinity theory. "It's a man's way of enslaving a woman, and I value my freedom far too much to just give it up like that." She snapped her fingers. "No thank you."

"I just thought that since Skye finally took the plunge, you might have mellowed to the whole marriage thing."

Xandra's oldest sister, Skye, had walked down the aisle six months ago and enslaved herself to the hottest, hunkiest driver to ever race a NASCAR series. Worse, she'd been ecstatic about the whole thing.

"Skye's still suffering from a major case of lust," Xandra told Albert. "It'll wear off eventually and she'll realize she's made a mistake."

That's what Jacqueline Farrel kept saying to any and every one who would listen. But Xandra had her doubts. Six months and her sister seemed happier with each day that passed. Content. Complete.

A pang of longing went through her. "My life sucks," she sobbed.

"You'll find someone else."

"I don't have time to find someone else. Do you know how hard it is to meet men? Dorothy from marketing has been dating for the last five years since her divorce and she still hasn't found anyone. I don't have five years to waste on dating, much less another eight years on top of that to get to my comfort zone." She shook her head. "My life *really* sucks."

"So do something about it."

"I am. I'm crying, and in another minute I'm going to go for the stash of cigarettes in my desk and start smoking. After that, I'm going to the candy machine down in the lobby and I'm going to buy every Snickers bar and eat them all."

"That's just a temporary fix."

True. Chocolate, even a lot of chocolate, would only

ease the pain. It wouldn't make it go away entirely, and it certainly wouldn't change the fact that she'd been dumped *and* she had a gray hair and the competition was snipping at her heels. She had to change things herself and get her life back on track.

Personally and professionally.

"You're right. I'm sitting here crying when I should be thinking about the future."

"The convention is next month. We need something to really wow everyone and draw our stable customers back to Wild Woman."

"I'm wasting my time agonizing over this relationship business when I should be washing my hands of it entirely."

"I wouldn't go that far. I was thinking more in terms of concentrating on work as a distraction until the pain eases. Then you can get back in the game with a fresh mind and find a new man."

"Forget it. That's the last thing I want. But I am going to come up with something really spectacular and kick this company up the next notch. In the meantime, I'm going to find the man."

"But you just said you didn't want a man."

"I don't." She smiled as she reached for her notebook and pen and scribbled the heading for her newest list. "I want *the* man." Her smiled widened. "The perfect man to father my baby."

THE EDITOR'S DIARY

Dear Reader,

You can find love—or more often, it can find you—in the strangest places and in packages you never expected. Just ask Steven Thatcher and Skye Farrel in our two Warner Forever titles this February.

Publishers Weekly raves that **Karen Rose's** first book *Don't Tell* is "as gripping as a cold hand on the back of one's neck" and we can promise that **HAVE YOU SEEN HER?**, her latest book, is so good it will make the hairs on the back of your neck stand on end. One by one, teenaged girls are disappearing from their beds at night, only to be found brutally murdered. Special Agent Steven Thatcher has sworn to find the serial killer responsible. But as his job pulls him one way, his family pulls him in another. A widower haunted by loss, Steven worries about his eldest son's failing grades and agrees to a parent/teacher conference. There he meets Jenna Marshall, his son's teacher, and the one person he shouldn't get involved with. But neither can deny their attraction. As the brutal murders continue, endangering her students, Jenna reaches out to Steven. But the killer has his eyes set on a new victim . . . Jenna.

Moving from spine-tingling suspense in North Carolina to hot days and even hotter nights in Dallas, we present **Kimberly Raye's** Warner Forever debut **KISS ME ONCE, KISS ME TWICE**. *Affaire de Coeur* calls

Kimberly Raye a "unique and special talent" and they couldn't be more right. For Skye Farrel, sex is business. Her Girl Talk seminars have professional women jumping at the chance to learn the art of sexual fulfillment. But while she teaches women to turn sparks into flames in the bedroom, her own love life is ice cold. Enter Clint MacAllister. As a sexy, six-foot plus NASCAR driver, Clint's speedy lifestyle hasn't left him any time for love. So, on the hunt for a wife, he can't resist Skye's proposal: her sex tips for his insight into the male mind. But soon, her new favorite student has put love on her mind and fear in her heart. Can Clint convince her to face her biggest fear and take a race down the aisle with him?

To find out more about Warner Forever, these February titles, and the authors, visit us at www.warnerforever.com.

With warmest wishes,

Karen Kosztolnyik

Karen Kosztolnyik, Senior Editor

P.S. Spring will soon be here and love is in the air so cozy up with these two Warner Forever titles, guaranteed to make your temperature rise. Mary McBride pens a fresh and funny contemporary about an advice columnist who's the target of a letter bomber and the undercover cop who's in charge of keeping her safe in **MS. SIMON SAYS**; and Wendy Markham delivers the witty and poignant tale of two people who try to set up their best friends at a matchmaking cyber café, only to find themselves hit by Cupid's arrow in **ONCE UPON A BLIND DATE**.

FREE NASCAR® JULY 4TH WEEKEND!

Win a trip for two to beautiful Daytona, Florida, for the Pepsi 400 race on July 4th weekend 2004. This grand prize includes coach airfare, hotel accommodations for two days and one night (one room, double occupancy), pit passes, and tickets to the exciting final. Five lucky runner-up winners will be randomly selected to receive a $100 gift certificate from Victoria's Secret and five second-place prizes of a $50 cookie gift basket will also be awarded. Just send us an index card with your name, address, and e-mail address to *Kiss Me Once* Sweepstakes, c/o Warner Books, Dept. MM, Ninth Floor, 1271 Avenue of the Americas, New York, NY 10020—or enter electronically at www.warnerforever.com! Enter any time between February 1, 2004 and May 1, 2004. Your entry must be postmarked by May 1, and you could end up being one of our truly romantic winners! Drawing will be held on May 10, 2004. Winners will be announced on our Web site on May 15 and notified by mail.

NO PURCHASE NECESSARY TO ENTER. See details and official rules on next page.

Complete this entry form or send us a 3x5 index card with the following information:

Name: _____

Address: _____

City: _____ State: _____ Zip: _____

E-mail: _____

Mail to: *Kiss Me Once* Sweepstakes
c/o Warner Books
Dept. MM, Ninth Floor
1271 Avenue of the Americas
New York, NY 10020

WARNER BOOKS
An AOL Time Warner Company

www.warnerforever.com

Official Contest Rules

PURCHASING DOES NOT IMPROVE YOUR CHANCES OF WINNING